sweet HEART

HEARTS OF SAWYERS BEND #2

IVY LAYNE

GINGER QUILL PRESS. LLC

Also By Ivy Layne

THE HEARTS OF SAWYERS BEND

Stolen Heart
Sweet Heart
Scheming Heart

THE UNTANGLED SERIES

Unraveled
Undone
Uncovered

THE WINTERS SAGA

The Billionaire's Secret Heart (Novella)
The Billionaire's Secret Love (Novella)
The Billionaire's Pet
The Billionaire's Promise
The Rebel Billionaire
The Billionaire's Secret Kiss (Novella)
The Billionaire's Angel
Engaging the Billionaire
Compromising the Billionaire
The Counterfeit Billionaire
Series Extras: ivylayne.com/extras

THE BILLIONAIRE CLUB

The Wedding Rescue
The Courtship Maneuver
The Temptation Trap

Contents

Chapter One 1

Chapter Two 9

Chapter Three 17

Chapter Four 27

Chapter Five 35

Chapter Six 41

Chapter Seven 49

Chapter Eight 59

Chapter Nine 65

Chapter Ten 71

Chapter Eleven 77

Chapter Twelve 85

Chapter Thirteen 91

Chapter Fourteen 97

Chapter Fifteen 105

Chapter Sixteen 113

Chapter Seventeen 121

Chapter Eighteen 129

Chapter Nineteen 137

Chapter Twenty 147

Chapter Twenty-One 155

Chapter Twenty-Two 161

Chapter Twenty-Three 169

Chapter Twenty-Four 177

Chapter Twenty-Five 185
Chapter Twenty-Six 193
Chapter Twenty-Seven 201
Chapter Twenty-Eight 209
Chapter Twenty-Nine 217
Chapter Thirty 225
Chapter Thirty-One 231
Chapter Thirty-Two 237
Chapter Thirty-Three 245
Chapter Thirty-Four 253
Chapter Thirty-Five 263
Chapter Thirty-Six 273
Chapter Thirty-Seven 281
Chapter Thirty-Eight 289
Chapter Thirty-Nine 297
Chapter Forty 303
Chapter Forty-One 309
Epilogue: Part One 315
Epilogue Part Two 323
Also By Ivy Layne 333
About Ivy Layne 337

Chapter One

DAISY

I SHOULD HAVE BROUGHT A SMALLER BASKET. I FUM-
bled, trying to balance the wide, woven basket
against my hip as I searched through the dark for
the staff entrance to The Inn.

Another of my bright ideas that didn't quite pan out the
way it was supposed to. Lately, I seemed to have a lot of them.
I'd been to The Inn at Sawyers Bend hundreds of times, but I'd
always come through the front as a guest of the restaurant and
bar.

Today, I was delivering what I hoped was a tempting selection of treats from my bakery, an example of the kind of thing I
might provide for The Inn to leave in guest rooms or sell in the
small shop by the front desk. Anything to expand my client base.
Right now, I needed every penny I could get.

I usually had a lull in the early morning after the first wave of baking was done and before our doors opened for the day. Grams could handle our first few customers, and I'd figured I could drop off the basket and get back to Sweetheart Bakery in time for the opening rush. And I might if I could find the staff entrance.

At the back of the enormous timber and stone building, I stared over the gardens, lit with spotlights here and there. Even in the dark, the gardens were beautiful, flowing from the back of The Inn, the gravel paths leading to benches, to soft grass perfect for a picnic, and further to the guest cabins scattered along the river.

Fatigue pulled at me, and for a moment, I wanted nothing more than to sink onto one of the pretty iron benches, unwrap one of my own cookies, and just take a break.

Not yet. Not for a while, maybe. I'd been running on too little sleep for too long, but I couldn't stop until I'd fixed the mess I'd gotten myself into.

Hitching the basket higher on my hip, I watched as tendrils of light from the rising sun crept through the garden. One more minute. Then I'd get it together, find the staff entrance, drop off my basket, and get back to work. As I soaked in the beauty of early morning in the mountains, the burble of the nearby river, and the mist rising off the gardens, I realized where I'd gone wrong.

Of course, the staff entrance wouldn't be at the back of the building. During the day this space was mainly used by guests. I'd passed through the guest parking lot as I'd walked from the bakery and had completely forgotten about the smaller parking lot on the other side of The Inn. That must be where I'd find the staff entrance.

My energy renewed, I awkwardly re-balanced the basket and started along the gravel path to the far side of The Inn, hoping I wasn't leaving a trail of prettily wrapped brownies and cookies behind me. Approaching the corner, I took the narrower path to my right, marked with a small sign that read STAFF ONLY, hoping I'd find the door I was looking for.

I wasn't expecting to run into a wall. With a yelp, I back-pedaled, scrambling as the basket tipped, trying to get my feet under me before I landed on my butt.

Not a wall. A man. Tall, in a hooded sweatshirt and jeans, he barreled into me, the cardboard box in his arms bumping my basket and sending it tumbling.

I winced at the thuds of brownies hitting the grass and shouted, "Hey, wait a sec," but the man flung out an arm, shoving me hard. So much for not landing on my butt. My feet flew out from under me, brownies and cookies raining down on the wet grass.

I stared in stunned amazement at the figure leaning over me, his features hidden by the deep hood of his sweatshirt. For the first time, my heart chilled. I'd assumed he was an employee coming in to work, or a guest out for an early run. That he'd apologize for bumping into me and we'd laugh and go our separate ways.

He said nothing, only loomed over me, face shadowed, radiating menace.

My heels kicked at the grass, hands scrabbling to pull me backward, away from this sudden threat. The man in the sweatshirt hesitated, his hands flexing on the box he held before whirling and racing around the corner, exactly where I'd been headed. He disappeared from sight, and I let out a breath of relief.

I should have collected what was left of my treats and gone back to the bakery to try again another time. Or brought what I could salvage to the front desk and dropped it off there.

I should have done anything other than follow the stranger with the box.

I don't know why I did, why I was so sure he was up to no good, or what I thought I could do about it.

I followed anyway. My life had given me good instincts for people who were up to no good. I didn't always listen—and wasn't *that* biting me in the ass these days—but when I did, I was usually right.

I rounded the corner of The Inn and found the man in the sweatshirt leaning over a metal square protruding from the side of the building. It looked like an HVAC vent or an air intake. He was opening the box, tilting it toward the vent as if getting ready to dump something inside. What the hell?

I fumbled for my phone. My pockets were empty. Crap, I must have dropped it when I'd hit the ground. That would have been the time to run, to head for the front desk and a working phone.

Running would have been smart. Smart, but too slow. If I ran, he'd be gone by the time I got the police on the phone, and it would be too late to stop whatever he was doing with that box.

He hadn't seen me. I still had time to get away. Instead, I called out, "Hey! Do you work for The Inn? I'm calling security!"

Stupid, I know. Alone in the dark with a stranger I'd already figured out was up to no good, and instead of going for help, I shouted at him.

Not my best move.

Not my best move, but it worked.

The cardboard box fell from his hands. In the growing light of the rising sun, I watched in horror as it spilled to the ground, a flood of shiny black cockroaches disappearing into the grass. Oh, gross.

Had he been about to dump those into the air intake at The Inn? The ramifications hit me in a split second. I ran an establishment that served food and beverages. I knew exactly how

4

bad a flood of cockroaches would be. On top of that, the sheer size of The Inn would make it nearly impossible to root them all out.

Plus, cockroaches. Yuck.

All of that hit me in a flash just before I turned to run. Where, I didn't know. He was between me and the fastest route to the front desk and a phone. I took off anyway. Anywhere was better than alone in the dark with a pissed off stranger.

I turned on my heel to bolt. I made it three whole steps before a hand closed over the back of my shirt, yanking me down to the ground. I landed hard, the breath whooshing from my lungs. The man in the sweatshirt was on me a second later, his arm raised, hand balled into a fist.

If he was thinking straight, he would have run. I guess that made two of us who weren't thinking. I twisted, trying to throw off his weight, but he held me down easily, muttering, "Dumb, nosy bitch fuckin' gettin' in my way."

He swung his fist, catching me on the cheekbone. Pain exploded, my head flying to the side, wrenching my neck. I'd never been hit in the face before. It hurt. A lot.

He swung again, his fist connecting. A moan slipped out as I struggled to raise my arms to protect my face, unable to knock him off of me.

I'm not tiny, about average size and weight, but he was a lot bigger. He hit me again, this time his fist bouncing off the arm I'd managed to pull free. I screamed with everything I had, knowing sound was my only defense.

Sucking in air for another scream, I braced for the next punch and rolled as his weight was gone, dragged off of me.

I heard a low, "What the fuck?"

I knew that voice. I stopped screaming and sagged into the damp grass, lungs heaving as I tried to catch my breath. A heavy fist struck flesh with a thud, followed by a pathetic moan.

5

Opening my eyes, I watched as Royal Sawyer pinned my assailant to the ground, one knee in the man's back, and wrenched both of the man's arms behind him.

"Daisy?" Royal asked, shooting a quick glance my way. "Daisy Hutchins? Are you okay?"

"I think so," I said slowly. "I was coming by to leave some cookies—Hope said I should drop them off with my card—and I couldn't find the door and I saw him. He—"

"Slow down, Daisy. Catch your breath for a second." His voice was low and soothing. Strong. I lay back in the grass, letting the absolute authority in his tone chase off my fears. No one was going to get through Royal. Everything was okay.

"Hope said you'd be by," he went on. "Why were you back here? Who is this guy?"

I took a deep breath, gathering my thoughts together, and sat up. "I thought I should come in through the staff entrance. I was going to leave the basket so someone could deliver it to your offices before you got in, but it was dark and I realized I didn't know exactly where the door was. I guess I was wandering a little, and then I saw that guy. Oh, God, I think he was trying to dump cockroaches into your air intake system. He was over there—"

I pointed at the spilled box on the ground by the HVAC equipment outside the building.

Royal swore under his breath. "Can you get up? Could you do me a favor?"

I nodded, still trying to get my bearings and, to be honest, a little intimidated by Royal Sawyer. As first meetings go, this wasn't the one I would have chosen.

I was hoping he'd get my beautifully presented basket of treats along with the brochure and proposal I'd tucked into the basket and ask me to The Inn for a meeting. I would have shown up dressed like the businesswoman I was, not in a flour-streaked t-shirt with my hair in a messy poof. I definitely would not have been covered in grass stains with a rapidly swelling cheek. Damn.

We'd never officially met, but I knew who Royal was. We'd both grown up in Sawyers Bend. We knew who everybody was. That's a small town for you. I'm Daisy Hutchins, granddaughter of Eleanor Hutchins, the owner of Sweetheart Bakery. My amazing baked goods aside, I wasn't anyone of importance.

He was Royal Sawyer, one of *the* Sawyers of Sawyers Bend. As his name indicated, around here he was practically a prince. Not that he sat around polishing the crown jewels. He and his brother Tenn ran The Inn at Sawyers Bend, and given the way it had taken off in the last decade, they did a hell of a job at it.

Maybe he wasn't actual royalty, but he was still a Sawyer. Wealthy, connected, and did I mention hot? There wasn't a single ugly Sawyer in the whole family.

Their father had been a bastard, but a handsome one, and he'd chosen his wives—according to Grams—mainly based on looks. He hadn't been able to hold on to any of his women for long, but they sure had made some pretty children.

Not that I spent a lot of time ogling male Sawyers. I was too busy for that.

If I did, I would have chosen Royal. Thick, wavy, dark hair he wore a little too long. Deep blue eyes. Broad shoulders with a lean, powerful build. A smile that was all dangerous charm, one he used easily and often.

I was kind of shocked he knew my name. I'll admit I was a little lightheaded, not just from getting punched in the face but from the focus in those blue, blue eyes narrowed directly on me.

7

Chapter Two

DAISY

"DAISY? YOU SURE YOU'RE OKAY?"

"I'm fine, really." I got to my feet, relieved my head stayed clear.

What a dork. There I was, sitting on my butt in the wet grass mooning over Royal Sawyer when there were more important problems at hand. Like the man in the sweatshirt and the cockroaches in that box.

"Can you grab my phone?" Royal asked, those sharp eyes locked on my face, narrowing as they took in the swelling of my cheek.

I nodded and spotted the phone strapped to his arm, the earbuds in his ears. Taking in his grass-stained running shoes and the athletic shorts currently stretched across his muscled thighs... *Pay attention, Daisy. Eyes off his legs.* Not easy with legs like that.

Royal must have been out for an early run, just like I'd thought the man in the sweatshirt was when I'd first seen him. I guess that explained how Royal kept that lean, strong body when he spent most of his day behind a desk.

Trying not to notice the clean, salty scent of him, I leaned in and unstrapped his phone from his arm. I definitely did not notice the bunch of his bicep under my fingers. Not at all.

"Would you pull up West in the contacts and give him a call, tell him we need him over here?"

I angled the phone at Royal's face to unlock the screen and found West in the list of favorites. Weston Garfield was the police chief of Sawyers Bend and apparently a friend of Royal's. With a few words, he was on his way.

"Do you want me to call Tenn?"

"If you don't mind," he drawled. The comment could have been sarcastic or impatient, but the smile curving his lips told me it was neither. How could he be smiling when he had sweatshirt guy pinned on the ground and that box a few feet away?

The box. Tenn answered, and I filled him in as I crossed the grass to the box, still laying where he'd dropped it, mostly on its side. As I'd hoped, a few cockroaches still scrabbled at the bottom. Gingerly, I nudged it upright to keep them inside.

I moved to hand Royal back his phone, then shoved it in my pocket when he shook his head.

"Hang on to that for now, would you? Do you have a few minutes before you have to get back to the bakery? West is going to want to take your statement."

"I'm good for now. I just have to find my phone and text Grams. J.T. is working today, so he can help her out." The guy who'd hit me was lying motionless under Royal, his chest jerking as he sucked in breath. "Why would he want to dump cockroaches into your air vent? Is he trying to get you shut down?"

"That's a good question," Royal said conversationally. "I'm sure we're going to have all sorts of questions for this guy. I'd like to know if this is the first time he's tried something like this. And if it was his idea or if he's working for someone else. But West is going to have plenty of time to ask while he's rotting in jail."

"Fuck you," came from the face shoved in the grass.

"Creative. I expected better from someone who was about to dump roaches into the HVAC."

Tennessee Sawyer came around the corner of the building, almost a carbon copy of his brother, except Royal's hair was more of an auburn brown and Tenn's was pure espresso. Tenn had the same build as Royal, the same perfect Sawyer bone structure, but he'd never done it for me the way Royal did.

Then again, Hutchins women were always a sucker for a charming smile. It was our downfall, generations deep. Royal's was so full of charm it was lethal. Tenn had a nice smile too, but he was straightforward. Serious. Royal had the kind of grin that had a girl out of her panties before she could think twice.

"What the hell is going on?" Tenn demanded, his brow furrowed with concern. "Daisy, are you okay? Hope said you'd bring some samples by, but it's barely dawn."

I gave an embarrassed shrug. "I'm up early to start the baking. I knew the kitchens would be open and I wanted to have the basket delivered before you both got to the office—"

All of a sudden, I remembered the basket of cookies and brownies I'd baked early that morning and had painstakingly wrapped in the ribboned packaging I'd decided on for The Inn, now scattered all over the side lawn along with my phone.

Before I called Grams to seriously underplay the reason for my delay, I had to find my phone.

I stood and looked around, catching sight of my basket by the corner of the building, upside down on the grass, the light catching the cellophane-wrapped treats that had spilled every-where. Dammit.

I tried not to think about my tired fingers tying all those ribbons into bows only hours before. I was supposed to make a good impression. To wow them with my delicious treats pre-sented so temptingly in their pretty basket with ribbons that matched The Inn's logo.

Instead, everything was scattered all over the grass. The brownies had probably held up, but the cookies would be a crumpled mess.

"One second," I said to Royal and Tenn. "I dropped every-thing when he ran into me. I have to find my phone."

I went to my knees in the wet grass, turning the basket upright and filling it with as many packages of cookies and brownies as I could find. Royal and Tenn spoke quietly amongst themselves. When I glanced up, I found Royal's eyes fixed on me despite his squirming captive.

I looked away, focusing on my task, surrounded by the disas-ter of my latest bright idea, the pain in my swelling cheek a tight throb. I wished I could disappear. I wished I'd never come here. If I were playing that game, I wished I'd done a lot of things differently.

I finally found my phone. I chickened out and sent Grams a quick text instead of calling.

Still at The Inn. Can you open without me?

She answered almost immediately.

On it, baby girl. See you when we see you.

Grams thought I was working too hard. If only she knew. Grams still lived in the house where I'd grown up. A few blocks from Main Street, it was walking distance to the bakery. I, on the other hand, lived in a small apartment above the bakery which made it easy to hide the long hours I'd been putting in.

Then again, I might be fooling myself. It was never easy to put one over on Eleanor Hutchins. She might be my grandmother, but she was still sharp as a tack. The second she saw my cheek, there'd be hell to pay. But that was a problem for later.

First, I worked on reassembling the cookies and brownies in the basket. With so many broken cookies it would never look as nice as it had when I'd packed it, but it would do. I'd take the broken cookies back to the bakery and put them to use in something else.

Rising slowly, my muscles aching in protest and my cheek throbbing, I walked back to where Royal and Tenn waited with our captive.

Royal's eyes were still locked on me, his charming grin nowhere in sight. Tenn only had eyes for the basket on my arm.

"That looks fantastic. You were going to leave that in our offices so the first thing we saw was that basket of treats?"

I swallowed hard and nodded. At the time, it had seemed like a good idea. Now I was wondering if it was just foolish.

"Pass over one of those broken cookies. I can't wait until I get into the office."

Mutely, I did as ordered, some of my embarrassment fading as Tenn's eyes rolled in pleasure at the first taste of one of my chocolate chip cookies.

"Why don't you go up to the offices with Royal and you two can talk about your proposal while you wait for West to take your statement? You need to get some ice on that cheek."

"You ready to take this asshole?" Royal asked, his grip tightening on sweatshirt guy's wrists, wrenching them up and driving the man's face into the grass.

"Let's go," Tenn agreed, and seamlessly, they switched places. Sweatshirt guy tried to roll as Royal stood, but he wasn't fast enough.

Once Tenn had him secure, Royal turned to me and held out a hand. "Let's get some ice on that cheek. Breakfast? Coffee?"

A little dizzy from the quick shift, I slid my hand in his and with the other gave him his phone. He had it at his ear a moment later. "Two Blue Ridge breakfasts in my office and a bag of ice." A raised eyebrow at me. "Eggs scrambled? Fried? Regular coffee, or do you want a cappuccino or latte?"

Dazed, I clutched my basket. "Scrambled and cappuccino, please."

Royal relayed my order.

"I could have waited with Tenn," I said. "You don't have to—"

"You need ice on that cheek. Considering you got beat up while trying to save The Inn from a cockroach infestation that would have been a monumental pain in the ass, the least I owe you is breakfast."

I couldn't argue with that. I kept an immaculate kitchen, but every time the health inspector stopped by my stomach was still in knots. So many details, so many things that were easy to forget. No one wanted a bad sanitation score hanging in their window.

I could have stayed with Tenn and sweatshirt guy to wait for West. I probably should have, but Royal's fingers were warm around mine. Strong. I let him lead me through the terrace doors and the lobby to the elevator, noting that he held each door, careful to make room for my somewhat rumpled basket of treats.

The executive offices were on the third floor, quiet and dark. It looked like Royal and Tenn's assistant wasn't in yet. Royal flipped on lights as we passed through the outer office, everything decorated with the same rustic elegance that dominated the rest of The Inn. The wide, tall windows in Royal's office looked out over the gardens. I peeked down to see West hauling sweatshirt guy to his feet, already cuffed.

"West is here," I said, needlessly.

Royal gave a quick glance outside before taking the basket from my arm and setting it on his desk. Using the light streaming in from the window, he tilted my chin and studied my swollen cheek. His thumb grazed my face so lightly it didn't hurt but sent a faint pulse of energy shimmering across my skin.

"He got you good, didn't he?" Royal asked, his voice tight. Gently changing the angle of my face, he murmured, "How many times did he hit you?"

"Twice."

Royal's thumb skimmed over my lower lip, his blue eyes dark, liquid with some emotion I couldn't define. Nerves skittering through me, I stepped away. "I'm okay."

"It could have been a lot worse. Why did you go after him? You could have just called West. You should have run inside. I don't know how far he was willing to go, but you could have been hurt, Daisy."

"I don't know why I went after him," I admitted. "I couldn't call West. I dropped my phone when he bumped into me. And he just—something about him was wrong. Then I saw him with the box at the air vent. I didn't know what was in it, but I knew it wasn't good. I just—I didn't think."

Royal shoved his hands in his pockets, his lips quirking into a facsimile of his charming grin. It didn't reach his eyes. "Good thing I came along, huh?"

"Very good thing."

Turning his gaze to the basket on his desk, Royal gestured to the seat opposite his own. "This your proposal?" He teased out the envelope I'd tucked beneath the brownies.

My throat suddenly dry, I nodded.

"Sit, take a load off while we wait for ice and breakfast. You're here, so we might as well do this now."

I tried not to fidget as he opened the envelope and scanned

my suggestions and cost projections for bringing a little bit of Sweetheart Bakery to The Inn at Sawyers Bend.

While he was reading, a sharp double knock sounded on the door. Without waiting for an answer, it swung open and a uniformed waiter rolled in a table, filling the room with the scent of coffee, sausage, and buttery biscuits. My stomach rumbled.

Royal looked up. "You can set it up on the desk, and please, give the ice pack to Ms. Hutchins." He winked at me and went back to reading.

Chapter Three

DAISY

I WANTED THAT CAPPUCCINO LIKE I WANTED MY NEXT
breath, but my cheek felt like it was the size
of a basketball and the whole side of my face
throbbed. I went for the ice first, carefully wrapped in a linen
napkin, and held it to my face, my eyes closing in relief at the
cool burn.

Wanting to have my cake and eat it too, I shifted the ice pack
enough to make room for a sip of coffee. Bliss. I hadn't had any
coffee since four o'clock that morning. I was way overdue for
more caffeine.

Royal set down my proposal and lifted the lids off our breakfasts. "I like how you coordinated your branding with The Inn's.
Looks good."

It did look good. The Inn's colors were dark red with accents
of navy and hints of gold. Years ago, when Grams had designed

the first logo for Sweetheart Bakery, she'd chosen a deep, rich pink, not far from the deep red The Inn used.

For my sample packets, I'd gone with navy ribbons paired with those of the same deep pink we used at the bakery and had added navy and gold accents to the Sweetheart Bakery logo on the sticker. It was still very much branded to Sweetheart Bakery but would fit right in at The Inn's gift shop.

"Thanks. I laid out some projections, and of course, we'll work with whatever you'd prefer, but I thought the third proposal would be the best fit."

"Supplying Sweetheart goods in our welcome baskets for suites and cottages as well as stocking a selection in the gift shop," he confirmed.

I nodded. "That's not a big commitment on your end and you gives you a chance to see how it goes. I'd also supply coupons for your regular welcome packets as well as the baskets to give your guests a discount at the bakery."

"We'd include those anyway. We try to promote local businesses as much as we can. I like proposal number three, but I'd prefer to do it on consignment rather than buying outright."

Nerves tickled my stomach. I love running my own business, but these kinds of negotiations were not my favorite thing. I'd known they might ask to put the arrangement on consignment.

That didn't work for me. First of all, the accounting would be way too time-consuming, and second, I couldn't afford to front the materials in the hopes I'd get paid for them eventually. Not right now. I needed to get paid when I dropped off my stock, not when they eventually sold.

"These are perishable goods, and on the low end of the price range. I don't think consignment makes sense. If you're worried they won't sell I'd rather start with smaller, more frequent orders and be paid when you receive delivery, not later."

"Is this a deal-breaker?" Royal sat back in his chair, folding his hands over his flat stomach.

"I think it has to be, yes." I wished I sounded more confident and authoritative. Wished I'd said *Yes, absolutely,* and wasn't terrified he was going to turn me down.

A regular order from The Inn wasn't going to change my life. It certainly wasn't going to solve my cash flow problem. Not on its own. But every little bit counted, and placement in The Inn's gift shop was added exposure to the many tourists who flowed through The Inn at Sawyers Bend.

The Inn was a local landmark, and a lot of people who couldn't afford to stay there still visited the restaurant, gift shop, and bar. They might not buy one of my treats at The Inn, but they'd see the package and recognize my sign when they walked through town.

My free hand curled into a fist in my lap, betraying my nerves. I forced my fingers to uncurl and reached for the cappuccino, pretending this was all no big deal. Like I regularly had breakfast with Royal Sawyer in his office at dawn. Sure, and I'd have tea with the Queen of England later in the day.

Nothing about this was normal.

Without saying anything, Royal unwrapped one of the brownies in the basket I'd set on his desk. Salted caramel. My favorite. He broke off the corner and popped it in his mouth, closing his eyes as chocolate and caramel melted across his tongue, the sharp bite of sea salt making the sugar sweeter. When he opened his eyes, he took a sip of coffee, swallowed, and shook his head.

"I can't say no to those brownies. And we owe you one. Let's do it, starting with orders twice a week. I'll expect you to coordinate with the gift shop to make sure you're keeping us stocked and adjust that timing as needed."

"I don't want you to say yes because you think you owe me," I said as every instinct for self-preservation urged me to shut the hell up. It didn't matter why he said yes, it only mattered that he did. If my foolish recklessness had helped me get their business, then everything had worked out for the best.

I couldn't help myself. My pride was stronger than that sense of self-preservation.

Royal flashed a grin that had me pressing my knees together, and this time that grin reached all the way to his deep blue eyes.

"I would have said yes anyway, but I would have pushed harder on the consignment thing. What you did this morning was incredibly foolhardy. It was also very brave. Sweetheart Bakery is a lot smaller than The Inn, but we both know what would have happened if that guy had managed to dump all those cockroaches into the building. You saved us a lot of trouble. I understand you don't want us to owe you, but the fact is that we do. And your proposal is a good one. It's a win-win. So, smile and say, *Thank you, Mr. Sawyer,* and finish your breakfast."

He winked at me. *'Thank you, Mr. Sawyer.'* I couldn't help the quirk of my mouth. I was impervious to flirting by handsome men. The wink, that smile—none of it would work on me. I absolutely did not smile back. This was business. That was all.

Dutifully, I said, "Thank you, Royal," deliberately using his first name to prove he didn't intimidate me.

Never mind that he did. A lot. Far more than I wanted to admit. Something about Royal Sawyer left me off-center. Restless.

To cover my discomfort, I took another sip of coffee, then set the ice back on the tray and picked up my fork. My last meal had been a long time ago, and The Inn's kitchen was one of the best in town.

Cinnamon-scented stuffed French toast, fluffy biscuits, scrambled eggs, and crispy links of local sausage. No way was I letting this go to waste. Royal took my cue and dug into his own breakfast. West didn't knock on the door until we were almost finished.

Sawyers Bend was a little busier than your average small town, given all the tourists that moved in and out on a regular basis, but Weston Garfield didn't typically see a lot of crime. That had changed since Royal's father died two months before.

Prentice Sawyer had been shot and killed in the family mansion. The second oldest son, Ford, was in jail for his murder. And Royal's black sheep of an older brother, Griffen, had inherited everything. Since then, the town of Sawyers Bend had skidded off the rails.

According to Hope—Griffen's new wife and one of my best friends—someone had tried to kill Griffen twice, finally breaking into Heartstone Manor with a gun, intent on taking out as many Sawyers as he could.

Added to the rumors that there'd been some trouble at The Inn, I was betting West Garfield had been a busy man.

He greeted Royal like an old friend and took the seat beside mine. Before he got started, he eyed the basket of cookies and brownies. "I know you're not gonna hoard all those for yourselves."

With a shake of his head, Royal passed over a packet with a crumpled cookie and one holding a brownie. West opened the cookie and fished out a piece. "It's a good thing you stay out of trouble, Daisy. I've never been susceptible to bribes, but these cookies might do it."

He sat back in the chair, his eyes fastened to my cheek. I couldn't see what it looked like, but it throbbed, and my skin felt stretched tight. Swollen. It was a good thing I had Grams and J.T. to work the front counter at Sweetheart. I didn't need customers seeing me like this.

"We have your early-morning visitor locked up. Unsurprisingly, he's not talking. He do that to you, Daisy?"

"It was dark, and I was trying to find the staff entrance—"
I ran West through the events of that morning. When it was
happening, it seemed like it took forever. In retelling it to West,
I realized only a few minutes had passed from the moment I
bumped into sweatshirt guy to Royal pulling him off of me and
pinning him to the ground.

West took careful notes, his face impassive, eyes serious. "Is
that everything?"

"That's it," I confirmed and drained the last sip of my
cappuccino.

West tapped his pen on his notebook before standing.
"What you did was very brave, Daisy. I know Royal and Tenn
appreciate you stopping him before he could cause them more
trouble, but the next time you run into a stranger in the dark
who's intent on committing a crime, you don't confront them.
You run the hell away. Understand?"

I hung my head. It wasn't that I didn't understand. I did. I
agreed with West. He was absolutely right.

And given the chance, I would have done the same thing all
over again.

I was only somewhat stupid, so I didn't tell West that.
Instead, I raised my head and said as contritely as I could
manage, "I understand."

West nodded. "If you think of anything else, let me know. I'll
talk to you later, Royal." He left, closing the door behind him.

Royal looked at me. "You just lied to the police chief, didn't
you?"

I shrugged a shoulder. "Maybe. If I'd had my phone, I would
have called for help." I thought about the man in the sweatshirt
holding that box up to the air intake vent, and I shook my head.
"No, I wouldn't. I mean, I would have called, but I also would
have tried to stop him. I'm not saying it was the smart thing to
do—"

"—but it was the right thing to do," Royal finished for me.

"It was the only thing to do."

I knew better than anyone that sometimes choices weren't about right and wrong.

Sometimes choices were about what you could live with.

I'd be living with this swollen cheek for a while, but if The Inn had to shut down because of a cockroach infestation all of us would suffer. There were other places to stay in Sawyers Bend, but none attracted high profile guests with money to spend like The Inn at Sawyers Bend.

Royal contemplated me, his gaze thoughtful as he took another bite of brownie. "What are your plans tonight?"

"What?" I asked, not following his abrupt change in topic.

"Tonight. What are your plans?"

"Um, dinner with my grandmother and J.T. and early to bed since I have to get up at four." It wasn't sexy or exciting, but that was my life.

"Have dinner with me instead," Royal ordered with a flash of that charming grin. The spark of light in his deep blue eyes would have brought me to my knees if I hadn't already been sitting.

My long-neglected hormones shouted YES!

My mouth opened, and instead, I asked, "Why?"

Royal's charming grin morphed into genuine amusement. "Because you're brave. And smart. And very, very pretty."

My jaw didn't exactly drop, but it was close. *Very, very pretty?* I didn't have to look down to see the grass stains on my jeans, the flour smeared across my shirt, and my cherry-cola curls falling out of the messy poof I'd stuck them in well before dawn.

At my best, I could pull off pretty. I had good genes to work with, after all. But after hours spent in the kitchen plus a fist-fight? No way.

I rolled my eyes. "I don't mix business with pleasure," I said, primly.

"Neither do I, usually," Royal countered.

I rolled my eyes again. "Right. You never date locals, only hook up with hot tourists who come through the hotel. If that isn't mixing business with pleasure—"

Royal's smile slipped. "Not the same thing. Are you saying you don't want to have dinner with me?"

I ignored his question. "Anyway, I have a boyfriend," I said.

Royal shook his head. "No, you don't."

"I do," I insisted.

"Who?" he demanded.

"J.T. Everybody knows that," I said. It was mostly true. Kind of.

Royal leaned back in his chair again, crossing his arms over his chest and raising one eyebrow. "And that's not mixing business with pleasure? He works for you, doesn't he? In fact, if you look at it that way, it's a harassment case waiting to happen."

I laughed at the thought. "J.T.'s been my best friend since middle school. He's not going to sue me for harassment." Realizing that made us seem less like the romance of the century, I looked away. "I appreciate the invitation. I'm flattered. But I have a boyfriend and I'm not interested."

"Lying again, Daisy?"

The heat that hit my cheeks had me standing. "Your first order will be delivered tomorrow. I'll include the invoice. It's been a pleasure doing business with you."

Royal stood and followed me out, his fingertips landing lightly on my lower back as he guided me through the door. "You sure about dinner tonight?"

"I told you, I'm not interested."

Royal's laugh followed me into the empty reception area, all the way to the elevator.

"If you say so. I'll be seeing you around, Miss Daisy."
I very much doubted that.
And I was very, very wrong.

Chapter Four

DAISY

"DAZE, YOU'VE GOT A DELIVERY." I KNEW THAT SING-song tone in J.T.'s voice. I finished adding the last flower petal on the cookie I was decorating and set the bag of icing down, bracing my hands on my lower back and stretching. I love icing cookies, but it's murder on the back.

A delivery? A delivery shouldn't have come to the front. My cheek felt better than it had the day before, but it looked awful. I wasn't leaving the kitchen. If J.T. wanted something, he'd have to come to me.

He did, pushing through the swinging double doors from the front of the shop. I looked up, expecting to see his handsome and well-loved face. Instead, an extravagant bouquet of flowers filled the doorway, so big it blocked most of my view of J.T.

"What did you do to deserve these?" he asked, crossing the kitchen to set the flowers on the small desk in the corner, away from the food prep areas. "I don't even want to guess what they must have cost."

Before I could stop him, he plucked the card from the front of the arrangement and opened it.

"Hey!" I lunged across the kitchen, but I was too slow. The door from the shop opened behind me just in time for Grams to hear.

"You're my hero, Daisy Hutchins. Don't think I'm giving up on dinner. R."

J.T. raised one dark eyebrow at me, but Grams said what he was thinking. "Dinner?"

I snatched the card from J.T.'s hand, trying to tamp down my thrill at the sight of Royal's dark, angular slashes of writing. I'd assumed his spontaneous invitation to dinner had been a whim. I took in the bouquet. Lilies, roses, and a few vibrant gerbera daisies in a blown glass vase I knew hadn't come from the flower shop.

J.T. was right, I didn't want to guess what they must have cost either. I only knew it was a lot.

"Dinner?" Grams prompted again, a gleam in her eye. Dammit. I knew that gleam.

"It's nothing. He's just... He doesn't mean it. He's Royal Sawyer." They both continued to stare at me, expectant. "You guys, he doesn't really want to go out with me. He's *Royal Sawyer*," I reminded them again.

Grams raised an eyebrow. J.T. shook his head at me. "Exactly. He's Royal Fucking Sawyer. I assume your eyes are still working. Let him take you to dinner. At the worst, it's a free meal, and Royal Sawyer is not gonna take you out for a bad meal."

"I'm not interested in being Royal Sawyer's piece of the week. He's nice to look at, sure. And he's grateful I helped them out with the thing the other day. He feels bad I got socked in the face. That's all. It's a small town and tourist season hasn't really kicked in yet. He's probably bored."

J.T.'s eyebrow was still raised. "That's a lot of protests there, Daze. You sure you're not interested?"

"I told him I have a boyfriend."

J.T. shook his head. "You know you don't have to—"

I cut him off. "That's not the point. I'm not going out with Royal Sawyer." I looked to Grams, waiting for her to back up J.T. and try to badger me into going out with Royal. She just looked from me to J.T. to the flowers and shook her head.

"You're wasting your life buried in the kitchen here, baby girl. You don't have to marry the boy, but I don't see the harm in letting him buy you a meal as a thanks for saving his bacon."

"I already got a thank-you. J.T. delivered the first order to The Inn, and they paid the invoice before lunch. That's all the thanks I need."

Grams shook her head again. I knew better than to think that meant she was dropping the subject. Grams knew how to bide her time. She also believed in letting people go their own way, so it could be she really was prepared to drop it. She'd speak her piece when she decided to and not a moment sooner.

In the meantime, I had to focus on my own problems, none of which had anything to do with Royal Sawyer.

"You should at least thank him for the flowers. That's just good manners," Grams added.

I should have known Grams couldn't let it go without getting the last word. Fine. She was right. It was a beautiful arrangement that required thanks. Later. I had special orders to fill, and more business to drum up before I could take a break.

A knock landed on the back door of the kitchen. Still lingering by the bouquet, J.T. was closest, and he moved to swing the door open. The slight figure in the doorway took me by surprise.

"Mom," I said, my heart giving a leap of hope.

If she was here, then maybe—

A smile crossed her face before her eyes skittered from mine to Grams.

And maybe not.

As always where my parents were concerned, that leap of hope flipped into a dive.

"Is Dad with you?" I asked carefully. J.T. and Grams waited along with me for my mother's response.

"Oh, he'll be along," she said vaguely. "He had some business to wrap up. I thought I'd come ahead and see if y'all needed any help in the bakery."

As she always had, Grams stepped into the void. "It's good to have you back, honey." She crossed the room and pulled my mom into a tight hug, rocking Sheree's form against her taller, broader one. "You have good timing. J.T. has a full load of classes this spring—he started in the culinary program at Tech—and we could use some help during the week. It's good to see your beautiful face."

Grams had a bottomless well of love for Sheree Hutchins. According to Grams, my father, her son, had shown up almost thirty years before with Sheree in tow, presenting her as his new wife and asking Grams to take them in after Sheree's own parents had cut her off for dropping out of college to marry a "shiftless white boy."

I'd never met my maternal grandparents, and I didn't want to, given the way they'd treated my mother, but after all these years, I had to admit—they might have had a point.

My father was the king of charming smiles. If he could hold onto a dollar we would've had a million of them because he could talk anyone into anything. People talk about being able to sell ice to Eskimos, but my daddy could sell an Eskimo the igloo he'd just built at a 50% markup.

He could have been a great salesman, but a loose acquaintance with the truth put him more on the end of a con artist. Combined with his need to spend every penny he got his hands on... Well, there's a reason my Grams raised me.

My dad liked to tease that I had no sense of adventure, but from what I'd seen, his *sense of adventure* had gotten my mom a lifetime of empty cupboards and middle-of-the-night moves when they couldn't make rent. Or worse. I'd take my stable, quiet life with Grams and the bakery any day.

My mother pulled away from Grams and crossed to me, stopping short when she took in my swollen cheek. "Oh, baby, what happened? Are you okay?"

"It's nothing, Mom. Just an accident." I wrapped my arms around her and held tight. She wasn't perfect, but she was my mom. Despite everything else, we loved each other. I rocked her back and forth, smelling the cocoa butter she used on her skin mixed with the vanilla scent she'd always worn. When I was a child I'd cried when I made cookies with Grams, the smell reminding me of my often-absent mother. Now it just made me smile. She was who she was. And so was I.

So alike on the outside and so different underneath. We had the same tawny skin. The same warm brown eyes. I'd always be grateful I'd inherited her full lips and long lashes. There the similarities ended.

My mother wore her dark brown hair straight to her shoulders. No matter how tight money was, she always managed to look classy and neatly put together. I could do classy and neat if I wanted, but I was more like Grams. I didn't go for her hippie style, but you'd find me in a T-shirt and cut-off jeans far more often than in a twin-set and slacks.

I got my tight curls from my mother, but I wore them chin length and natural, except for the color. Lately, I'd been playing with color, so even there our hair was different. After an unfortunate mistake with yellow, and another with orange—my bright idea of going around the color wheel with hair dye—I'd settled on a shade of cherry-cola with hints of hot pink. It was wild, but every time I looked in the mirror, it looked like me.

My mom toyed with a hot pink curl springing from the poof on top of my head. "I like the color, baby. It suits you. I missed my gorgeous girl." She cupped my face in her hands, gentle on my swollen cheek, and kissed my forehead.

Pressing my cheek to hers, I murmured, "I missed you too, Mom."

I meant it. I had missed my mom.

I always missed my mom, even when she was right in front of me.

How could I not when she always, *always* picked him first.

Straightening, she looked around and spotted the bouquet on my desk. "Flowers? Wow, who are those from?" She looked at J.T., and he shook his head with a wry grin.

"Those are a little out of my budget, Sheree. Daisy got those from Royal Sawyer."

I shot J.T. a look. *Thanks for nothing*, my eyes said. His grin widened and he shrugged.

My mother's face fell. "You're not getting mixed up with the Sawyers, are you Daisy? They're nothing but trouble for a girl like you."

I bit back the response that jumped to my lips. Like she could talk. She was married to Darren Hutchins, a man who defined trouble.

And what did she mean *for a girl like me*? Because I was half-black or because I wasn't rich? I didn't want to fight with her when she'd just come home, but something inside me couldn't let it go.

Royal had been nothing but kind to me. Just because his father had been known as an asshole didn't mean Royal was too.

"Royal isn't like that, Mom. I did him a favor, and he sent the flowers as a thank-you, that's all."

"What kind of favor?" she asked and raised a hand to touch the bruise on my cheek. I stepped back, shaking my head.

Chapter Five

DAISY

HIS WASN'T ROYAL'S FAULT. I WAS IN THE RIGHT PLACE at the right time and I kind of stopped a break-in. Sort of. It's complicated. And I'm not getting mixed up with Royal Sawyer. He's not my type." I hoped that would be the end of it.

J.T. looked at his feet and murmured, "Royal's everybody's type."

Before I could glare at J.T. he did what we'd been doing for each other since middle school and saved my ass. Winding his arm through Sheree's, he turned her to the double doors leading to the front of the shop. "Come on, Sheree, let's get you back in an apron. We have customers, and we can't let Daisy out front looking like that. She'd scare them all away, right? Anyway, she's got orders to fill."

Grams gave my arm a squeeze and followed them out.

We'd had a momentary lull when the flowers came, but it didn't last long. The sounds of a busy shop leaked through the doors as I worked. It was a good thing my mom had shown up when she did. I had my hands full filling orders, prepping for the next day, and trying to figure out my next target for expansion now that I'd locked down The Inn.

I couldn't forget scheming a way to get my mother alone. I needed to know about Dad, and I couldn't ask in front of Grams or J.T. They still didn't know what I'd done. With every day that passed, it got harder and harder to tell them.

Who was I kidding? It didn't get harder, it had started out impossible and only got worse.

I couldn't tell them. I wouldn't.

I was just going to fix the problem and then no one ever had to know. Every time I hit that train of thought my stomach squirmed with unease. Making excuses for my own bad judgment sounded too much like my father.

Not telling is a lie. I knew it, but every time I opened my mouth to come clean the words disappeared.

I had a plan. And maybe, just maybe, my dad would come through.

J.T. and I followed Mom and Grams back to the house after we closed. As J.T. said, "Might as well get a free meal if Grams is cooking."

I usually settled for a sandwich in the evenings, hastily assembled while I finished up the day's work, or did paperwork at my desk. I could use a decent meal, and I hadn't seen my mother in months. If I went to dinner at the house I might have the chance to catch her alone.

Sheree had learned a few things in her decades of marriage to my father. She proved elusive, always managing to be right next to Grams or J.T. every time I tried to catch her eye.

She knew I hadn't told them.

By the end of dinner, I found myself wanting to stomp my foot like a thwarted child. Sheree was always so sweet and kind and affectionate. It's true, she was all of those things. She also used them to hide her wily side.

I finally pinned her down while she washed dishes in the kitchen and J.T. had pulled Grams aside to ask her about something he was studying in class.

Grabbing a pot to dry, I tried to act casual. "Mom, how was Charlotte? Did you like it?"

"Charlotte?" she asked as if she'd never heard of the biggest city in North Carolina. Crap. That wasn't a good sign considering that's where Dad had said he'd find his big business opportunity.

Cautious, not wanting to spook her, I pressed a little harder. "Yeah, Charlotte. I thought that's where you guys were."

"Oh, of course. It was nice. I don't care for it in the winter, though, so we headed down to Tampa."

"Is, um, Dad planning on coming for a visit?"

My fingers curled into fists behind my back. I wanted to demand information. Considering the position they put me in, I didn't think a little straight talk was out of line. Not going to happen. My mother and straight talk were not acquaintances.

"He'll be along, I expect. He had some things to wrap up."

I swallowed hard and braced, keeping my voice low. "And the money, Mom? Do you know if Dad's planning on paying me back? He was supposed to have it by Christmas, remember?"

She refused to meet my eyes, scrubbing hard at the casserole dish in the sink. "Daisy, baby, you know I don't handle things like that. I'm sure your father has it under control. You ask him when he gets here, and he'll get this sorted out for you. Hasn't he always taken care of you?"

No, I wanted to shout. *He's never taken care of me. Grams took care of me and now the three of us have screwed her over.*

I didn't yell. Not just because it would draw Grams and J.T.'s attention. I didn't yell because this was all my fault and yelling at my mother wouldn't fix a thing. Her lower lip would start to tremble and her soft eyes would fill with tears.

She wasn't manipulative. Not really. It had taken me a long time to understand that she truly believed my father would make everything right despite the fact that he almost never did.

And honestly, who was the fool here? The woman who'd been happily married to him for over thirty years or the one who'd handed over her dreams and somehow expected this one time her dad wouldn't let her down?

Yeah, I knew the answer to that question. Sheree had chosen her delusion and lived happily inside it. I'd stepped out of my comfort zone for mine and reality had torn it away.

Still, I had a little hope. If Sheree was here, then my dad would probably show up eventually. I might go easy on my mom, but with my dad, I could take a more direct approach. There was always a chance he was going to come through.

Later that night, J.T. and I lay in the double bed in my small apartment over the bakery, my head on his T-shirt-covered shoulder, his fingers in my hair, tugging at my curls.

"What was up with you and your mom?" he asked. "She seemed extra squirrelly."

For just a second I was tempted to tell him everything, but I couldn't bring myself to admit how stupid I'd been, even to J.T.

"Nothing, I was just annoyed that she wouldn't tell me where Dad was."

"I thought they were in Charlotte."

"Apparently not. Mom decided she wanted to winter in Florida."

J.T. laughed, the rumble familiar under my ear. "Why didn't we think of that?"

"Right? Silly us working our asses off going to school and running a business when we could've been hanging out on the beach. Too bad we have all those bills to pay."

J.T. tugged a curl, drawing my eyes up to his. "You gonna tell me why you've been working so hard?"

I rolled into him, wrapping my arm around his chest as I tried to think of an answer he'd accept. I had nothing, so I went with option two—a counterattack. "Are you going to tell me where you're staying when you don't come home during the week?"

As expected, J.T. didn't answer. It hurt my heart that he didn't trust me enough to say. That after all these years he didn't know deep down that I loved him no matter what. I'd always loved him and I always would. There was nothing he could say or do that would change that. But I couldn't make him believe. I had to hope he'd tell me when he was ready.

At a stalemate, J.T. changed the subject. He tugged another curl before he said, "You should go out with Royal."

"Are you kidding me?" I pulled away and rose up on my elbows. "Going out with Royal is the last thing I should do. First of all, he's not serious. I don't have time to waste on some guy who just wants to get laid."

"Getting laid wouldn't be the worst thing in the world, Daze. I've heard it's nice."

"Like you don't know," I muttered under my breath.

"I'm starting to think you don't remember. It's been so long I think you've got cobwebs in your vag."

I poked him in the ribs right in his tickle spot, and he flinched away, laughing. "I'll have you know my vag is in excellent shape. I'm just taking a break from sex."

"Is that what you're calling it? A break? When was the last time you slept with anyone who wasn't me?"

I flopped on my back and stared at the ceiling. "I'm not going out with Royal," I repeated.

"Why not? Every single woman in town—and half the married ones—would kill for the chance to get a date with Royal Sawyer. He'll ask you again. Why not just say yes? What harm could it do?"

"He reminds me of my father," I admitted, turning my head to look at J.T. He looked back at me in confusion.

"What? How the hell does Royal remind you of your father?"

"It's all that charm. I bet he flashes that smile and gets whatever he wants. I don't have time for a man like that. One in my life is more than enough."

J.T. stared up at me, his eyes sad and serious. "Daze, I love you. You're the best woman I know aside from Grams, but sister, you have got some issues. Every charming man is not your dad. And if you look at Royal and see Darren Hutchins, I don't even know where to start with how wrong you are."

"You're one to talk about issues," I said lamely, feeling like we were thirteen again. "You don't even know Royal."

"I know he's not your father. And I know you should give him a chance. I also know you're not gonna listen because you're a stubborn bonehead."

I poked him in the ribs again, and when he was done giggling I settled back in, my head on his chest and my arm across his waist, the way we'd fallen asleep so many times over the years.

"I'm not the only stubborn bonehead around here," I murmured as I let my eyes slip shut.

J.T. didn't answer, just trailed his fingertips up and down my arm, keeping his secrets and holding me close as we both fell asleep.

Chapter Six

ROYAL

"So, we're agreed." Tenn tapped his pen on the resume between us.

I sat back, staring down at the cream linen page with the name *Forrest Powell* printed at the top. "I like him. He's got the experience, and he seems ready for a new challenge." I crossed my arms over my chest. "The real question is do you like him? Are you sure you're okay with this?"

Tenn dropped his pen on top of Forrest's resume and sat back. "I told you I'm good with it. You've been restless for a while. I get why you didn't want to work with Dad. Fuck, Ford was the only one who could put up with him."

"Griffen is different. He's not Dad."

Tenn barked out a laugh. "No shit. For one thing, he's not a raging asshole. He did skip out on us for fifteen years—"

"He didn't exactly 'skip out' on us."

I'd never forget the sight of my oldest brother walking down the long drive from Heartstone Manor, a worn backpack slung over his shoulder. It was the last we'd seen of him until the day we buried our father.

"I know Dad threw him out," Tenn said with a jerk of his shoulder. "But he could have come back."

"Maybe we should have tried to stop him from going in the first place."

There was no maybe about it. We should have stopped it. It was easy to forget that I'd been only seventeen at the time, Tenn and Avery barely fifteen, and the others just children. Except Ford. He'd already been working with Griffen and our father.

None of us had expected Ford to be the architect of Griffen's exile. Growing up, they'd been closer than brothers. The idea that one would betray the other was unthinkable.

Ford had done it. In one afternoon, Ford had gone from the second son to our father's right-hand man, complete with his ring on the finger of Griffen's fiancée. And Griffen had disappeared.

"It's ancient history," Tenn said, "and there's nothing we can do to change it. Griffen's home now. If he's willing to bring you into Sawyer Enterprises, you should do it. It's what you want. Anyway, we're better off with someone on the inside keeping an eye on him. Just in case he's looting the company or running it into the ground."

"Griffen isn't going to loot Sawyer Enterprises." I shifted in my seat, not liking the idea of spying on Griffen.

Tenn jerked his shoulder again and looked out the window. "You don't know that. And we don't really know him."

Tenn was right. We didn't really know him. But Griffen had been more than fair to all of us since he'd been back. We didn't have any reason to think he was up to no good.

Tenn knew me better than anyone on earth. We'd taken over The Inn at Sawyers Bend as a team and had spent the last decade making it the thriving resort it was today. I'd loved every minute of it, but lately, I'd found myself looking for more, for something new. I just didn't want to lose a brother in the process.

I should have known better. Tenn always had my back. "You'd have to pry me out of this place with a crowbar," he said, "but that doesn't mean you have to stay here with me. I like your plan. We'll hire this Forrest guy to take over for you, and you can split your time between The Inn and learning the ropes of Sawyer Enterprises with Griffen. If you like the way it's going we can always ease you out of The Inn completely if that's what you want. Or you can keep doing part-time on both. And if this guy doesn't work out, we'll find somebody else."

"I'm planning on mornings at The Inn and afternoons with Griffen and Hope, but I may need more flexibility, depending."

Tenn waved his hand, dismissing the problem. "We'll work it out, man. Seriously, we have enough to worry about without you stressing over the schedule."

He wasn't wrong. "Did West have anything to say about cockroach guy?"

"Nothing useful. It was exactly like the guy who shot at Griffen. He was paid, doesn't know who sent the money, yada yada."

Dumping cockroaches in our HVAC system was only the latest attempt at sabotage. So far, the problems had been more annoyance than catastrophes. Missing luggage, guest rooms broken into, room service orders diverted.

A few hundred cockroaches set loose in The Inn? That was far more than an annoyance. We had to figure out who was behind it before things got any worse.

A quick double-knock sounded on the door to my office. Tenn and I looked up to see our assistant hovering. This couldn't be good. Penny didn't hover. Penny threw problems at us like fastballs, usually followed by solutions of her own devising.

I wasn't surprised when she said apologetically, "The front desk called. Your aunt Ophelia has a... Complaint."

Tenn and I shared a look. He called, "Tails," pulling a quarter out of his pocket. I nodded in agreement. The quarter came up heads. Fuck. I guess that meant I was the lucky one who got to deal with Aunt Ophelia and our cousin, Bryce.

"Sorry, man." Tenn clapped me on the back with a grin. "We can table the rest of this until you get back."

Whatever it was, I was determined that it wouldn't take long. Ophelia and Bryce had been a time-suck since they'd shown up in Sawyers Bend fresh on the heels of my father's murder.

It might have been a simple matter to get rid of them, but nothing about my father's death was simple. He'd changed his will constantly, so often that none of us bothered to keep up with his latest machinations. Still, we'd all been shocked as hell when the family lawyer had proclaimed my oldest brother Griffen the sole heir of everything.

While he'd lived, my father had retained ownership of the various Sawyer businesses, The Inn at Sawyers Bend included. Tenn and I had been running the place for over a decade, but the company itself had been owned by our father. Despite our birth, Tenn and I were no more than salaried employees. That hadn't changed with our father's death.

No, that's not right. Everything had changed when Prentice died.

According to the terms of the will, my siblings and I had to move back into the family home, Heartstone Manor, and live there full-time for five years. If we did and Griffen was satisfied with our behavior, he'd release the contents of our trust funds at the end of the five years. Assuming there was anything left to release.

The will gave Griffen complete control over every penny we might inherit.

Griffen was as stuck as we were for the next five years. Only time would tell if he'd walk away at the end, free of his family, his pockets flush with the cash our father had left us.

If we didn't follow the terms set out in the will, our cousin Bryce would inherit everything, and we'd all be out on our asses.

It was an effective threat. Generations of Sawyers had made this corner of North Carolina their home, amassing vast wealth and standing in the community.

Bryce would drain the coffers dry in less than a year.

He was exactly the kind of asshole who'd buy a mega-yacht and a fleet of exotic cars. Who'd attract hangers-on and throw lavish parties until there wasn't a penny left.

I don't think a single one of us felt any loyalty to our father. He sure as hell hadn't shown any to us. The town was a different matter.

Sawyer Enterprises owned most of the real estate and businesses in the town of Sawyers Bend. If Bryce got his hands on the company, he'd take the town down with him. We weren't going to let that happen.

The family attorney claimed Bryce and Ophelia didn't know the details of the will or what they stood to gain from it. I wasn't sure I believed that. They'd missed the funeral but had shown up not long ago with a letter from our father, mailed days after his death, inviting them to move into Heartstone Manor. The letter didn't explicitly promise them anything beyond a roof over their heads, but it implied there would be a reward for sticking around.

For reasons no one understood, my father had let Heartstone Manor fall into a state of benign neglect over the last few years. While it made living there a pain in the ass until renovations were complete, it also gave us a solid excuse to keep Ophelia and Bryce from moving in. We'd stuck them in a suite at The Inn, deciding it was worth the cost if it meant they weren't at the breakfast table every morning.

It had seemed like a simple solution. In reality, it had proven anything but.

I left the elevator on the top floor and knocked on the door of their suite. Bryce swung it open and stood back, gesturing for me to enter. His mouth was twisted in a sulk, reminding me vividly of the toddler he'd been. If memory served, Bryce had two expressions in his arsenal, a smugly satisfied grin and an annoyed sulk. I'd take the sulk any day.

Bryce didn't say a word, just closed the door behind me and crossed his arms over his chest, glaring, his lower lip pooched out in an almost feminine pout.

He looked a lot like my younger siblings, Sterling and Braxton. Spun-gold hair and the Sawyer blue eyes, an athletic build and chiseled cheekbones. If Bryce had had any kind of work ethic he could have made a living as a model or a B-movie star.

As it was, he was a professional mooch. Considering the designer labels on his back and his current circumstances, he was doing a good job at it.

Aunt Ophelia fluttered into the room wrapped in a pink organza dressing gown even though it was close to noon, her frosted blonde hair in an elaborate twist and her makeup perfect. Diamonds winked at her ears and glittered on her fingers and wrists. She always had liked her diamonds.

"Royal, darling," she gushed, "I'm so glad you're here to straighten out this little mess."

"What can I do for you, Aunt Ophelia?" I asked, adding a flash of the grin that always seemed to work when I needed to get out of trouble.

"You can tell your staff that we have an open tab. So far, they haven't given us any trouble about ordering in meals, but when

I tried to order a bottle of champagne, they told me we hadn't been approved for alcohol over a hundred dollars a day. And you must fire that girl working in the gift shop. She insisted we provide payment when I tried to pick up a few things. I thought this was a family company. We are family, aren't we?"

"Of course, we're family," I assured her. "It didn't occur to me that you wouldn't know the company policy. No freebies. I'm afraid with a family as big as ours, that was the only sensible approach."

"I don't understand," Ophelia said, her perfectly manicured hand fluttering to cover her chest.

"I can see how you'd be confused," I said smoothly, "considering that you're staying here for free. But given my father's invitation for you to reside at Heartstone Manor and the lack of guest rooms there right now, it only seemed fair that we cover your room and board. But retail and the bar…" I gave a helpless shrug and another flash of my most persuasive smile. "It's not as if we have a bar or a gift shop at the Manor."

Considering some of the vintages available in the restaurant and bar as well as the designer gear we stocked in the gift shop, Ophelia could have run up thousands of dollars in room charges in minutes if we'd let her. I had no doubt that's exactly what she'd been planning to do.

"So, you're just going to starve us out?" Bryce challenged. Ophelia liked to play the ditzy ingénue, but Bryce was more demanding in his entitlement.

"I think I just specified that you wouldn't be starved. Room and board, as guaranteed by Prentice. The rest of your upkeep is on you."

I didn't bother with charm for Bryce. I had a small reserve of patience for Aunt Ophelia. I suspected she was far more intelligent than she pretended to be—after all, she'd lived in luxury for decades without a day of work—but she was mostly

47

harmless as long as it wasn't your bank account she was draining dry. And she'd always been kind to me when I was a kid.

Bryce, on the other hand, had been a little asshole.

Not much had changed.

Chapter Seven

ROYAL

"THIS IS BULLSHIT." BRYCE SHOVED HIS HANDS IN HIS pockets and strode to the window, taking in the view of the gardens and the mountains beyond. "I don't see why you all should get everything, and we have to beg for scraps."

I took a deep breath, reminding myself that losing my temper wouldn't get me anywhere. My goal was to extract myself from the situation until the next time when, hopefully, Tenn would lose the coin toss and he'd have to deal with Bryce and Ophelia.

"I know this has been explained to you," I said dryly, "but let me try again. Technically, no one has inherited anything yet, except for Griffen. I don't own The Inn. I just work here. That's how I pay my bills. Actually, for the time being, I got the exact same thing from my father that you did. Room and board. If that's not enough I suggest you do what the rest of us have done and get a job."

Unlike Ophelia, Prentice Sawyer had never believed in lazy children. My sister Sterling aside, all of us had worked since we were kids. Summer jobs in various family businesses, chores around the house—anything that would keep us busy. We'd all been given positions in family companies after we graduated from college, but none of it had come for free.

"Fine, then," Bryce said, holding his sneer too long, letting it slide from darkly handsome to bratty. "Why don't you give me a job here?"

I resisted the urge to laugh. We had a waiting list of resumes for positions at The Inn. We paid well, treated our employees fairly, and had great benefits. We were always hiring—being in a tourist town meant higher than average turnover—but I doubted Bryce was qualified for anything at The Inn.

"I didn't know you were looking," I said. "Why don't you tell me a little bit about your qualifications. Have you ever worked in hospitality?"

"I've stayed in plenty of hotels," Bryce shot back.

"So, no hospitality experience. Have you ever worked in an office? Answered phones or handled customer service? We have an opening in event coordination and one on the housekeeping staff. Do you have any experience with cleaning?"

The blank look Bryce gave me almost broke my composure. I couldn't help pressing further. "What did you study in college? If you have a business degree, I might be able to put you to work."

Bryce gritted his perfectly straight, white teeth before forcing out, "Communications."

"You did that minor in Italian," Ophelia added unhelpfully.

I vaguely remembered Bryce spending his junior year in Italy. He'd almost gotten kicked out of college for not attending classes, but I wasn't sure he'd learned any Italian. Unable to resist, I said, "Hai le braccia corte."

Bryce stared back at me with a look of blind confusion. Guess none of that Italian had stuck. It was probably good he didn't know I'd just called him cheap. Somehow, I didn't think Bryce would find it as funny as I did. I gave another helpless shrug.

"I'm sorry, I can't help you, Bryce. It wouldn't be fair to the other applicants to hire someone so unqualified. Unless you'd be willing to wait tables. Or maybe I can give you a few shifts with housekeeping and see how you do."

"I'm not working housekeeping," Bryce protested, the look of shock on his face priceless.

"Every single one of us did at least one summer scrubbing toilets and changing sheets. A little hard work never hurt anyone. I bet you'd learn a lot."

Bryce tossed his gleaming, golden hair. "You've always been an asshole."

"Bryce!" Ophelia looked at me and shook her head. "I'm so sorry, Royal. I don't know what's gotten into him. It's just that we're a little short right now. Gerald's alimony check hasn't come through and—"

I could never figure out how much of Ophelia was naïve entitlement and how much was calculation. It didn't really matter. I had no intention of subsidizing her lavish lifestyle at my own expense and neither did any of my siblings. I knew Griffen wouldn't do it, so they were on their own.

On their own in a luxury resort, eating gourmet meals three times a day. Everyone should be on their own like Bryce and Ophelia.

I shook my head gently. "I'm sorry about that, Ophelia. Maybe you should give him a phone call. In the meantime, you have a roof over your head and three meals a day. Once we have the house fixed up you can move over there, but for now, The Inn is one of the most beautiful spots in the Carolinas. Enjoy. I've got to get back to my office. I'm late for a meeting. I'll see you at Sunday dinner, if not before."

I made my escape, ignoring Bryce's protests as they followed me down the hall.

I got back to the office to find Tenn standing behind his desk, his phone to his ear, his brows drawn together in frustration.

"Yeah, okay. Royal just walked in. One of us will be down there in a few." He hung up the phone. "Did you deal with Ophelia and Bryce?"

"Just had to set them straight on a few things."

"What did they want?"

"Only an open tab for alcohol and at the gift shop," I said mildly as if that were no big deal.

Tenn gave a short laugh. "Oh, is that all? I shudder to think how much they could have charged to the room if we hadn't thought to cut them off from the start."

"I know. I told Bryce he should get a job."

This time Tenn burst out with a genuine laugh. "Bet that didn't go over well."

"You'd win that bet. What was up with the phone call?"

Tenn let out a long sigh. "The produce order was canceled."

I stared at him. "Canceled? How did the order get canceled?"

"Someone called in and canceled all the orders from The Inn for this week."

"And the vendor just canceled it? Without calling us? That's insane."

"It was our bad luck that a new hire was on the orders desk when the cancellation came through. Whoever it was gave the head chef's name and said there'd been some changes. The new hire didn't know enough to check and went ahead and canceled the order."

"Fucking hell. Do they have a plan?"

"They're working on it. Waiting on one of us." Tenn pulled the quarter out of his pocket.

I backed up a step. "Oh, hell no. I just got Ophelia and Bryce. This clusterfuck is your problem."

Tenn shook his head. "We flip every time. That's the deal."

Since he was right, I didn't argue. This time I called tails. Mercifully, the quarter fell heads up.

"Damn," Tenn swore as he pocketed the quarter.

"I have to get over to Heartstone anyway. I told Griffen I'd be there in time for lunch. If you need extra hands on deck to get the produce situation sorted out, give me a call."

Striding out of Tenn's office, I stopped abruptly. Penny was braced in the center of the room, her small frame pitted against another—this one taller, stronger, and far more determined.

"I told you, Ms. Sawyer, you can't come in without an appointment."

"Let go of me, you little bitch." Vanessa Sawyer looked up and saw me watching. With a toss of her shining black hair, she demanded, "Royal! Tell her to let me go. I'm your sister-in-law. I have a right to be here."

I resisted the urge to roll my eyes and ignored Vanessa.

"Thanks, Penny. You can let her go. Tenn and I will take care of her from here."

In a quick, fluid move, Penny dropped her grip on Vanessa's arms and stepped to the side, out of reach. Grabbing her purse from her desk drawer, Penny announced, "I'm taking an early lunch," and sailed out the door to the elevators.

"Why are you here, Vanessa?" I asked, sliding to block her entry into Tenn's office. "You're not our sister-in-law. Ford divorced you years ago. And I know I'm not the only one who wishes you'd find another husband and stop using our name."

Vanessa tossed her hair over her shoulder again and propped her hands on her hips in a posture she knew thrust her full breasts into prominence.

Vanessa was gorgeous, I'd give her that.

With her pale skin, red lips, and black hair, she was like an evil version of Snow White. It was no wonder Griffen had fallen so hard for her all those years ago. He'd been determined to marry her—right up until our father convinced her to switch allegiance to Ford when he'd exiled Griffen from Sawyers Bend.

Vanessa had been more than happy to trade Griffen's ring for Ford's. As long as she got to marry the Sawyer heir, Vanessa was happy. Or as close as Vanessa got to happy.

Tenn came to stand beside me, crossing his arms over his chest. "We heard about your visit to Griffen and Hope. You're not going to have better luck with us."

Vanessa drew in a shuddering breath, but I wasn't buying it. I doubted she was capable of genuine tears. Though, to be fair, if anything could push her there it was her current situation.

"You know with Ford in jail and not working there isn't any alimony. I know I should've saved, but I... I just didn't. And now my car payment is due, and my mortgage, and I don't know—"

I looked over my shoulder at Tenn. My brother was always a sucker for a damsel in distress, even one as soulless and conniving as Vanessa.

"Why don't you head downstairs," I suggested. "I can handle this."

Tenn was out the door a second later, Vanessa staring after him with longing. She knew her best chance at walking away with a check had just left.

"Vanessa, I don't have anything for you. I'm not going to give you any money. The Sawyer family has paid out enough over the last decade. We're done. If you need cash, sell your car and the house and downsize. That should get you by until you find a new cash cow. Or—I can hardly believe I'm suggesting this—get a job. That seems to be my mantra for the day. You want money? Get a fucking job. You want a handout? Try somewhere else. I have enough mooches under my roof right now. The last thing I need is another."

Vanessa sniffed. "You have no compassion, Royal Sawyer."

I told Vanessa the truth. "I have plenty of compassion, Vanessa. And if I believed for a second that you'd ever loved Ford, that you wanted anything from him other than a direct line to his wallet, I might feel bad for you. I might even help you out. But I know you didn't love Ford any more than you loved Griffen. You're only here to see what you can squeeze out of us now that the alimony well has run dry."

Vanessa went stiff, her jaw hard. "If you were smart, you'd write me a check to get rid of me. That would be the easy way. Fifty grand, and I'll leave Sawyers Bend. You'll never see me again."

I didn't bother to hide my laugh. Fifty grand? I wouldn't have given her fifty dollars. Not after everything she'd put my brothers through.

"Not a chance. The rest of the family knows what you're up to, so I wouldn't bother working your way down the list. The Sawyers are done with you."

Vanessa glared at me, furious tears brimming in her blue eyes. "You're going to regret this, Royal Sawyer. You think you're done with me? You think you can treat me like trash and throw me away? You're wrong."

"Is that supposed to be a threat? Because I'm only going to warn you once. If you come after us, Vanessa, we will bury you. And that's not a threat. That's a promise."

She whirled on her spike heel and stormed out, leaving a smothering cloud of perfume behind her. Her departure left me strangely deflated, sorry, and sad at what my brother's marriage had come to.

Ford sat in jail for murdering our father, a crime none of us believed he'd committed, and the wife he never should have married was still hanging around, hoping for something from us.

Everyone had a hand out.

Everyone wanted something.

Trying to shake off my mood, I stopped in my office to grab my bag before heading to Heartstone Manor for the second half of my day. Pink and navy ribbons caught my eye. One of Daisy's brownies.

And just like that, my bad mood washed away.

Daisy.

I wished I had time to stop by the bakery, to see her smile and have her tell me once more how she wouldn't go out with me.

She would, eventually.

Daisy liked me, no matter how much she said she didn't.

I wasn't going to give up.

Lately, I was surrounded by people who wanted things from me they hadn't earned.

Not Daisy. Daisy put herself at risk to protect The Inn, to protect me, and all she'd gotten out of it was a business deal I would have agreed to anyway.

She didn't use what she'd done to push for more. She didn't ask for favors or try to take advantage. Daisy had done what she thought was right, had put herself in danger, and hadn't even pressed her advantage.

To say she was a change of pace was a vast understatement.

But it wasn't just that. It was her wide smile and the light in her brown eyes. Her round curves, her energy, her soft cherry-cola curls, and the sound of her laugh.

I was trying to play this slow. To give her space. I wanted her, but I didn't want to stalk her. It was a fine but distinct difference.

I unwrapped the brownie as I walked to my car, Daisy firmly rooted in my mind. It occurred to me that Hope would be working with Griffen and me this afternoon.

Hope, Griffen's new wife, was also Daisy's best friend. If anybody could give me the inside scoop on the supposed boyfriend, it was Hope.

Before I left for Heartstone, I had a stop to make. I didn't have time to see Daisy, but fuck it. For Daisy, I'd make time.

With a new spring in my step and the taste of rich chocolate filling my mouth, I turned back to The Inn. The chocolate had given me an idea.

Food was Daisy's thing, and I had the best kitchen in town at my disposal. I had a feeling I'd need every one of my advantages to win Daisy over.

Good thing I had a lot of them.

Chapter Eight

DAISY

*C*AREFULLY, SO CAREFULLY, I CARRIED THE TRAY WITH THE wedding cake to the cooler in the back of the kitchen. Ready with a day to spare, the cake would feed a hundred guests at a garden wedding the next day.

All in white, embellished with delicate violets and green vines, it was gorgeous, if I did say so myself. I made sure the cake was settled neatly in place and closed the heavy door to the cooler, turning to evaluate the kitchen and figure out what to do next.

My mother had run back into the kitchen and slapped a note on the desk while I was working on the candied violets.

Low on toffee-chip cookies, orange-cranberry muffins, pie—all of them!—and chocolate cake.

Looks like I had my afternoon cut out for me.

I already had more toffee-chip cookies ready to go. Ditto on the chocolate cake. I hadn't expected the run on orange-cranberry muffins or pie. Everyone in town must be in the mood for pie. Checking the clock, I saw it was past time for lunch. No wonder my stomach was growling.

I thought of the leftover casserole in my fridge upstairs. Not appealing. Still, a girl had to eat. When she was pinching every penny, a girl had to respect leftovers.

A quick double-knock fell on the back door to the kitchen. I was moving to open it when the handle turned. Royal stood there, a paper bag in his hand. He held it aloft and said in greeting, "Pastrami on rye? The Inn kitchen had fresh-cooked kettle chips."

I didn't quite snatch the bag from his hand. Not exactly.

I could smell the pastrami, salty and rich. Calories. Yum.

As usual, I'd started my day on a cup of coffee, planning to eat breakfast, and had somehow never made it there. My feet hurt, my hair was an explosion of frizz, and I was pretty sure my sweat had passed the glowing stage. Royal just smiled at me, his eyes tracking past me to where the bouquet he'd sent crowded my small desk.

"Did you like the flowers?"

I raised my head from peeking in the bag and glanced over my shoulder at the flowers. "They're beautiful. I've been debating the appropriate way to say thank you."

Royal's eyes skimmed me from head to toe, slowly, deliberately, heat blooming in their wake. Oh, I knew what he was thinking. That way lie danger. For me, not for him. I shook my head in a negative, trying to hide the smile that wanted to curve my mouth.

I expected him to say something suggestive. Proposition me or ask me out again. Instead, he gave me an easy smile. "I'm sure you'll think of something. In case you were wondering, your brownies aside, I'm partial to pie."

"What kind?" I asked before I could stop myself.

"Oh, pretty much all of them."

"But what's your favorite? Just asking out of curiosity."

"Anything with berries."

"Good to know," I said and stood there like a dork holding the sandwich bag and staring at him. He was just so much. He filled the kitchen with his maleness, with that dark hair and strong jaw, his broad shoulders and blue, blue eyes.

Maybe it was his pheromones. That was it, he was using his body chemistry to make me crazy. It wasn't my fault. Any woman would be attracted to him.

"Am I interrupting?"

"No—I, um, I just finished a wedding cake, and I was thinking about lunch, actually, and how I really didn't want to eat the casserole upstairs, so this is very much appreciated. But, um, why are you here?"

Royal leaned his hip against one of my worktables and shoved a hand in his pocket. He shrugged one shoulder. "To be honest, I don't really know. I had a crap morning and I'm headed to Heartstone for what will hopefully be a better afternoon. I tried to tell myself I didn't have time to see you, but here I am. Because I really wanted to see you."

"But why?" A dumb question, I know, but really, I didn't get it. What was there to see? It was just me and my apron, my hair sticking out in every direction, streaked with flour. Why me?

Royal straightened and closed the distance between us, his blue eyes focused on my face. Plucking the sandwich bag from my hand, he raised his own and extended one finger to trace over the curve of my cheekbone.

Leaning down, he murmured, "Because you're you, and seeing you feels good. I could try listing all your good qualities. I did that on Friday, but it doesn't seem to have sunk in. So, I'm

61

going to go with the easy answer. Being near you makes me feel good. And I can't stop thinking about doing this."

Royal set the sandwich bag on the table behind him and turned, cupping my face in his hands. I knew what he was going to do. I could feel it coming.

I should have stepped back. I should have told him not to.

I should have told him I had a boyfriend.

I didn't do any of that.

I didn't want to step back.

And I didn't really have a boyfriend.

But I did want Royal to kiss me.

I might as well see what it was like, I reasoned. Royal would lose interest and move on eventually, so I should kiss him while I had the chance.

At that moment—my heart beating a fast rhythm in my chest, his hands warm on my face, his mouth dropping to mine—kissing Royal made complete sense.

His lips brushed mine, soft and warm. Gentle but coaxing. He wasn't all tongue and saliva like the last guy I'd kissed. He'd been enough to put me off kissing for—had it been a year? Maybe J.T. was right. It had been too long.

My thoughts faded as Royal tilted his head to the side and deepened his kiss, his lips nudging mine apart, his tongue dipping in to taste.

Chocolate. Royal Sawyer tasted like bittersweet chocolate. Like chocolate and heat and man.

I rose to my toes, winding my arms around his neck, and pressed my body to his. So much strength. And big, bigger than me. His arms closed around my back and my toes left the floor. Before I had a chance to panic, Royal turned and set me on the worktable, making space between my spread knees, his mouth still on mine, his kiss hungrier.

Demanding.

I did the only thing I could—I tilted my head back and gave him more. Who knew Royal Sawyer could kiss like this?

Royal's mouth tore from mine, his breath coming in harsh pants. "Daisy," he breathed, "I knew it would be this good." His mouth skimmed along my jaw, settling beneath my ear with a light suck that sent another wave of heat shimmering through my body.

"You taste like dessert." His lips were back on mine, his tongue stroking until my head spun so hard I thought it would roll right off my body.

I could have kissed Royal all day. Somewhere in the back of my mind I thought about dragging him up the stairs to my little apartment and stripping off his suit. I wanted my hands on all those hard muscles. I wanted to taste him all over. I wanted…

A thud against the swinging door to the shop broke through my haze of lust. Royal was already moving. By the time Grams walked into the kitchen, we were standing five feet apart, Royal unpacking the lunch he'd brought me.

Flustered, I tried to cover like I hadn't just been about to strip him naked in the middle of the bakery kitchen.

Pretending I didn't see Grams, I said, "You didn't bring anything for yourself. Are you going to keep me company while I have lunch? Do you want a drink?"

Grams set down a stack of empty trays on the worktable, her eyes popping between the two of us, bright with curiosity.

"Royal Sawyer. Those are some nice flowers you sent my granddaughter. And now you're bringing her lunch?"

"How are you, Ms. Hutchins?" he asked with a deferential dip of his head. Grams shot me a look. I could practically hear her voice. *The boy has pretty manners.* He did.

"I'm good, Royal, I'm good. Even better now that Daisy's mama is home. All we need is her daddy and I'll have all my chicks in the nest, so, I'm pretty damn fine." Grams pulled her long gray braid over her shoulder and crossed her arms over her tie-dyed Phish T-shirt. "You courting my girl, Royal?"

"Yes, ma'am, I am. Or I'm trying to. She says she's not interested."

"Oh, I'm sure my Daisy is smart enough to know a good thing when she sees it. She's a clever girl. She's taken over running the bakery, you know. And she has plans for expansion. Outdoor seating, sandwiches for lunch, and new ovens. She set the budgets, figured out how to put aside the money and everything. We're almost ready to start, right, baby?"

My stomach clenched. We *would* have been almost ready to start. Except the money was gone.

DAISY

F I HAD THE GUTS, I'D HAVE TOLD GRAMS RIGHT THEN.
I even opened my mouth, drawing some strange
sense of reassurance from Royal's presence at my
side. Why that was, I didn't know.

I didn't want Royal to know how dumb I'd been, did I?

I didn't. I didn't want anyone to know I'd been stupid enough
to give my father money, but somehow, I felt like Royal would
understand.

I closed my mouth and said nothing, just listened to Grams
describe how we were going to turn the scrubby patch of
grass on the side of the building into a deck with pretty, black
wrought-iron tables and chairs and umbrellas for shade in the
summer. I already had in mind the exact planters I'd put out, the
summer blooms to fill them. Bright and pretty, so they'd catch
tourists' eyes from the sidewalk.

My chest ached to know it wouldn't happen this year.

It's okay, I reminded myself. I'd made a mistake. Eventually, I'd get the courage to tell everyone, and I wouldn't make the same mistake again. Nothing else I could do but move on.

If only reminding myself of all that made me feel better. It did, a little. Mostly, I still felt like a gigantic dumbass.

"You've gone silent with hunger," Grams said, giving me a funny look. "I'll leave you to your lunch. I'm just going to grab that chocolate cake from the cooler."

"I'll get the toffee-chip cookies lined up on the tray for you," I said, glad to have something to do other than talk about our plans for the bakery.

Grams swung open the door to the cooler and let out a gasp. "Daisy, these violets are a work of art. Royal, come look at this and see how talented my Daisy is. You'd never believe those flowers were made of sugar."

Royal looked over her shoulder into the cooler and then back at me. "You made that? The flowers and the vines and stuff? Out of sugar?"

I concentrated on lining up toffee chip cookies on the tray, a little embarrassed at the way they were raving over the cake. I'd always loved decorating cakes, and I was pretty good at it.

"Some of the violets are actually real violets that I candied. The rest of the violets and the vines and leaves I made from sugar and a kind of gum paste and then painted with edible color. It's for the wedding over at The Inn tomorrow evening."

"The garden wedding?"

"Do you have more than one weekday wedding?" I asked, curious. Most of our wedding cakes were for Saturdays, but the date was important to the bride and groom, and they didn't care if their wedding was on a Tuesday.

Royal laughed. "Not this week. Three over the weekend, though. The event planning staff is going a little crazy."

I handed off the tray of cookies to Grams and watched her hustle through the kitchen door to the shop. "Is that what messed up your morning? The weddings?" I asked.

Royal looked away and let out a breath. "No, that was my aunt and my cousin. And my former sister-in-law. Long story. Family." He shook his head.

"Family's always complicated," I said, knowing better than anyone how family could turn a great day upside down.

Royal unpacked my lunch from the paper bag as Grams came back in holding two glass bottles of sweet tea. Royal took his with thanks and Grams left, saying over her shoulder, "Make sure she eats every bite, Royal. She's been skipping too many meals."

I tried not to fall on my lunch like a ravenous fiend, but I'm pretty sure I ended up with mustard on my apron and plenty smeared across my face. After I got the first few bites in my stomach, I remembered to use my napkin.

Royal was smiling at me again. I wiped my face one more time just in case I'd missed a glob of mustard.

"I like watching you eat," he said.

My eyebrows knitted together as I thought about that. "That's interesting. Do you have some kind of food fetish?" I was mostly kidding.

Royal's rich, full laugh filled the room again. I was starting to really like that sound. "No food fetish," he said, still laughing. "I just like the way you eat. Full throttle. It's sexy."

I smirked. Saying I was a full-throttle-eater wasn't the kind of flirting I was used to.

But it made me smile, so maybe it was the kind of flirting I needed. "I'm pretty sure I still have mustard all over my face. Maybe you have a mustard fetish."

"I think I have a Daisy fetish."

At that, I shoved a chip in my mouth. I didn't trust my own

response. Royal was just too easy to talk to. He made me forget to be careful.

"What kind of family situation do you have that's complicated?" he asked. "It seems like you get along pretty well with your grandmother."

I glanced at the swinging door between the kitchen and the shop. It was soundproof, but it did swing open without warning. "I do get along well with Grams. She raised me, for the most part. I love her to pieces." Another glance at the door. "The rest of it is—better saved for another time, I think."

"Fair enough," Royal said. "I'll tell you about my morning instead."

He launched into a story about his aunt and weasel of a cousin who were trying to milk The Inn for every penny they could charge to the room they weren't paying for. Every family had one, I guess. At least Royal and Tenn were smart enough to cut theirs off before they handed them a chunk of cash like I had with my dad.

"And the ex-sister-in-law?" I asked. "What did she do to ruin your morning? Was she Tenn's wife?"

Royal let out a bark of surprise before he grinned. "Oh, hell no. Vanessa was engaged to Griffen, then dumped him to marry Ford."

"Oh, *that* sister-in-law." I shook my head. "I don't know her, but I heard the story. Why is she bothering you? I thought your brother divorced her years ago."

"He did. She's been living off our name and his alimony all this time. But their divorce decree said the alimony was based on Ford's income."

I didn't need Royal to fill in the blanks. "And he's not collecting a salary from jail, right?"

"Exactly."

My eyebrows shot up. "And she expected you and Tenn to do what? Give her a job?"

Royal busted out with a belly laugh, his eyes so bright they made my chest hurt. He laughed until his eyes teared. Wiping them with the back of his hand, he said, "Damn, I needed that." He shook his head, still chuckling. "No, Vanessa didn't want a job. Vanessa doesn't work, except at the gym. She wanted a big fat check."

"Ugh. So, you spent the morning getting hit up for money? That doesn't sound fun." At least he had practice saying no. I needed to get some of that. If I'd been prepared, maybe I would have sent my dad packing like Royal had his own moochers.

"It wasn't. Hopefully, there won't be any surprises at Heartstone."

"Why are you going over there? I thought you worked at The Inn?"

"I'll tell you if you go to dinner with me."

"I have a boyfriend," I said.

No, you don't, a little voice whispered in my head.

I do, I reminded myself. *J.T. Sweet, loyal J.T. Funny, cute J.T.*

J.T., who I'd only kissed once a long, long time ago.

J.T., who'd told me to go after Royal.

See? He's not your boyfriend.

Yes, he is!

Fine, then he's a boy-friend. Royal is a man. You don't need a boy-friend, you need a man-friend.

"You're staring into space. I can't tell if that's a yes or a no," Royal said, the side of his mouth quirked up in a bemused grin.

I wanted to kiss him again.

No, I'm not dating Royal Sawyer.

I thought you just decided you needed a man-friend, mocked the little voice in my head. She could shove it. I opened my mouth to turn him down and nothing came out.

Royal took a step closer and raised his hand as if to touch my face. It hovered in the air in front of me for a moment, magnetic, drawing me closer.

I almost leaned in to close the distance myself. Royal's hand dropped to his side.

"Daisy," he said slowly, his voice low and private. "I'm in an odd position here. Every instinct I have is telling me to pursue you. To ignore you every time you tell me no. To chase you down until you're mine. But I don't want to scare you or make you feel cornered. If I'm making you uncomfortable and you want me to leave you alone, I need you to tell me. I'm persistent, but I'm not a stalker."

"Are you always this persistent?" I had to ask. Some guys get off on the chase. Maybe Royal was one of them. Maybe if I went to dinner with him he'd lose interest.

"Not usually. In business, yes. Not with women."

"Just with me?" I asked, my voice thin and high-pitched in my ears.

"So far, just with you." When he lifted his hand and stroked his fingertips over one of my unruly curls it felt like he'd given in to a need he'd been denying. "Am I scaring you, Daisy?"

"No. I think I might be scaring myself. And I need to think about dinner."

Royal studied me for a long moment before he nodded. "Understood. I'll just take this and go." He dipped his head and ran his lips across mine, the brief taste drawing me closer. So sweet. I could've reached up and—before I finished the thought he was gone, stepping back and turning for the door.

I stared after him, my lips cold, missing him already. I looked down and spotted the pack of cookies I'd put aside for Hope when I made up the tray. "Royal! Wait a sec."

"Change your mind?"

"For Hope."

I shoved the cookies into his hand and leaned up to press a quick kiss to the hard line of his jaw. "I'll see you later," I said before practically pushing him out the door and closing it behind him.

Chapter Ten

ROYAL

G RIFFEN AND HOPE WERE WAITING FOR ME IN GRIFFEN'S office, a lunch tray taking up half of the desk. It was hard for me to think of it as Griffen's office. For most of my life, this had been my father's place, the massive leather chair a throne from which he lorded his power over the rest of us.

I hated this room. I hated the trophies hanging on the walls, animals he'd hunted himself—though I had my doubts about the bear. Prentice wasn't above a little cheating when it suited him, along with taking credit for somebody else's achievements. I'd always had a feeling the hunting guide had taken down the bear.

The look on the majestic bear's face had always struck me as sad. Trapped. Forced to spend eternity nailed to a wall when he should have been free to roam the mountains. Prentice's children hadn't been much different from those animals. We were trophies to him. Evidence that unlike our Sawyer ancestors, Prentice was capable of producing more than a paltry few offspring.

Prentice had packed the family tree, though he'd gone through three wives and a mistress to do it. By the time someone broke into the Manor and shot him dead, most of us had moved out to get away from him.

These days, I was coming to regret our hasty departure. Our father had been largely alone in Heartstone Manor over the last few years, and everything had gone to hell. He'd been so proud of the house, one of the finest examples of Jacobean architecture in the United States and one of the very few Gilded Age mansions still used as a private home.

Once, Heartstone Manor had been a showpiece. It would be again when Griffen finished with it. I'd never been able to uncover the truth of what had gone wrong. I only knew that one day Prentice had been hinting that a new Mrs. Sawyer would be moving in, had completely renovated the master suite of the house for her, and then... nothing.

The new Mrs. Sawyer had never arrived, and Prentice had changed. If possible, he'd grown even more cruel and demanding. Even Ford had moved out of the house by then, saying he could put up with Prentice for the sake of the company, but even he needed a break by the end of the day. Miss Martha, the housekeeper who'd practically raised us, had quit and refused to return.

And Prentice, who had taken such pride in Heartstone Manor, let the house fall into a state that could best be described as benign neglect. The gardens were choked with weeds. Most of the rooms in the house were still coated with dust, furniture and art missing, the house barely habitable.

Griffen was determined to change that. He and Hope had hired Savannah Miles, Miss Martha's daughter, as housekeeper.

Like her mother, Savannah was efficient, hard-working, and she didn't take crap off anyone, all skills necessary for managing both Heartstone Manor and the Sawyer family.

In the office, the savory scent of soup filled the room. A tray held three steaming bowls sitting beside two plates with thick roast beef sandwiches and one with a neat stack of saltines.

Hope was newly pregnant and morning sickness was kicking her ass. Seeing me in the doorway, she looked up with a smile. "Royal, you're here. The front gate called when you came through and Savannah brought in lunch. Beef and barley soup, sandwiches for you two and saltines for me."

I took a seat in front of the desk. "Stomach still bothering you?"

Hope shook her head ruefully. "Sometimes I can barely choke down water and sometimes I think I could eat a horse. Today is one of those days I don't want food."

I slid the packet of toffee-chip cookies across the desk. "Daisy sent you these. For when you think you can eat something."

Hope's eyes widened as she reached out and snatched up the cookies. I'd already known they were her favorite, and apparently, so did Daisy. That's what best friends were for. "Royal, you brought me Daisy's cookies? Today, you're my favorite brother-in-law."

"Just today? Why not every day?"

"Well, Finn made me that carrot and ginger soup the other day when I couldn't keep anything else down. That day he was my favorite."

That soup had been amazing, especially considering I'd thought it would be disgusting. I'm not a fan of carrots. "Fair enough. What about the soup today? Did Finn make that too?"

Griffen and Hope shared a look. Sometimes I thought they had whole conversations with a single glance. Hope shook her head. "The new cook, Ms. Haverty, complained to Savannah

73

about Finn, and Savannah banned him from the kitchens unless it's Ms. Haverty's day off."

I leaned in and inhaled the scent rising from the steaming bowl. It smelled pretty good. Still, since he'd come home for Prentice's funeral, I'd learned that my younger brother Finn was a genius in the kitchen. So far, neither of the Heartstone Manor cooks had been able to meet his high expectations, a fact he didn't keep to himself. I wasn't surprised he'd been banned from the kitchen, more that Ms. Haverty had lasted this long before booting him out.

"Try the soup and saltines, Buttercup." Griffen reached over to rub a soothing hand down Hope's back. "And after, maybe a nap?"

"Maybe," Hope conceded. "Only if you tuck me in."

I smiled to myself at Hope flirting with Griffen. I'd known her since I was a kid, when her uncle Edgar had taken her in. Edgar had worked closely with Prentice for years, and Hope had been his assistant after she graduated from college. Between the three of us, Hope knew the most about Sawyer Enterprises. She'd been invaluable in keeping the company thriving with Prentice dead and Ford in jail.

She'd always been quiet and shy. I don't think I'd ever seen her flirt with any guy, much less Griffen. They'd been close as kids despite their six-year age difference, and it was common knowledge that she'd had a crush on Griffen forever, but she'd never dared to flirt with him.

It had been Hope who'd spilled the beans about Griffen and Vanessa's planned elopement all those years ago, giving Prentice half of the lever he'd needed to force Griffen out of the company. And the family. She'd been wracked with guilt over the part she'd played, but once done, it couldn't be undone.

If you'd asked me, in a million years I never would have thought Griffen would end up married to Hope. They'd been friends, but she'd barely been a teenager when he'd been exiled. Given what she'd done, I'd figured he hated her. Maybe he had, but he didn't now.

Looking at them, you'd never guess he hadn't been in love with her most of his life. He was fiercely protective. Over the moon that she was having his child. If it weren't for all the bullshit going on—our father's murder, Ford in jail, someone trying to shoot Griffen—Griffen and Hope might still have been on their honeymoon.

As it was, the newlyweds were making the best of the situation. I watched as Griffen dipped a saltine in the soup, urging Hope to take it. Her face looked green as she nibbled. Griffen noticed me watching. "Sometimes a little food makes the nausea better."

"And sometimes it doesn't?"

"And sometimes it doesn't," Griffen admitted. "How are things at The Inn?" he asked, picking up a sandwich.

I pulled my chair closer to the desk and reached for my own plate. "Someone called our produce supplier and canceled all of our orders," I told him, "and Vanessa stopped by to extort fifty grand out of me. Also, Ophelia and Bryce demanded an open tab at the bar and gift shop. So, all in all, not too unusual these days. But bookings are strong, and we've laid out the sites along the river for the new cottages. Foundations are already going in."

"That's good news," Griffen said. "If Vanessa comes back, let me know."

"I will. No offer to help with Ophelia and Bryce?" I asked and took a generous bite of my sandwich.

Griffen laughed and shook his head. "Savannah has had her team putting in all their extra time on the guest wing. Soon you'll be free of those two, and they'll be my problem. Until then, you can deal with them."

"Can't argue with that," I agreed. I glanced at Hope and saw that the stack of saltines was halfway gone. She still looked a little green. "Before we jump into business, I have a question for Hope."

Hope set down her spoon, tilting her head to the side, her eyes thoughtful as they rested on me. "Is it about Daisy?"

"It is. Are you going to claim girl-code and refuse to talk?"

Hope took another spoonful of soup before she answered. "I don't know yet. Why don't you ask, and I'll tell you if I'm going to answer?"

"Does she have a boyfriend?" I was pretty sure I knew the answer, but I wanted to hear it from Hope.

Hope nibbled on a saltine. "Why are you asking?"

"Because I asked her out, and she said no."

"Maybe she just doesn't like you," Griffen threw in.

"Maybe, but I think she does. I think she wanted to say yes."

"Then why didn't she?" Griffen asked.

I looked to Hope. "Did she say no because of the boyfriend?"

Hope hesitated, then shook her head. "If you tell her I said this, I'll smother you in your sleep." She glanced at Griffen. "Or I'll have Griffen do it for me. Understood?"

"Understood. I protect my sources. Now, spill."

"First, tell me why you're asking. Why do you want to go out with her? I know your reputation, and I know the last time you had a serious girlfriend was pretty much never. I love Daisy. She's one of my closest friends in the world and I'm the first person to say she could use a date. But not with some guy who just wants to sleep with her and move on. You know what I mean? So, if that's you, start with the moving on and skip the sleeping with her part."

Chapter Eleven

ROYAL

I TOOK ANOTHER BITE OF MY SANDWICH, CHEWING AS I thought. I definitely wanted to sleep with Daisy. I wanted to get her naked, wanted to lick every inch of her smooth, soft skin, wanted to see her eyes light with desire. I needed to know what her face looked like as she crested into orgasm. Had to see her sated and sleepy after. I wanted all of that.

But not only that. Not only sex. I wanted to see her laugh. A lot. I wanted to talk to her. To be with her. Sex optional—for now.

And wasn't that a new one for me? I usually started with sex and hoped for a quick getaway. Not with Daisy.

"I can't make any promises," I said carefully. "I don't know her well enough to do that. Not yet. But I know I want to know her better. I like her. I'm absolutely attracted to her, don't get me wrong. Very attracted. But it's not just physical. I'm attracted to *her*. You know what I mean?"

Hope nodded. "Then I'll tell you this. The boyfriend isn't a boyfriend. Not like that. I can't explain why because it's not my story and it's not your business unless J.T. decides to share. They love each other, but it's not romantic."

She looked up at the ceiling for a long moment and took a breath, letting it out in a puff of air. "I think it's habit more than anything at this point. And I think you're right. I think she does like you. Knowing Daisy, that probably scares the heck out of her."

A weight lifted from my chest at the knowledge that the boyfriend wasn't really a boyfriend. I wasn't the kind of guy who poached on someone else's territory, but the idea of bowing out had burned.

I wanted Daisy. I couldn't stand the idea someone else had gotten there first, had claimed her before I even met her.

If the field was clear, it was time to make plans.

"Any advice?"

Hope shook her head slowly. "Don't give up. Don't push too hard, but don't give up."

"Thanks, Hope."

She smiled and took another spoonful of soup before setting the spoon down with a clink. She rose, a little unsteady on her feet. Griffen shot up beside her, reaching out to wind his arm around her waist, steadying her.

"I'm sorry. I'm okay. I'm not going to get sick," she said for Griffen's benefit, "but I need to go lay down. I'm sorry. My list is on the desk."

"I'll walk you up," Griffen said, already steering her to the door.

"You don't need to do that, I can get myself upstairs."

"Shut it, Buttercup." Griffen looked over his shoulder at me. "I'll be back."

"Take your time."

When they were gone, I dug into the roast beef sandwich and soup, pulling Hope's list in front of me to get a jump on the afternoon's agenda.

For most of my life, Sawyer Enterprises had been made up of the businesses in Sawyers Bend and various larger concerns, including a logging company, several quarries, furniture manufacturing, and commercial real estate all over the Southeast.

Over the years, Ford and Prentice had sold off the quarries and the logging along with the furniture manufacturing, choosing instead to invest in a diverse array of businesses across the country.

For the most part, Brax oversaw the company's real estate investments. Tenn and I handled The Inn at Sawyers Bend, Avery the brewery, Quinn her guide business. Prentice and Ford had focused on managing the company's assorted investments. With Prentice dead and Ford in jail, Griffen and Hope had spent the last six weeks getting up to speed. Now it was my turn. I couldn't wait.

Sawyer Enterprises offered an array of continually shifting challenges. So did The Inn, and I loved it there, but this was on a bigger scope, going beyond the hospitality industry to everything from tech to emerging resources to manufacturing. It was fascinating, and I was grateful Griffen had so easily agreed to let me join him.

I was ready when Griffen came back.

"She okay?" I asked.

He sank into his chair looking a little green himself. "Her doctor swears this is completely normal. If that's true I have no fucking clue how women do it. You have any idea how many times she's puked today?"

I shook my head. I didn't know, and I didn't want to.

"Too many, man. Too fucking many." Griffen sighed and picked up his sandwich. "Hopefully, she'll sleep most of the afternoon and wake up starving for dinner. Did you take a look at her list?"

"I did. Do you want me to cover The Inn business while you eat?" Griffen nodded and I picked up my own list.

Before I could get started, our younger sister Sterling strolled in, throwing herself into the chair beside me. "I figured you two would rate better than soup and sandwiches. I hate to agree with Finn, but the new chef sucks."

"You're welcome to take on the job if you think you can do better," Griffen said, the corner of his mouth curled up in a half-smile. I expected him to deliver a set-down, but Sterling and Griffen seemed to have reached a semi-affectionate truce.

The youngest of the Sawyers, Sterling had a raw deal from the start. By the time she started school, her mother was dead, Prentice's final wife, Darcy, had also died, and Prentice decided he was done with parenting. Not that he'd done much of that in the first place.

Sterling was mostly left to run wild. Miss Martha had done her best, but she'd had a house to run and the rest of us to distract her. Sterling had no one. She'd made it through high school mostly because the boarding school where all the Sawyers went was too afraid of losing Prentice's generous donations to kick her out. She'd been thrown out of three colleges before she managed to graduate and had spent her time since then drinking and spiraling out of control.

Griffen had taken her in hand when he moved into Heartstone Manor, and since then, she'd been a lot better. I hadn't seen her drunk in over a month. That was saying a lot for Sterling.

I had a disorienting moment of déjà vu when she looked at me—her golden hair, blue eyes, and perfect bone structure so like our cousin Bryce's—and said, "There isn't any money in my bank account."

"That's unfortunate," Griffen said mildly. "What are you going to do?"

Sterling stared at him, nonplussed. "I'm going to ask you to put money in it. Obviously."

"You can ask all day, but it's not going to happen." Griffen set down his pen, his eyes on her patient. Gentle.

"What do you mean it's not going to happen? Dad always gave me money." She leaned forward, ready for a fight, her eyes flashing.

"I'm not Dad," Griffen said, still calm, refusing to give her the argument she wanted. "You've had a free ride for long enough. You want money, get a job."

"That seems to be the theme for the day," I added. Sterling raised one perfectly arched eyebrow in my direction. "You're third in line today. Fourth if you separate Ophelia and Bryce into two people."

"Who was number three?" Sterling asked, distracted by her curiosity.

"Your former sister-in-law."

Sterling's eyebrows shot up. "That bitch had the nerve to ask you for money?"

"She did, right after Ophelia and Bryce hit me up. And I told all three of them the same thing Griffen just told you. You want money? Get a job."

"Are you going to give me a job? Or do you expect me to go all over town putting in resumes?"

I glanced across the desk at Griffen, who raised an eyebrow at me in question. I shrugged in answer. "Do you want to work at The Inn? It *is* tradition. The rest of us all put in time at The Inn when we were growing up."

"Are you going to stick me in housekeeping?" Sterling's upper lip curled in a sneer that again reminded me of Bryce. While I hadn't had a shred of sympathy for our cousin, who'd grown up with every luxury including his mother's doting affection, I did have some sympathy for my baby sister.

"I don't know. If you don't want housekeeping, what do you think you'd be good at? I expect you to do whatever job you get, not just clock in and collect a paycheck. You understand that, right?"

"Duh. You're way too much of a hard-ass to make it that easy." She slouched back in the chair and eyed me appraisingly. "I don't know what I'm good at. I've never really done anything."

"What do you think you'd like?" I had something in mind, but I wanted to see what Sterling would say first.

"I don't know." She stared up at the ceiling, thinking. "I don't think I want to wait tables. Or work the front desk. Are there any jobs in the office? I'm good at organizing things."

Griffen and I stared at her in disbelief, both of us remembering the state of her bedroom when we'd moved back into the house. It had been filthy, so disgusting that Griffen had refused to let our own housekeeping staff touch it until Sterling cleaned it herself.

Sterling shrugged a shoulder and straightened in the chair. "Okay, fine, I get why you guys are giving me those looks, but it's true. I was always in charge of throwing parties at my sorority, which takes a lot of coordination, even if it doesn't look like it. I know word processing and spreadsheets. I'm not totally useless."

"I didn't think you were," I said, hoping my idea was a good one. "Our head of event coordination has an assistant, and that assistant is about to go on maternity leave. She may be back, she may not, but the person we hired to fill in for her just decided to take a different position. If you're interested, show up at The Inn tomorrow by 8:30. I'll introduce you to Marcy, and we'll see how it goes. It doesn't pay a lot, and Marcy will work you hard, but I think you'll like it, and her."

Sterling sat frozen for a long minute. "Really? You'll give me a job at The Inn?"

"I'll hire you on a trial basis. In the end, it will be up to Marcy."

Sterling stood and nodded. "I'll kick ass in event coordination, you'll see."

"I can't wait."

Sterling's smile was a little shy when she said, "Can I, um, ride in with you tomorrow? I don't have any gas in my car, and I guess I won't have any money to fill it until I get a paycheck."

"I go in at eight, and I'd love to give you a ride."

"I can't remember the last time I got up that early," Sterling said. She leaned over and gave me a quick hug. "Thanks, you're the best, Royal. I swear I won't fuck this up."

"What about me?" Griffen said, sounding affronted.

Sterling sent him a saucy wink. "You're not bad, but Royal just gave me a job, so he's my number one brother right now. If he fires me I'll give the spot back to you."

"If he doesn't fire you because you have a job you like and you're doing well at it, then I'm happy to take number two. As long as you don't put Tenn ahead of me."

Sterling laughed, a sound I realized we didn't hear enough. For a party girl, she never seemed to be having that much fun. A moment later she was gone, closing the office door behind her.

ROYAL

*T*HAT WAS UNEXPECTED," I SAID.

"You okay with giving her a job?" Griffen asked, noting something down on the pad in front of him.

"I guess that depends on how it ends up working out. But I never would have thought she'd slow down the drinking the way she has. Who knows? She seems a lot less angry. Less reckless. That means a lot. And unlike the rest of them, she didn't revolt at the idea of working for a living."

"Always a good sign. I assume Bryce wasn't interested in a similar offer?"

"I didn't exactly make Bryce a similar offer," I admitted. "Mostly because he's still an asshole, and he's not my little sister."

"Well, we have to put up with them living in the house once the guest wing is ready, but nothing in the will says we have to support them. If Bryce decides he's willing to lower himself to employment, maybe we'll find something for him."

"You still haven't gotten to your lunch," I said, stacking my empty dishes on the tray. "I'll run down The Inn business while you eat."

"Works for me," Griffen said, picking up his sandwich again. "I'm starving."

"Tenn is going to make an offer to Forrest Powell. If he works out, he'll fill in for the time I'm spending here and put us a little ahead."

Griffen ate as I went over construction details on the cottage expansion. While I was talking, my phone beeped. A quick look showed a message from Tenn.

Produce emergency averted. I don't care what the coin says, next crisis is yours.

"Tenn said he covered the latest emergency. We have to figure out who's behind the sabotage at The Inn before it gets any worse. At first, it was canceled reservations and guests who thought things were missing from their rooms. Then the guy with the cockroaches—"

I shook my head as I remembered the swelling in Daisy's cheek. That was on me. I wasn't the one who'd hit her, but she should have been safe at The Inn.

"Tenn will have the purchasing staff call all of our major vendors, letting them know to double-check any unusual changes. But narrowing it down seems impossible. West arrested cockroach guy and it still didn't get us anywhere."

"Lately, all we have are dead ends," Griffen agreed. "West still doesn't have anything on the nutcase who tried to run me off the road and broke into the Manor. Same story—somebody paid him to do it, but he doesn't know who it was. I believe him, but that doesn't fucking help us."

"I'm not even sure I can narrow down the suspects," I said. "Dad had so many enemies one walked right into Heartstone Manor and shot him in the head. I'm not sure they see much of a difference between him and the Sawyer family in general. Do you think—" I stopped, not sure I wanted to put my thoughts into words.

"What?" Griffen prompted.

"Any chance Vanessa has anything to do with it?"

Griffen let out a long sigh and stacked his now-empty plates, pushing the tray to the corner of his desk. "I don't want to think she does. She's not my favorite person, but hiring someone to kill me seems a little extreme. Still, I don't think I can exclude her. Same for Ophelia and Bryce. I don't see them committing murder, but the issues going on at The Inn? That's just the kind of petty bullshit I could see Bryce thinking up. Or maybe I just still hate him from when we were teenagers."

"He hasn't gotten much better, from what I can see."

"The investigator at Sinclair Security keeps hitting dead ends, too," Griffen said, shoving his hair off his forehead in frustration.

"They put their best guy on it, and he couldn't find anything that didn't point straight to Ford as Dad's killer. And he dug deep. Then I had them put their best forensic accountant on tracing the missing artwork. She's been more successful. She's found some sales, some records of where the money went. But she hasn't uncovered the whole picture. Whatever Dad was up to, it wasn't straightforward."

"Nothing with Dad ever was," I said.

"True. He was always up to something." Griffen picked up Hope's list. "Okay, some of this is going to be a little harder without Hope, but let's dig into some ongoing business. Cole

Haywood will be here at four. We should try to make some headway before then."

That name rang in my ears as I pulled out my own laptop and moved to the chair Hope had occupied beside Griffen.

Cole Haywood was our brother Ford's defense attorney. He'd been pushing for Ford to plead guilty to our father's murder and take the deal the prosecutor was offering. Cole didn't care that Ford was innocent, that if he took that deal he'd spend years in prison for a crime he hadn't committed.

All Cole cared about was winning.

No, that wasn't fair. Cole had reminded us repeatedly that pleading innocent and being found guilty could mean the death penalty. It was possible the Sawyer name would protect Ford from a murder conviction. It was just as possible it would make him more of a target. According to Cole, the prosecutor was a pit bull and a crusader.

She was the last person who'd be swayed by wealth and power. Griffen had pushed Cole to put her off, to give us more time to find some evidence to exonerate Ford. And we'd looked. Sinclair Security's investigator had looked. Griffen had looked. West had looked. Cole had been searching for evidence since the beginning. No one had found a thing.

If Cole was coming here, I could only assume we were out of time.

The afternoon passed far too quickly. Before I knew it, Griffen's phone rang with an alert from the front gate. Cole Haywood was here. I didn't know him well. Prentice had worked with him some, I think.

They'd known each other through business, though I wasn't quite sure how. Cole was a criminal defense attorney. As far as I knew Prentice had never been prosecuted for anything, but I wouldn't have put it past him to hide something like that from the rest of us.

Cole paused in the doorway, taking in Griffen and me sitting side by side, the papers and laptops spread across the desk. "I won't take much of your time," he said, his voice heavy. Tired.

I'd first met Cole years before when he'd been newly married. His wife had been gorgeous, not a surprise since he was a good-looking guy. Kind of like Bryce, Cole was almost too good-looking with his designer suit and chiseled jaw. At least, he had been back then. I hadn't seen Cole smile since his wife had died in childbirth, taking their son with her.

His face had taken on hard lines, grief wearing grooves in the sides of his mouth and his forehead. He was leaner these days, the polish of social charm worn away by pain, leaving him with a dangerous edge.

He didn't bother to sit, though he did close the office door behind him. The words I'd dreaded filled the room. "We're out of time. The prosecutor is done delaying. Either Ford cuts a deal, or we go to trial."

Griffen tapped his pen on the heel of his palm. "What's the deal?"

"It's not for you to approve," Cole said, abrupt and annoyed. Griffen didn't seem to care. For all the reasons he had to hate Ford, Griffen didn't believe he'd killed our father.

"I understand that," Griffen said, his patience strained. "I know you're Ford's lawyer, not mine, but you're here so you might as well tell us. What's the deal?"

"She offered ten years with a chance of parole after five. She'll include time served, though that doesn't amount to much."

"Ten years?" Griffen said, his voice low. Pained.

"It's first-degree murder, Griffen."

"A murder Ford didn't commit," I reminded him. "The prosecutor might not care, but you and I both know he didn't do it."

Cole looked out the window, avoiding both of our gazes. He seemed to sag into the door frame behind him, his voice exhausted when he spoke.

"I told you, it doesn't matter what I know. What I believe. It only matters what I can prove. Ford doesn't have an alibi. Eyewitnesses put him near the Manor at the time of the murder. They found the goddamn murder weapon in his closet. I'd love to get your brother off, especially considering that I don't think he did it. I'm not a fucking magician. Your father is dead. Someone needs to pay for that. The prosecutor isn't going to wait for us to find another suspect when they already have one in jail."

He straightened, holding his briefcase in front of him like a shield. "Look, I only stopped by out of professional courtesy. Ford already agreed to the deal. The wheels are in motion. There's nothing you can do except show up at the next visiting day."

Cole strode from the room without another word, his footsteps echoing down the hall.

Chapter Thirteen

ROYAL

here's nothing you can do.

The words rang in my ears. *Nothing.* Ford was locked up, and he wasn't getting out. Not for at least five years. Maybe longer. The injustice of it burned in my gut. Ford wasn't perfect, but he hadn't killed our father. I knew that without a doubt. If he had, he wouldn't have been stupid enough to hide the murder weapon in his own closet.

Five years in prison for a crime he hadn't committed while whoever did it ran around free.

Five years.

Somewhere in the back of my mind, I'd been sure we'd get him out of jail. Sure that at the last minute, someone—Sinclair Security, West, Griffen—would find the evidence we were looking for, and they'd have to let Ford go.

I'd never really believed we'd give up, never believed Ford would take the deal.

"Fuck." I leaned over, bracing my elbows on my knees, sucking in one breath, then another.

The burning in my gut spread to my chest, my head. My vision blurred with tears of rage. This wasn't how it was supposed to go.

This wasn't right. Wasn't fair.

A low sound, almost a growl, came from beside me. I raised my head to see Griffen motionless, staring down at the top of his desk, his jaw clenched so hard the muscles bunched below his ears.

Without warning, he flew from his seat and let out a primal scream, the sound filled with every ounce of his frustration and rage, filled with the helpless fury that had snowballed since the moment we'd learned of Ford's arrest.

With another bellow of raw emotion, Griffen reached out an arm and swept everything from the desk, sending our laptops and papers crashing to the floor.

He spun around, arms raised, the anger surging through him, needing a target. I understood what he felt on a visceral level, knew the need to let out his fury, the pain of knowing that despite trying our best, our brother would still suffer.

The course of Ford's life had changed when our father had been killed. We'd tried to stop it. We'd failed. We'd failed our brother.

Before I knew it, Griffen was climbing onto the desk. Feet planted on the shiny surface, he lunged at the trophy buck hanging on the wall, grabbed both antlers, and tore it to the ground.

Something broke through my own rage, something clean and pure. The bare spot on the wall was a little bit of my father stripped from the room. It felt right.

I didn't care that technically this was Griffen's office. Griffen's house. It was mine too, and I wanted every reminder of my father gone. I dragged over one of the heavy leather chairs and stood on the arms, reaching up to rip that poor bear's head off the wall. It deserved better. I added it to the growing pile Griffen had started, watching as he tossed a stuffed mallard on top.

"Any attachment to these curtains?" I asked with a grunt as I tore them to the ground.

"I fucking hate them. The curtains, the trophies. That goddamn painting of Prentice. I want it all out."

Together we stripped all signs of my father from Heartstone's office. Griffen swung the French doors wide, and we carted all of it to a clear spot in the grass behind the house, piling it high. I whirled at the sound of movement behind me to see Sterling standing there, her eyes wide with fascination.

"I'll be right back," she breathed and took off at a run into the house.

I didn't know Sterling could move that fast. She was back only minutes later with what looked like yards of white satin shoved under her arm, a half-full bottle of vodka in one hand, a lighter in the other.

Sterling tossed the bundle of fabric on the top of the pile and upended the vodka bottle, watching with an exuberant grin as the vodka soaked into the pile. When it was empty, she tossed it in the grass behind us and flicked her lighter, setting it to the closest bit of white satin. Flames ate at the heavy fabric, greedy, growing by the second.

If we'd wanted to take it back, it was too late.

The three of us stood there side by side and watched it burn, these memories of our father and the mark he'd left on the house. On us.

Finn turned up, taking a spot beside me, his arms crossed over his chest, one dark eyebrow lifted. "Redecorating the office?"

"Taking out the trash," I answered. Finn was as much a stranger to me as Griffen had been. He'd left home not long after Griffen, choosing the military over life with our father. His constant bitching about the household cooks was entertaining but other than that, I didn't know him very well. Now was as good a time to start as any.

"Anything you want to add?"

Finn stiffened as if arrested by the thought. I wondered what was going through his head when he turned and jogged back into the house as Sterling had. He was back seconds later, half-shoving and half-dragging the throne-like leather chair that had sat behind Prentice's desk as far back as I could remember. Griffen grunted in approval, moving to grab the other side of the chair. Together they hefted it to the top of the pile, dodging sparks as it settled.

"I hate that chair," Finn murmured from beside me.

"Me too," Sterling agreed. "The way he'd sit there and stare down at me, telling me what a disappointment I was. How I'd never amount to anything. I always figured—why bother trying? Nothing I did was ever good enough. Not for the mighty Prentice Sawyer."

"You know it wasn't just you, right?" I asked.

Sterling looked over at me. "But he let you and Tenn run The Inn."

I shook my head. "Only because he thought we'd fail and he could sell it off. He told us so many times we were going to fuck it up and the whole town would know what losers we were. Then we didn't fuck it up, and he took all the credit."

"Sounds like Dad," Finn said. "When I joined the Army, he told me never to come back." Finn glanced over at Griffen. "I didn't come back often, but I did come back. You could have if you wanted to."

Griffen's teeth clenched. The fire absorbed his gaze for a long moment before he answered. "I didn't want to at first. Later—it just seemed impossible." He was silent again, staring at the flames.

In a low voice I could barely hear, he said, "I imagined what he'd say, how he'd take all the things I'd accomplished, everything I'd made of myself, and break it down until I ended up feeling two inches tall. I should have come back. For the rest of you, if not for me. I'm glad I never had to see Prentice again, but I'm sorry for leaving my family."

"We should have looked for you," I said. It hurt to make the words real, to take that heavy guilt and make it concrete.

Griffen hadn't wanted to, but he'd come home. He could have ignored the will, could have stayed in the life he'd built in Atlanta with the Sinclairs helping to run Sinclair Security.

Griffen hadn't owed us anything, but he'd given us all a chance. He was giving me a shot at the job I'd always wanted, and he'd helped Sterling more than anyone had in years. He was making Heartstone Manor a home again. He deserved the truth. We all did.

"We should have tracked you down," I said. "We should have stopped him from kicking you out in the first place."

"Ford should have stopped it." A crystal tear rolled down Sterling's cheek. "He regretted it," she said, her voice thick. "I know he did. He tried to make up for it with the rest of us, but he should have stopped it. After he divorced Vanessa, he should have found you, should have apologized and brought you back. I think he couldn't bring himself to face what he'd done. And now—" She choked out a sob. "He's not coming home, is he?"

I reached out and pulled her into my arms, holding her close as I hadn't in too many years. "He is. He's coming home. Just not right away."

"What's going on?"

Chapter Fourteen

ROYAL

I GLANCED OVER MY SHOULDER TO SEE PARKER framed by the French doors of the office, looking ready for a garden party in her pink linen dress. Her brow furrowed as she stared at us, ranged around the bonfire as if we were going to pull out marshmallows to roast.

That was an idea. I wondered if there were any marshmallows tucked away in the kitchens.

Parker's husband loomed behind her, looking over her shoulder, his lip curled in disgust, then in alarm as he spotted the edge of a picture frame being devoured by the flames.

"What the hell are you idiots doing? Don't you know how valuable some of that stuff is?"

Finn shot out an arm, blocking him before he could reach in and pull out the burning painting of our father. "We're not the idiots here, you moron. That painting's on fire. If it was worth anything before, it sure as hell isn't now."

"The lot of you are insane. I can't wait until I can get out of this place and go back home." He stormed into the house, slamming the French doors behind him so hard they rattled.

I couldn't help but notice that he'd said, *I can't wait until I can get out of this place.*

Not *we.*

I.

He hadn't said he wanted to take Parker home with him.

Parker had always been a good girl. She did what Prentice told her, never attracted attention. She was beautiful, the perfect image of her mother, Darcy, the only one of Prentice's wives who'd ever mothered any of us.

Parker had gone to college in New England. She'd met Tyler Kingsley in her junior year and married him the following summer. Once she was his wife, she'd never really come home again. Not until Prentice died.

I didn't know her well these days, but I'd always loved her. I wished I could say the same for her douchebag of a husband. From what I could tell, he was an asshole through and through.

Parker must have been used to his attitude because she ignored his tantrum, taking a place beside Finn. "When did you decide to redecorate?" she asked mildly, in a tone more suited to the garden party she was dressed for than a bonfire in the backyard.

"Just today," Sterling answered in the same tone. "Anything you want to add?"

Parker contemplated the flames. "Is that the skirt of your debutante gown I see?"

"It is," Sterling said, her lips curving into a wide smile. I couldn't remember if I'd ever seen her smile like that before, as if a weight had lifted from her heart. "I hated wearing that dress.

Hated the creepy guy Dad set me up with, and all the manners, and rules, and people giving me the side-eye because they said my mom was trash and so was I. I like the dress much better now that it's on fire."

"You looked beautiful for your debut, but I agree. It looks better on fire." Another moment of silence before Parker said, "Excuse me," and headed back inside.

I figured that would be the last we'd see of her until Sterling murmured, "I wonder what she wants to burn?"

I was distracted from Sterling's question by the sight of Hawk Bristol—our head of security and head groundskeeper—storming around the corner of the house. "Griffen, what the fuck? We don't have enough security problems without you setting a huge fire in the middle of the lawn?"

Griffen shrugged a shoulder. "We've had plenty of rain and the fire isn't close to the woods or the house. You can grab a hose if it makes you feel better, but I think the rest of us just want to watch this fucker burn."

Hawk scanned the group of us, and I wished for one crazy moment that Tenn, Avery, Quinn, and Brax were here, too. I had no doubt they had their own memories they'd like to burn to ash.

Parker came striding out of the house, her sleek blond hair streaming behind her, her arms overflowing with white satin and tulle. She tossed the mound of fabric into the fire where the flames licked and consumed, flaring higher as they devoured her contribution to rebellion.

Parker took a spot next to Sterling, wrapping an arm around her younger sister's shoulders. "I always hated my deb dress, too."

Sterling looked up at Parker, her eyes wide. "Really? You looked like the perfect princess. I was overblown. Too obvious."

She gestured to her figure, as lush and abundant as her mother's had been, even when she'd been a young teenager. "I looked like a porn star wrapped up in satin, but you were like a porcelain doll."

Parker snorted. I didn't think I'd ever heard her make such an inelegant sound. She tightened her arm around Sterling and shook her head.

"I felt like a porcelain doll. I smiled and behaved myself and did what I was supposed to because that was the best way to keep Prentice's attention off me, but I didn't feel like the perfect princess. I felt like a tool. I think that's why I got married before I graduated from college. I didn't want to come back here." She looked back up at the house where her husband had disappeared. "I thought it would be an escape."

"But it wasn't?" Sterling asked quietly, her eyes on Parker's face and the shadows that hid there.

Parker only sighed and watched the fire burn.

The air smelled of burnt hair and chemicals. Not quite as comforting as a campfire. Now that the stench really hit me, I rethought my plan to find marshmallows.

A throat cleared and I turned to see Daisy standing there, a covered dish in her hands and a confused look on her face. In the late afternoon sun, her cherry-cola hair was a burst of color, streaks of hot pink and auburn twined together, her curls pulled back with a wide band to bare her face.

Hope was behind her, wide eyes taking in the scene. Hope looked far better than she had the last time I'd seen her, her face rosy with health instead of green. She must have had a good nap.

"What's going on? Is that a bear on fire? And curtains?" Daisy looked up at me. "What are you guys doing?"

"Just a little spring cleaning," I said.

"Are you sure that isn't going to reach the woods?" She eyed the flames nervously.

"Hawk went to get a hose, but I think we're clear. There isn't any wind."

I'd thought Hope would head straight for Griffen, but she stood behind Daisy, typing on her phone. Maybe sensing my attention, she looked up. "You should take Daisy for a walk in the gardens."

The three of us looked behind me into the mostly dead, very overgrown remains of Heartstone Manor's formal gardens. Hope gave me a pointed look. She was up to something. I didn't know what, but I couldn't wait to find out.

"That's a great idea, Hope." I hooked my arm through Daisy's elbow, steering her in the direction of the gravel path to the gardens. "Did you stop by to see me?" I asked, hoping the answer was yes.

Stopping in the shade of a tree, Daisy turned and held out the covered dish. "I baked you a pie. To say thank you for the flowers."

"You didn't have to." I stepped closer and plucked the covered dish from her hands.

"I wanted to. The flowers were beautiful."

"I'm glad you liked them," I said, holding on to the dish with my free hand, the scents of fruit and sugar drifting up now that we were far enough away from the bonfire. "What kind of pie did you bake me?"

"Mixed berry," she said, shifting her weight as if preparing to flee.

I hooked my arm through hers again, drawing her deeper into the gardens. Everything back here was a mess. My father had let them go and Hawk had been too busy to move his small landscaping crew back here. Someday they'd be restored, but for now, they were at the bottom of Griffen's renovation list.

I led Daisy to a wrought iron bench, and we sat in the shade of a tree looking out over the scrubby remains of Heartstone Manor's formal gardens.

"Why mixed berry? Was that the pie of the day?"

Daisy glanced up at me and thought for a minute before saying, "You struck me as a man who appreciates variety and a little tart with his sweet."

"You'd be right. And maybe I should be embarrassed to say so, but I'm hiding this pie, so I don't have to share it with everyone else."

Daisy laughed, the sound a relief after the tension of the past few hours. "I wouldn't want to share it either. I'm greedy when it comes to pie."

"Would you think less of me if I tell you I've been hoarding your brownies?"

I'll admit I asked just to get another laugh out of her. She didn't disappoint me, the sound of it soaking into my soul just as the first laugh had. I could spend all day just making this woman laugh.

I looked down to the curve of her lip, the length of her gracefully crossed legs. I wanted to run my hands over all of her smooth skin. I liked to make her laugh, but I'd like it even more if I could do it while we were naked.

One thing at a time, I reminded myself. She still wasn't sure she wanted to be here. The last thing I needed was to scare her off before she made up her mind, which made my next move debatable. But there was no reward without risk, and Daisy was worth taking a chance.

"Why don't you stay for dinner?"

She shifted on the bench, putting more space between us. "I—I wouldn't want to impose. I didn't think about it being so close to dinner. Grams is handling closing, and I thought I'd run over here and give you the pie after Tenn said you were here and not at The Inn, but I couldn't impose for dinner."

"Do you have other plans?" I probed.

"Not really, but I'm not dressed to eat dinner... here." She looked over her shoulder at the imposing rear view of

Heartstone Manor. Even with the gardens a mess, the house was beautiful, towering above us, the wings extending to the sides of the main building like arms embracing the gardens.

"We don't dress for dinner anymore." I thought of Parker in the cocktail dress she'd worn the night before. "Well, most of us don't dress for dinner. Sterling was wearing pretty much the same thing you are."

Daisy wore khaki shorts and a pink polo shirt with the bakery's logo embroidered on the chest. She looked casually professional and far more presentable than the way some of us had shown up to dinner.

"Hope will be there. She didn't have a great day. She's been sick as a dog, and I'm sure she'd love to see you."

I wasn't above using Daisy's friendship with Hope to get my way. I didn't know why she was so gun shy, but I had every intention of finding out.

First, I had to get her to trust me.

Chapter Fifteen

ROYAL

"W HY DON'T WE GO BACK IN THE HOUSE, I'LL STASH THIS pie somewhere secret, and we'll get you a glass of wine. Or beer. Or whatever you want. Except the vodka Sterling used to start that fire."

"She poured vodka on it to get it started?" Daisy laughed again. I was getting addicted to the sound of her laugh, the spark in her eyes when she was amused. "It's fitting, I guess. Sterling pouring out the vodka to burn—what did she burn?"

"Her debutante gown. And the vodka."

"And you? What did you burn?"

"The trophy of a bear my father lied about killing. When I was a kid, I always wanted to set that bear free."

"And now you have. Did it feel good?"

I stretched out my arms along the back of the bench, one hand landing barely an inch from Daisy's shoulder, and tipped my head back to look at the sun-dappled branches above us. "Yeah, it did. It felt fucking great."

"Good." Daisy leaned her head back to rest against my arm and joined me in staring up at the tree. "Why did you decide to start a bonfire in the yard? Why now?"

I found myself telling her the truth. "Ford took a plea deal. No trial. No search for the real killer. Just murder one on his record and the next chunk of his life in prison."

Daisy sucked in a breath. "I'm sorry."

"And it's weird," I went on, hardly aware of what I was saying but feeling like with Daisy I could spill out the jumble of emotions inside me. "It's weird because I know it's not my father's fault. He was the one who was murdered. Obviously, it's the fault of whoever killed him and set Ford up to be blamed. But still, it feels like this is on Prentice. It feels like he did this to all of us."

"And he's dead, so you can't get back at him. But the bonfire's a pretty good substitute. Isn't it?"

"I think it might be, yeah."

We sat in silence, soaking up the warm air and the sounds of birds and insects, the rustle of the tree leaves above our heads. From the corner of my eye, I saw Hawk point a hose at the bonfire. He was all business, no appreciation for mayhem. Probably a good addition to the Heartstone Manor team considering the rest of us, but I could have let that fire burn all night.

"So, do you want a glass of wine before dinner?"

Daisy looked up at me, considering. "I think I might, yes."

Out of nowhere, Hope appeared, Sterling and Parker behind her. Parker lugged a wicker picnic basket and Sterling carried what looked like a bottle of white wine in a marble cooler and two wine glasses.

Without a word of explanation, Hope spread a blanket across the grass under the tree, Parker set the basket on the corner, and Sterling arranged the bottle of wine beside it, laying the two glasses gently on the blanket.

Parker sent me a gentle smile and Hope winked before they turned to go. Sterling said, "Enjoy," with that laugh in her voice I hadn't heard often enough. Then she was gone along with the others, leaving Daisy alone with me.

Daisy stared at the blanket and picnic basket with wide eyes. "What just happened?"

"I think they were the picnic fairies. And I think we're going to owe them a big thank you." I stood and reached for Daisy's hand. "Shall we see what they brought us?"

I left the pie on the bench and joined Daisy on the blanket, picking up the wine that one of our picnic fairies had thoughtfully opened and re-corked. Daisy pulled out crackers and cheese, neat slices of cured sausage, and a small container of olives. Next, she withdrew two individual quiches, still steaming from the oven.

"Wow." My stomach rumbled as I surveyed our haul of food. "No dessert. I guess that means I only have to share the pie with you."

I handed Daisy a glass of wine and took the small plate of crackers, cheese, olives, and sausage that she'd prepared for me.

I waited until she was munching on her own cheese and crackers before asking, "Tell me about your family. I saw your mom is working at the bakery now. Are you two close?"

Daisy took a long sip of wine. "Not really. I'd like to be. I wish we were. I'm closest to Grams. She pretty much raised me."

There was a lot of history in that statement. I wasn't used to digging into the heavy stuff on the first date. Really, I never dug into the heavy stuff with the women I dated. With Daisy, I wanted to know. I wanted to unravel the mystery of her family and J.T. I wanted to know all of her secrets.

"Why didn't your mom raise you?"

Daisy hesitated. I wanted to know, but not if she didn't want to tell me. "If you don't want to talk about this, that's okay."

"It's not that. Well, it is, but like I said before, it's complicated."

"I'm a good listener," I said, "but I meant it. If you don't want to talk about it, we can talk about something else. But if you don't want to say because you're afraid of what I'll think... Just consider that when you showed up, the Sawyer family was burning their father's treasured possessions. We're pretty fucked up over here. There probably isn't much you could throw at me that's worse than the skeletons in our closets."

I managed to startle a laugh out of Daisy, giggles chasing the pensive expression from her face. When she could talk, she said, "Good point. Basically, here it is. My dad is one step up from a con artist on a good day. He's insanely charming, and handsome, and he's excellent at talking himself out of trouble. Which is good because he's also excellent at finding trouble."

She nibbled on another cracker, lost in thought. I waited, not wanting to push now that she was talking.

"When I was a kid he was always on the move, always looking for the next big score, the business deal that was going to make us rich. My mom loves him. She believes in him. He lets her down over and over, and she always thinks this time it'll be different. The way Grams tells it, my dad got a job offer when I was just a baby, and she was supposed to watch me until they got settled. They didn't come back for two years. By then, Grams didn't want to give me up."

Daisy took another long sip of wine before she spoke again. "Honestly, I doubt they asked her. They love me. I know they love me. They're just not very interested in parenting. Grams was everything I needed."

"I know all about being raised by someone who isn't into parenting," I said. "Prentice was pretty much hands-off. He let his wife of the moment take care of us, and Miss Martha did her best, but Prentice didn't take much interest unless it was to berate us for something. My own mom barely stuck around after she had Avery and Tenn. Apparently, having twins wrecked her figure, and she wasn't going to ruin the rest of it raising us. Prentice wrote her a fat check, and I never saw her again. He married Darcy a month later."

"And your mom just never came back? Mine wasn't around a lot, but at least I see her now and then."

"She's married to some guy twice her age. They live in Palm Beach. And Darcy was a great mom while we had her." I felt my throat close as the words left my lips. I looked down into my wine, not wanting Daisy to see the grief I knew was in my eyes. All these years later and I still missed Darcy like a hole in my heart.

"I'm sorry about your mom," Daisy said. "And Darcy. Hope told me Darcy was wonderful." Daisy shot a quick look at my face and changed the subject.

"I kind of always figured my mom stuck with my dad because he needed taking care of more than I did. And I'm grateful they left me with Grams. With Grams, I had hugs, and food on the table, and school. Grams taught me to bake and tucked me in every night. Grams taught me to dream like my dad, but she also taught me how to work hard and make those dreams come true."

"She sounds amazing." I wished we'd had a grandmother like Daisy's when we'd been kids.

"She is," Daisy agreed.

I took her empty plate, slid her quiche onto it, and handed it back. "Finn complains about every cook we have, but I think this one's not too bad. Fingers crossed the quiche is good."

"It smells fantastic," Daisy said and took a bite. I took one of my own. Maybe the quiche wasn't as perfect as one Finn might have made, but it was pretty damn good. We ate in silence for a few minutes.

I wanted to ask about J.T., but I didn't want to push my luck and remind Daisy of her kind-of, sort-of, not-really a boyfriend. I'd save that for another time.

"So, Grams taught you to bake? Sweetheart Bakery has been open as long as I can remember."

"She taught me everything I know," Daisy said. "I wanted to go to school for it, the culinary program that J.T.'s in at Tech, but there wasn't money and then Grams needed more help at Sweetheart, so I never did. I did get an Associates in business—I did night classes at the satellite campus in town—and that's probably been more helpful in running the bakery than culinary school would've been anyway."

"Do you wish you'd gone? Do you still want to?" It must be hard to watch J.T. chase a dream she'd wanted for herself.

"Kind of?" Daisy looked up at me through her lashes. Popping a bite of quiche in her mouth, she chewed thoughtfully. "When J.T. talks about his classes I want to know everything he's learning. But the schedule is a killer. I'd have to leave Sweetheart and Grams can't run the place on her own. I wouldn't want her to. And the truth is it's not practical. Even if I saved up for the tuition, it's not a program you can do part-time, and I don't need a fancy degree on my resume because I already have a job. Sweetheart Bakery isn't going to buy me a Ferrari, but we do a pretty solid business."

She shrugged. "Culinary school is one of those things I dream about but I'm not working for. I think I'm too practical for that."

"If he works for you, how did J.T. swing the tuition? Is he loaded down with student loans?"

"He's paying tuition with blood money." Daisy shook her head. "His parents kicked him out when we were in high school. They didn't talk to him for years, but they came back a while ago, said they felt terrible and missed him, and they wanted to make it up to him. They still barely see him, but they forked over the cash for his tuition, so that's something."

"Why'd they kick him out?"

Daisy shook her head again. "Some things aren't mine to tell, you know?"

"I do." I had a suspicion, but I wouldn't push. "When are you going to start adding on to the bakery?"

I'd figured that would be an easy question to lead us away from J.T.'s secrets, but it looked like I'd hit a sore spot. Daisy's thick lashes lowered, and she took another bite of the quiche.

Interesting. She'd gone quiet at the bakery when Grams had been talking about her plans for expansion. There was something wrong there, but I'd pried enough already.

"It smells like Hawk made them put out the fire." At the obvious change of subject Daisy's eyes cleared of worry. The air had cleared as well, the odor of burnt hair and chemicals faint but present all the same. The last few minutes it had cleared, chased off by the scent of wildflowers and damp grass. Much better.

"That was quite a fire. Anything you wish you'd thrown in while you had the chance?"

Chapter Sixteen

ROYAL

I TOOK A BITE OF QUICHE AND THOUGHT ABOUT IT. "I think we hit the major spots in the office, but I wish the others had been here. I'm sure they had stuff they wanted to see go up in flames."

"Is it weird? All of you living at home again? Hope told me it was part of the will. I'm sorry if it's awkward that I know these things because of her. She's one of my best friends, so—"

"I don't mind. I'm used to people knowing way more about my family than they should."

Daisy looked away, her shoulders stiff. I reached out to close a hand over her arm and gave her a gentle shake.

"I don't mean you. I'm just saying I'm pretty much an open book. I don't mind you knowing stuff. I trust Hope's judgment, and I want to get to know you better. It wouldn't be fair if I asked you about your family and then got annoyed that you know about mine.

"And to answer your question, it's extremely weird to have all of us back home again. Griffen is practically a stranger. So is Finn. And I don't know the rest of them that well either, aside from Tenn. Prentice was always setting us against each other. What we should have done is team up against him, but by the time we were old enough to figure that out, we'd spent most of our lives getting played by Prentice. I don't think it occurred to a single one of us to work together. Watching Ford betray Griffen felt like an object lesson."

"Wasn't your father behind that? Didn't he talk Ford into it? Hope said—" Daisy stopped herself. "It just seems like maybe an object lesson was the point. Maybe it wasn't only about Ford and Griffen. Maybe your dad wanted to prove to the rest of you that you couldn't trust each other."

I stared at her. Why had that never occurred to me? I'd figured out that Prentice had been behind Ford's betrayal of Griffen. It had been obvious at the time. Prentice hadn't even bothered to hide his machinations once they came out. But it had never occurred to me that he might have been making a point to the rest of us.

If that was his plan, it had worked.

Daisy watched the realization bloom on my face. Reaching out, she closed her hand over mine. "Sorry to bring it up. Your dad was a real asshole."

I barked out a laugh. Goddamn, this woman was good for me. "And then some." I leaned over and dropped a kiss on her lips. Immediately, I wanted more. After dessert. Soon.

Daisy looked over my shoulder at the rear elevation of Heartstone Manor. "At least you have plenty of room to avoid each other if you want to. You could probably stash a football team in there and no one would notice."

I followed her gaze. The house was massive, it was true. "You'd be right, except half of the bedrooms aren't even furnished. Prentice let the house go to hell, and none of us were living here, so we didn't know."

"Why would he do that?"

"Your guess is as good as mine. He was a miserable bastard most of the time. The only one of us who had regular contact with him was Ford, and Ford claims he doesn't know what Dad was up to. I don't know how they could work together all day and not know anything about each other's personal lives, but apparently, that was the case."

"Whatever happened with cockroach guy?" Daisy asked suddenly. "Did he say why he was messing with you guys?"

"Like every other asshole who's come after our family lately, he claims he was paid by someone else."

"And you don't know who?" Daisy ate the last bite of her quiche and set the plate down beside her empty wine glass.

"No clue," I admitted.

"I bet this is driving West nuts."

"West and the rest of us. Especially Griffen. Hope probably told you he spent most of the time he was away working for one of the best security companies in the country. Even they haven't been able to find anything." I picked up the bottle of wine I'd corked. "Another glass?"

"I'd better not. I have to drive home, and more wine will put me straight to sleep. I still have to prep for tomorrow, and I was up at 3:30."

"Do you always get up that early?" It had been a while since I'd seen three-thirty am. I hadn't gotten to bed that late in years, and I sure as hell wasn't getting up that early.

"No, not usually. I've been working on some extra projects and getting up early is the easiest way to fit them in. I'm not a late sleeper anyway. You can't be and run a bakery, but even I have to admit I could do without the 3:30 wake up call."

"Then we should have dessert so you can get to bed on time." I rummaged in the picnic basket and came up with two clean forks. "I hope you don't mind sharing the pie."

I repacked the picnic basket and set it aside. Grabbing the pie from the bench, I sat back down, leaning against the tree. "Come over here, and I'll feed you some pie."

Daisy's eyes were cautious. For a second, I thought she'd claim her fork and turn me down. Triumph swelled in my chest as she came to sit beside me, hip to hip, and leaned back into my chest.

Just the feel of her that close was everything I wanted. The weight of her body against mine, the scent of her hair, sweet with fruit and flowers. She fired me up and calmed me down at the same time.

I wanted to toss the pie aside and get my hands on her, but she was skittish enough as it was. Instead, I forked up a bite of the mixed-berry pie and carefully brought it to her lips. She took it and chewed slowly. I took my own bite, my eyes closing in bliss as the tart, sweet berries exploded over my tongue.

I fed her another bite and then another. I loved to watch this woman eat. The way her tongue flicked across her lips, her eyes closing as she gave herself over to experiencing the food. The little noises of pleasure she made in her throat, just like she did when I kissed her.

Maybe I could have behaved myself if we'd been sitting across from each other at the dining room table. If we hadn't been alone.

I'd planned to share more of the pie. I swear I had, but I couldn't take it anymore.

I set the pie plate on top of the picnic hamper and tossed our fork into the grass. "Pie later. I need to kiss you now." Pulling Daisy into me, I tilted her face to mine, already lost in the heat of her warm brown eyes.

Daisy's fingers slid into my hair, closing in a firm grip, pulling my face to hers. Daisy's mouth on mine was all the answer I needed. I lost myself in the kiss. In the taste of her lips, the feel of her in my arms. So sweet and so right. Everything about her felt like she belonged exactly where she was.

Daisy didn't protest when I rolled us to the blanket and stretched out. She arched into me, kissing me harder, as lost as I was. I skimmed my hand under her shirt, my fingertips drinking in the soft silk of her skin, the weight of her breast in my hand through her lace bra.

I wanted to strip her clothes from her body, to spread her legs and taste her everywhere. To fill her with me. To make her come. Somewhere in the back of my head, I managed to remember that while we were alone, we weren't that far from the house.

If anyone was nosy enough to go up to the second floor or happened to be in their bedroom, they could look right out the window and see everything that was happening on the picnic blanket.

No matter how much I wanted her, I wouldn't embarrass Daisy like that. I could settle for just kissing. I could have kissed Daisy all night. For just a second, I thought about sneaking her into the house and up to my room, my thought process not that different than it had been at sixteen.

No. Not this time. I already knew she wasn't ready. For the first time, it wasn't about the end game. I wanted Daisy in my bed, but more than that, I wanted to keep her there.

Rushing might get me a fuck, but it wouldn't get me Daisy.

She shoved at my shoulder, and with a rush of disappointment, I rolled back to let her go. I didn't expect her to follow, pushing me to my back and leaning over me, one leg hitched over my hip, grazing my hard cock. Soft breasts pillowed on my chest as she brushed her lips against mine, her fingers again buried in my hair, her palm nudging my head back into the perfect position for a slow, deep kiss.

The brush of her leg against my cock was almost enough to push me over the edge. But it wasn't just that, it was her taking control, leading the kiss. So far, I'd been the one to initiate. I hadn't realized how it would feel for Daisy to turn the tables and seduce me.

Her fingers busy on my shirt buttons, I skimmed my hands up her back and flicked open her bra, filling my palms with her breasts, loving the hum of pleasure in her throat at my touch. It wasn't until she spread my shirt open that she sat up, her nipples peaking beneath her polo shirt, teeth sunk into her swollen bottom lip.

Her fingers stroking down my chest, voice husky, she said, "We're outside, aren't we?"

I grinned up at her as she looked around, eyes dazed with lust as if wondering how we got here. "We are. And there are a lot of windows aimed this way."

Her teeth sank into her lip again, the obvious regret on her face the most beautiful thing I'd ever seen. Curling up to sit beside her, I nuzzled her cheek, reaching behind her to refasten her bra. "Next time I want you somewhere private. Somewhere it's just us."

"I want that too," Daisy admitted. "Not tonight, but soon."

"Not tonight, but soon," I agreed.

Letting her go—packing up the picnic and carrying it back to the house, walking her to her car and sending her off with just one more kiss on her sweet, perfect mouth—it was all so much harder than it should have been.

It was a date. A date with a pretty woman. I'd had countless dates and not a single one of them had meant anything. I'd walked away from every one of those women without a second thought.

I hadn't taken Daisy to bed. She hadn't even agreed to go out with me or confessed that she didn't really have a boyfriend, and still, saying goodbye was a bitch.

I wanted her to stay. I wanted her in my house. In my bed. I just fucking wanted her.

Now, I knew she wanted me, too. I could have walked away if I thought she wasn't interested. Really, truly wasn't interested.

Now that I knew she wanted me almost as much as I wanted her?

Nothing was going to scare me away.

Not even Daisy herself.

Chapter Seventeen

DAISY

FOR TWO DAYS, I WAS WALKING ON AIR. ALL I COULD think about was Royal.

I tried not to. God knows I had plenty to keep me busy.

I'd managed to put Grams off on the expansion, and while I hadn't come close to replacing the money, I was making progress. I tried not to look at each entry in my spreadsheet and think about what it was costing me in time and sleep and worry.

I tried not to think about how far I was from my goal and that eventually, I was going to have to explain to Grams and J.T. why our pretty little deck wasn't going to happen this year. So far, I'd added another regular account with the gift shop on the other end of Main Street, and the pop-up grilled cheese stand I'd done for lunch on Tuesday had been a hit.

I was exhausted, tired all the way to the marrow of my bones, and still, all I could think about was Royal.

I couldn't get my head around the idea that he liked me. More than liked me.

He was Royal Sawyer. He was smart, and funny, and successful on top of just being a Sawyer. And handsome. So freaking handsome. Just looking at him—hell, just *thinking* about him—made my knees weak. It was everything. Those blue eyes. His smile. That body.

I'd barely gotten a good look at it the other night under the tree, but what I'd seen—wow.

I wanted to see more. A lot more.

I had to face the truth. I wanted Royal Sawyer.

It would be easier if I could tell myself I just wanted to sleep with him. J.T. had been right, it had been a long time for me. Whether I wanted a relationship or not, I could do for some physical contact of the sexual variety.

If I was going to face the truth, I had to admit that I wanted a lot more than that from Royal. He was so easy to talk to. To be with. He didn't judge. I'd wondered if he would look down on me for not having gone to college like he had or for not going after culinary school like J.T. was, but it felt like he completely understood.

He listened, really listened instead of waiting until I was done so he could talk. When I was with him, I felt like I could tell him anything. It wasn't until I was alone that the doubts crept in.

"Daisy? Do you want to talk about this now?" Grams' voice cut through my fog of distraction. My cheeks went hot as I thought she wanted to talk to me about Royal. No way I was discussing him with Grams.

I already knew what she thought on the subject. If I asked her, she'd probably drop me off at his door in lingerie with a fistful of condoms. Grams did not approve of my date-free lifestyle.

"Huh?" I set down the pan I'd been drying for at least three minutes too long and turned around. Grams stood in front of me, concern in her eyes.

"You look tired, baby." She ran her fingertip beneath one eye, stroking the puffy circle I knew was there.

"Just not sleeping well," I lied. Not sleeping enough was more like it. "I can't get used to J.T. being gone during the week."

Grams raised an eyebrow at me, not buying my bullshit. "It's been over four months since he started at Tech, and he's been staying in town during the week for half of that at least. You should be used to it by now. I'll give you an herbal tea blend. You need your sleep." A grin spread across her face that I knew meant trouble. "Maybe you should ask Royal Sawyer to tuck you in."

"Grams, butt out."

"I'm your grandmother. I'm not going to butt out. It's my God-given right to be nosy about my granddaughter."

"Not about my sex life," I protested, busying myself with cleaning up the kitchen and prepping for the next day.

Grams propped a hip against one of the worktables and crossed her arms over chest. "Well, the day you get a sex life, let me know and then I'll proceed with being nosy."

"Smart-ass," I muttered under my breath.

"Who's a smart-ass?" my mother asked from the doorway to the shop.

"Daisy says I am because I'm teasing her about Royal Sawyer," Grams said. "Shop all closed up?"

"Everything's done up front," my mom said, adding, "I think she's a smart girl if she's being cautious about Royal. The apple doesn't fall far from the tree, you know."

I bit my tongue before I could demand to know what she meant. Grams got there first. "Sheree, what makes you say that? Prentice was a bastard, and Ford could be cold, but I haven't seen any sign that the Sawyer children take after their father. More like they take after their grandfather. Now, Reginald was a good man. I always thought Prentice drove him into an early grave."

"Drove him into an early grave? How?" I asked, curious. I got most of my Sawyer-related info from Hope, but suddenly, it occurred to me that Grams had been born in this town, and she probably knew more of the old history than Hope did.

"Well, Prentice talked his father into signing the company over to him when he was in his 30s and then pushed his father out completely. Said it was an early retirement, but Reginald was born to work. He just wasted away after Prentice put him out to pasture. Died not long after. I don't know where Prentice got all his mean, but it doesn't run in the blood, that's for sure."

My mother crossed her arms over her chest, her jaw set mulishly. "I'm just saying you can't know that. There's nothing wrong with Daisy guarding her heart. Royal is a player. Everyone in town knows it. And he may put on a good act, but he's still Prentice's son."

I turned to study her, realizing that this wasn't my mom suspicious of a man who had an interest in her baby girl. This wasn't really about me. It was something more.

"What do you have against the Sawyers? What did they ever do to you?" I couldn't imagine. My mother hadn't spent that much time in Sawyers Bend despite her long marriage to my father. They flitted in and out of town, but they were never here long enough to make friends or cause any trouble.

My mother lifted that set jaw in my direction. "Prentice Sawyer took advantage of your father in a business deal not long after you were born. I don't care if he lived in that big house and wore a fancy suit, he was still a thief. When your father tried to get back the money Prentice swindled out of him, Prentice had him arrested."

"Sheree!" Grams cried, "Why didn't you ever tell me this? I could have helped! I could have—"

"It's ancient history," my mother said quickly, and I could tell she regretted letting so much slip in front of Grams. "It happened right after Daisy was born. We might not have had to leave town for so long if it hadn't been for that."

Maybe I was bitter about my parents' frequent absences. I tried not to be. I tried to focus on everything I had instead of the things I was missing, but I couldn't help thinking that if Prentice Sawyer had swindled my father out of money it was probably done before my father could swindle him out of the same.

For the life of me, I couldn't imagine any business Darren Hutchins could have with Prentice Sawyer that was aboveboard. Possibly because I'd never known my father to have any business that was aboveboard. Except the one he'd pitched to get my money.

I tamped down the sick feeling that rolled in my stomach, the revulsion at hearing my mother complain about being swindled out of money when she and my father had done exactly that to me.

I wanted things to be simple. I just wanted to love her and have her love me and leave it at that.

I couldn't help resenting the easy way she slipped through all of it.

How could she stand here and look me in the eye knowing we were both lying to Grams? Knowing she and my dad had effectively stolen from me, stolen from Grams?

If I managed to pin her down she'd just wiggle her way out, telling me to talk to my dad, that it wasn't what I thought, that nothing was what it looked like, and everything was okay.

I wasn't going to confront her about the money, not with Grams right here, but I couldn't ignore her comments about Royal.

"Mom, I get why you think you have a reason not to like the Sawyer family. That's your business. But Royal is a good man, and I'm not going to listen to you say otherwise. If he breaks my heart, feel free to call him all the names you want. Until then, I don't want to hear it."

I squirmed under the pitying look in her eye. Her phone beeped just as she started to say something else. Snapping her mouth shut, she looked down at the screen and everything about her changed. Her eyes brightened and her smile stretched wide. It was as if a sunbeam cut right through the ceiling of Sweetheart Bakery and illuminated my mother.

Shit.

She stood there, her face wreathed in smiles, eyes glowing, and all I felt was dread. I knew what put that look on my mother's face. I wasn't ready.

Deciding to take a page from her book, I shoved my misgivings away and looked at Grams. "What did you want to talk about when you came in? I was distracted, and I wasn't really paying attention."

Grams shot a concerned look at my mother, then shook it off. "I wanted to know if you're ready to talk about the next lunchtime pop-up. I can't believe how fast we sold out of those grilled cheeses. I was thinking it would be fun to do chili with bread bowls. Though that's really more of a winter thing. Or Paninis! We could have two or three options and put the press behind the counter. What do you think?"

My mother slipped out to the front of the shop, leaving us to strategize. I decided not to worry about what she was up to and told Grams my latest brainstorm. "Do you remember me telling you that I had a picnic with Royal the other night? Well—"
Ignoring the flush that hit my cheeks at the thought of that picnic, I told Grams all about the single serving quiches Royal's chef had prepared.

"It's in our wheelhouse considering it's basically a pie. It's easy to keep warm without drying out and cook ahead of time. We can have samples outside like you did with the grilled cheese."

"Oh, Daisy, you're brilliant. I love it! I'll do some research and come up with a few options. We can try them out and decide which ones—"

The door between the shop and the kitchen swung open with a flourish. My father strode through, arms spread wide.

My heart swelled and my stomach sank. He was here, finally.

Maybe now I'd get the answers I needed.

Maybe, but I doubted it.

Chapter Eighteen

DAISY

MY FATHER'S GRIN MATCHED MY MOTHER'S. "MY girls! I have all my girls together. I've missed you so much."

I was struck dumb by his presence, by the sheer force of him and, uncomfortably, by his resemblance to Royal. Just like Royal, he filled the room. All that charisma wrapped around us as he pulled Grams into a hug and rocked her back and forth, half-dancing her across the kitchen until they reached me.

Then I was in their embrace, smelling my father's familiar cologne, his arms strong as he rocked me back and forth like he had Grams. I wanted to stay there in my dad's arms, soaking up his love, as fragile and illusory as I knew it was.

With a tight squeeze, he said, "My beautiful baby girl. I've missed you so much." Leaning back, he took in my face and touched the same spot under my eye that Grams had. "Such a pretty girl shouldn't work so hard. I'm sending all you girls to the spa. You need a day off. You need a vacation! I'll get it all set up."

I wanted to ask where he was getting the money to pay for us to go to the spa and if he had it could he please pay me back. Obviously, I couldn't do that because a) I doubted he had the money to send us to the spa, and b) if I asked for it I'd have to tell Grams why he owed me money.

Out of the corner of my eye, I took in Grams beaming at my father, and I knew that I wasn't hiding his debt just because I didn't want her to know I'd been stupid enough to lend him money.

I was partly doing it because I didn't want Grams to know her son had sunk low enough to scam his own daughter.

Maybe he didn't scam you, I tried to convince myself. *Maybe he has the money—or at least some of it—and everything is going to be fine.* I wanted to believe that was true.

I stepped out of his embrace and looked away, fiddling with the knot I'd tied in my apron. As soon as I was out of his immediate sphere he turned back to Grams and Mom, soaking in the love and approval beaming off both their faces. Grams was so happy to see him, she couldn't contain herself.

"Darren, Sheree didn't tell us you were coming today! I'm so glad I made a special dinner anyway. We've just about got the shop closed up, why don't you come back to the house with us, and we'll have a family dinner. You can tell us all about your adventures while we eat."

My chest ached at the hope in her voice, hope I knew echoed in my own heart.

I could see the end from the beginning.

He was going to disappear along with my mom as abruptly as he'd appeared, and everyone would be the worse for his visit but him.

I'd told myself so many times that this is just who he is. I can't take it personally. That he isn't capable of loving like other people. I'd been able to live with those lies to myself right up until I'd let him sell me on his business plan and had handed over all that cash.

I'd believed for months that he'd come through. Now, looking at him, I wanted to hold on to that last shred of hope that everything was going to work out.

Dinner was excruciating. My father sat in Grams' spot at the head of the table telling story after story. People he met in Tampa, a card game where he won big, and the bulldog puppy in the final pot that he'd almost brought home with him. My mother and Grams hung on every word. I watched my mother's face, rapt with love and admiration, and wondered if I looked at Royal like that.

Was I just one more Hutchins woman to fall for a smooth, charming guy with nothing underneath? Was Royal really everything he seemed? Or did I just find him so attractive because a part of him reminded me of the Dad who was never quite there for me?

Was I really falling for Royal, or did I just have daddy issues?

For a second, I wished my dad had never come back, even if he did have my money.

Royal was not my father.

I knew that. I did. And still, seeing my dad—his thick, dark hair, similar build, and wickedly charming smile—all I felt was doubt.

I waited until dinner was over, until my mother and Grams had picked up their plates from the table and headed for the kitchen. My father stayed where he was, handing me his plate as I approached, so I could clear it for him. I took it, holding back the impulse to slam it over his head.

Aware of my mother and Grams only a closed door away, I didn't bother to soft-pedal. "Dad, you haven't been answering my calls. Do you have the money to pay me back? You said you'd have it months ago, and I'm running out of excuses for Grams."

Annoyance flashed across my father's face. He gave a shake of his head as if flicking it away. In a blink, his smile was back. "Daisy, honey," he said in a low tone that wouldn't carry to the kitchen, "I don't have it yet, but I will. I promise. That's why I'm here. To see my girls and do a little business."

Ice spread through me at those words. "Dad, not here. Not in Sawyers Bend. Grams and I have a business here. Can't you just visit and then—"

Hurt filled my father's eyes. "You don't want me around? You aren't happy to see your dad?"

"It's not that, Dad. Of course, I want to see you. But I never told Grams I gave you that money. And it was from the business. You know that. I can't keep covering up—"

"Sure, you can, baby. I know how smart you are." He stood and gave me a long hug. "You're my beautiful, brilliant girl, and I know you can give me just a little more time. I won't let you down."

Taking the plate from my hands, he sauntered into the kitchen, leaving me with another flash of his grin and more problems than I'd had at the start of our conversation.

Typical.

I heard laughter through the kitchen door and fought back tears. I wanted to be on the inside, laughing with Grams and my mom. I didn't want to be standing here alone, angry at my parents and unable to look Grams in the eye. I piled the rest of the dishes in my arms and pushed through the kitchen door.

"I'm sorry to leave you with the dishes, Grams, but I still have to finish setup for tomorrow." I dumped the dishes in the sink, avoiding my grandmother's eyes.

"You go on, baby. We've got this. Don't stay up too late, okay? You need your sleep."

"I won't," I lied, and pressed a kiss to her cheek. I'd do anything for Grams. Anything except tell her the truth about her son and the money he almost certainly wasn't going to pay back.

I walked home with my head down, studying the screen of my phone. Out of habit, I'd started to text J.T., but as I pulled up our message thread, I realized the person I really wanted to talk to was Royal. I didn't know why. My best friend would understand about my dad without any explanation. So, why did I want Royal?

I pushed away the desire to hear Royal's voice and texted J.T.

Guess what? Dad showed up tonight. Says he has business in town.

Nothing for an endless minute. I walked down the block, seeing tourists pass me by, spotting the Sweetheart sign all the way at the other end of the street. I'd lied to Grams a little. I was done with setup, I'd just needed to get out of there.

Finally, three dots appeared on the text screen.

WTF? Do you want me to come home? I know things have been tense with him...

Yep, J.T. knew things had been tense, though I hadn't told him why. He figured it was the usual. In some ways, it was. The money just added an extra layer to the complicated relationship I had with my parents. I was debating my response when the phone rang in my hand. J.T.'s face showed on the screen.

"Hey," I answered. "How's school?"

"It's great. Are you okay?" His voice sounded muffled like he was keeping it low for privacy.

"I just left family dinner at Grams' house. Dad spent the whole time bragging about Tampa and the poker games he won. Telling us he was going to send us to the spa."

J.T. laughed. I could picture him shaking his head as he usually did when it came to my dad. "Did he hit you up for your credit card for the spa before or after dinner?"

"I think he's waiting on that. He said he has business in town. I asked him not to get into any trouble but—"

"Fuck. That doesn't sound good. Since we know it's not like he got a job."

"I know. I just, I don't know, J.T.—"

A voice filtered in from the background on J.T.'s end. "Hey man, you want me to tell them we're gonna be late?"

I wanted to ask J.T. who he was with and where they were going. Not to be nosy, just because he was my friend and I wanted to know about his life like I used to. *Patience, Daisy*, I reminded myself. "I'm okay if you need to go, J.T."

"You don't sound okay, Daze. You sound like shit. I can come home. I have to get up early for class, but I'll come home, and we'll raid the bakery case for cookies and watch a movie."

That sounded so good, but I couldn't take him up on it. It wasn't much after six, but it would take almost an hour to get here from Asheville and J.T. had to be at class at six-thirty in the morning.

I loved that he loved me enough to come home anyway, and I loved him enough not to let him.

"It's a date for the weekend," I said. "I'm going to try to go to bed early. And it sounds like you have something fun on for tonight. I don't want you to miss it for me."

"You sure? You know if you need me all you have to do is call."

I knew he meant it, and that was enough to have tears springing to my eyes. I missed him now that he was gone so much, but a part of me was fiercely glad he was out there forging a life for himself. He'd been hiding away with me and Grams for way too long.

"I know. I love you. Go have fun."

"Love you too, Daze."

We hung up and I kept walking, feeling like I'd lost

something, which was stupid because J.T. was still my best friend, and he always would be. He absolutely would have come home if I needed him to, just like if he needed me I'd drop everything to get to him.

But he had that friend waiting for him. The friend he still hadn't told me about.

I wasn't going to be the one to hold him back. And I wasn't going to ruin his night so I could whine about my shitty relationship with my parents. I'd survive, and one of us should have some fun.

I drew closer to Sweetheart Bakery but stopped in the middle of a block to check out the menu posted in a restaurant window. I wasn't going to try a full lunch service out of the bakery, but I had my eye open for simple ideas I could add to a modified lunch menu.

Once I got that little deck built and put out tables and chairs, I'd be able to serve sit-down meals for a good chunk of the year. If I could afford to cover part of the deck, I could use clear curtains and a space heater to extend the season.

A pang hit me when I thought about the change in schedule and all the money I had to save all over again.

Get over it, I ordered myself. *You made this mess. Now you have to live with it.*

The phone rang in my hand and I looked down to see Royal's name on the screen. I answered before I could talk myself out of it.

Chapter Nineteen

DAISY

"Hey," I said, way too eager for the sound of his voice.

"Hey back. What are you doing?"

With uncharacteristic honesty, I blurted out, "Walking home from family dinner at Grams' and feeling sorry for myself. How about you?"

"Sitting at my desk, also feeling sorry for myself. Want to come have a pity party with me? I have truffles and a split of champagne."

"You have truffles and a split of champagne at your desk? Maybe I should have you come over to the bakery and stock my office. Why are you feeling sorry for yourself? Did you have a bad day?"

"I'll tell you all about it if you come to The Inn. Did you walk past it already?"

I had, kind of. The road from Grams' house hit Main Street in the middle. The bakery was on one end and The Inn on the other. Going to The Inn would mean retracing half my walk, plus adding another few blocks. I didn't care. I wasn't that tired. Especially not if Royal was my destination.

"I'm on my way."

"See you soon," Royal said, sending a thrill of anticipation through me.

Getting involved with Royal might be a bad idea. I wouldn't know until it was too late. But it didn't *feel* like a bad idea, and when it came to Royal, I was going with my gut. I sure as hell wasn't taking my mom's advice.

Just because Grams had fallen for a fast-talking older guy who left her pregnant at 16 and my mom had let my dad talk her into dropping out of college to marry him didn't mean I was going to pick a loser, too.

Royal was anything but a loser.

My feet moved faster on the way back toward The Inn. I could hardly believe it when I looked up and spotted Royal coming down the street toward me. He turned just as he pulled even with me, reaching out to take my hand. We walked side by side back toward The Inn, his fingers wrapped around mine, saying nothing.

I didn't need words just then. His presence at my side was enough to smooth the rough edges left by dinner with my parents. When we reached The Inn, Royal guided me around the side, through the parking lot.

"It's a nice night, so I thought I'd show you the gardens. I promise the gardens at The Inn are much better than Heartstone's. And I want to show you the project I've been working on."

"That sounds great," I said. "I'd love to see The Inn's gardens." As we rounded the building and stepped onto the gravel path, a young woman in an Inn uniform strode up and handed Royal a basket. With a nod at Royal and me, she disappeared.

Royal hooked the handle of the basket in the crook of his arm but didn't say anything about the contents. I resisted the urge to ask what was inside, hoping it was the truffles and champagne. I asked the other question I wanted answered. "Did you have a bad day?"

Royal's smile was rueful. "Not the worst day ever, but frustrating and way too long. I was late getting out to Heartstone this afternoon because I was getting our new CFO settled in. I think he's going to be a great fit, but I underestimated how long it would take to show him the ropes. Then Savannah ran into an electrical problem at the Manor, which ate up half of our afternoon, and worse, is delaying getting Bryce and Ophelia out of The Inn."

"Is that why you were back in your office?"

"Things came up this afternoon while I was at Heartstone that I needed to deal with. I guess it wasn't a bad day so much as too long. I like the ending, though."

Another smile, this one leaving me breathless. He was so handsome when he smiled. Royal was handsome all the time, but when he smiled, really smiled, he was blindingly gorgeous.

Looking up at him, I wondered how I could have thought he was anything like my dad. In looks and charm, yes, absolutely. My dad and Royal had both to spare. But my dad never would have put in a long day doing any kind of work, much less juggling two businesses and family at the same time. My dad couldn't even clear his own fucking plate from the table.

I squeezed my fingers around Royal's and smiled back. "I like the ending, too."

I have to admit I was barely paying attention to the gardens other than to register that they were green, filled with flowers, and beautiful. As the sun slowly set, fairy lights twinkled to life in some of the trees and glowing spotlights illuminated the path.

We passed the first of the cottages by the river, built in the same stone and timber style as The Inn itself. I'd never stayed in one, being a townie and not having a massive bank account, but I'd heard they were gorgeous on the inside. And very, very expensive. Some of them were lit up already, guests home for the evening and enjoying their private sanctuaries.

The river burbled through the trees, the scent of water drifting into the garden, twining with the scents of flowers and other growing things. We passed the last cottage, which had its porch lights on but was otherwise dark. After that, there was a short gap and then what looked like a foundation, already poured. Beyond that foundation was another and yet another.

"Are you adding new cottages?"

Royal drew to a stop and turned so we faced the newly poured foundation. "We are. Tenn and I planned this out years ago but couldn't get Prentice to approve it. Griffen looked at our business plan and gave us the go-ahead. The Inn has high occupancy rates year-round, but the cottages are booked to capacity most of the time. We charge a premium, even more in the summer and fall, and people keep showing up. It seemed a waste not to use the land."

I studied the new foundations dotted along the river and had no doubt these cottages, too, would be occupied year-round. It was peaceful here, the existing cottages rustically gorgeous. The perfect spot for a vacation in the mountains.

"How long until they're ready?"

"Maybe by late fall, early winter if we don't run into any trouble."

"That's great, Royal. If they're anything like the others, it's going to look beautiful."

"That's the plan," he said and turned us back the way we'd come.

I wasn't ready when he took me to the porch of the nearest cottage and led me inside. Nerves thrilled through me as we walked through the main living area, past the wide-open doors to the bedroom, but Royal ignored the temptation of the big bed and brought me to the covered back porch overlooking the river.

"We've kept this cottage closed while we're under construction to give paying guests a buffer from the noise. I thought we could sit on the porch and drink some champagne."

"That sounds perfect," I said, a little dizzy from the romance of it. I sat on the wide porch swing facing the river and propped my feet up on the railing. Royal took the spot beside me and did the same, the heat of his body against mine easing the tightness I'd had in my chest since dinner.

Royal poured me half a glass of champagne. "Tell me why you were feeling sorry for yourself."

I both regretted having said anything and wanted to tell him everything. I settled for something in the middle.

"My dad's home. It's good to see him, I guess, but he... Well, I told you about him. He's full of big stories, and smiles, and hugs, but he says he has business in town and he—"

I almost told Royal that my dad owed me money, but I couldn't do it. It wasn't just that Royal was wealthy and I wasn't comfortable pointing out how very much I wasn't. It was more that Royal saw me as a businesswoman. In a way, as a peer. I didn't want him to know how foolish I'd been and think less of me.

"It just got to me all of a sudden," I went on. "The way my mom and Grams hang on every word he says and never question any of it."

"I used to feel like that about my dad. He'd go on and on bragging about how he'd outsmarted everyone, when I knew being smart had nothing to do with it. He'd probably lied and cheated to get his way."

I let out the breath I'd been holding. I'd been right, Royal did understand.

"I usually feel like I have my life under control," I went on, "and then my dad shows up and it all starts slipping away. I feel guilty because I just want him to leave and let me go back to my peaceful, organized life. But he's my dad. I want to love him and I want to want him around, but I don't. Grams is so happy when he's here. I don't want to spoil it for her, so I just keep my mouth shut and go along."

"I wish I could fix it for you," Royal said, "but parents are the kind of problem you can't fix."

"I guess you know that better than anyone," I said and took a sip of champagne before leaning my head on his shoulder.

"I guess I do," he agreed. "Here, try this."

Royal stroked a dark chocolate truffle over my bottom lip, the bittersweet scent filling my nose. I bit in, my taste buds prickling as the potent ganache melted across my tongue. A low hum vibrated in the back of my throat, my brain lighting up with pleasure.

Champagne and chocolate definitely improved the end of my day, but not as much as Royal himself. I opened my eyes to see Royal studying me, absorbing every change of expression, every sound I made.

"Are you watching me eat again?" I asked, my voice husky with embarrassment but more from the look in his eyes as he watched me.

"I'm thinking about feeding you truffles naked. Does that count?"

My mouth dropped open. I'm not sure what I would have said if Royal hadn't popped the other half of the truffle into my mouth. His lips grazed my ear. "Do you want me to feed you chocolate naked? If it helps, I'd be naked too." He sucked at the spot beneath my ear that always made me dizzy. Liquid heat flooded between my legs at the rhythmic pull of his lips on my skin.

"Naked is good. I want to see you naked," I breathed, my head spinning. Reality intruded, my thoughts skipping to something other than lust. "My life is complicated right now."

"So is mine," Royal countered. "Life is always complicated if you do it right." His lips skimmed down the side of my neck. "That's part of what I like about you."

"That I'm complicated?" All the blood in my body was somewhere other than my brain. I wasn't getting it.

"I always thought complicated was too much work. But not with you. Complicated is worth it with you."

"What if I'm too complicated?" I asked, not sure why.

Royal moved his mouth from my neck, kissing my jaw before he sat up and topped off the champagne I'd barely sipped.

"I don't know, so far, you haven't scared me off, no matter how hard you've tried. And I'm not exactly simple. There's my family, for one thing. Complicated doesn't even cover them. And there's your boyfriend."

For a second, I had no idea who he was talking about. Oh, yeah. J.T. Wasn't it time to come clean about that? I couldn't tell him the whole story. That wasn't mine to share. But I could tell him the truth that was mine.

"I don't have a boyfriend," I admitted, waiting for him to pounce on the words with some version of *I told you so* or *I knew it.*

"Since when?" he asked, sounding curious rather than vindicated.

"Since a long time." I took a sip of the champagne, the tart sparkle washing away some of the chocolate. Spotting the box of truffles beside Royal, I took one out and lifted it to his mouth, watching with rapt attention as his eyes lowered when he bit in, his thick lashes dark fans across his tanned cheeks.

"I think I just got used to saying J.T. was my boyfriend. People assumed, and we let them because it was easier and neither of us was looking for someone else."

Royal swallowed, and when his eyes opened, they fixed on mine. "Did you sleep with him?"

"Actually sleeping? All the time. Sex? No."

"Never?"

It wasn't really his business—it's not like I was going to grill him on his sexual history—but I understood. Where J.T. was concerned, it *was* his business. A platonic friend I loved deeply was one thing. A friend I loved deeply who I'd also had sex with was a totally different thing.

"Never. We kissed once when we were in middle school and it wasn't worth repeating." I set my champagne on the railing and turned to face Royal, knowing it was essential that he understand if we were going to move forward. "I love J.T. He's more family to me than most of my actual family, and I'm the same to him. I'd do anything for him. Anything. But we don't love each other like that, and we never have."

"Okay."

"Okay? Just like that?" I don't know what I expected. An argument? An ultimatum? Anything but this easy acceptance.

"Just like that. You haven't given me any reason not to trust you. And I understand friendship. I'm looking forward to getting to know him."

"He can't wait to meet you," I said. "He was almost as excited by the flowers you sent as I was. He would have dressed me up and delivered me to The Inn on the spot if I'd let him."

"Now I really can't wait to meet him," Royal said, sending me another of his blinding smiles. "I need someone on my side."

"Hey!" I swatted the back of my hand at his chest before picking up my champagne and taking another sip. "I'm on your side."

"Are you?"

It could have been a playful, teasing question. It would have been simpler if it had been. Royal's eyes were deadly serious, and I knew my answer was important. This was more than flirting.

For all the running away I'd done, Royal needed me to stop. I didn't know why, I just knew that it was time.

Chapter Twenty

DAISY

I HAVEN'T DATED IN A LONG TIME," I ADMITTED. "OVER two years. I don't trust my own judgement with men, and you're exactly the kind of guy I've always avoided."

"Why? What is it about me that scares you off?"

The hint of vulnerability in his eyes cracked the shell around my heart. I couldn't be the one who made him feel less. I wouldn't. Reaching out, I wrapped my fingers around the back of his neck and leaned in to press my lips to his.

"Nothing," I said, withdrawing just enough to meet his gaze. "There's nothing about you that scares me off. Not really. It's me. I like everything about you, Royal. That's what scares me."

I sat back and put my empty champagne glass on the railing. Royal waited, his guard still up. If he needed more, I'd give it to him with the blunt honesty he seemed to bring out in me.

"Grams always talked about the Hutchins women having bad luck with men. Not just her with my grandfather, who took off long before dad was born, but her mother and her grandmother, too. They all had stories of charming men and broken hearts. And watching my mom and dad together made me cautious about falling for someone. My mom may be a Hutchins by marriage, but she fits right in. She's so blinded by my dad she buys all the bullshit he hands her and asks for more.

"I can't stand the idea of losing myself like that. I dated some, had a boyfriend for a while a few years ago, but he moved away for a job, and when I didn't miss him, I started thinking I was better off on my own. J.T. had his own reasons he wasn't interested in dating, so we made do with each other."

"Without sex? I can see how being with J.T. would be almost the same as having a boyfriend, but didn't you miss sex?"

The laugh escaped before I could stop it. "If you'd known my last boyfriend you'd get why I thought I could do without."

Royal raised an eyebrow, possibly seeing a challenge in my words. "That bad?"

"I figured it was me. No one before him was any better. I thought I was just bad at it." I looked at Royal through my lashes, flirting and shielding myself at the same time. My heart sped with nerves. "After you kissed me, I realized it might not be me after all."

I swear Royal's grin made my panties wet. Wetter. Yep, there was nothing wrong with the way I responded to Royal. Nothing at all.

"That good, huh?" he said, that sexy grin just a little bit smug.

"You know it was. So good it got me thinking."

"About what, exactly?" Royal probed, his guard slowly melting away.

"That maybe it's time to take a risk." In case it wasn't clear, I added, "With you."

That was all I needed to say. Royal hauled me onto his lap, satisfaction and anticipation glowing in his eyes. "Took you long enough."

"Hey, I had stuff to work through."

Royal brushed my hair back from my face, cupping my cheek in his hand. "I'll try to make sure I'm worth the effort."

I closed the distance between us, putting my mouth to his ear. "I already know you are."

I could spend the rest of my life kissing this man.

That was the last coherent thought I had.

Royal turned on the long swing, taking me with him, and propped his back against the padded arm, me on top of him. Our legs tangled, his mouth took mine, our kiss tasting of chocolate and champagne.

Royal's hand slipped under the hem of my shirt, fingertips stroking my skin. I wanted skin. I wanted to touch. I wanted to feel him all over, to satisfy the ache between my legs. The hard bar of his erection pressed between us.

I wanted to slide my hand there, to stroke and squeeze, but the narrow porch swing didn't leave me enough room. Royal's hips rolled into mine, his hardness trapped against my heat, my breath coming in pants.

My body was liquid, my lips moving on his out of instinct, my brain shut off in favor of sensation. His hard hands on my hips, his soft lips, the way his mouth owned mine. I needed more, my long-ignored sex drive coming back to life with a vengeance. I didn't just want sex. I wanted Royal. My hips rolled into his, knees spreading wider, his hard length pressing exactly where I needed it.

Abruptly, Royal pulled his mouth from mine and tipped his head back, staring at the ceiling of the porch, his own breath short and fast. "We have to stop," he muttered, blinking rapidly as if he found his words as crazy as I did.

"Stop?" I repeated, dazed.

"I didn't bring you here for this, Daisy." His hand stroked down my back, resettling my shirt before he corrected, "Well, I brought you here partly for this. But not for more. Not yet. Not here."

I could barely believe it when I reminded him, "There's a bed inside."

Royal's laugh was rough-edged. "Don't remind me. I want to get my hands all over you, believe me. Just not yet."

"We don't need to wait," I offered, not sure I understood.

Royal nuzzled that spot beneath my ear, sending a bolt of lust all the way to my toes. "Yes, we do. I do. I need to wait. When I get you naked, I want time and privacy. And I want you to know that it means something."

"You don't have to prove anything to me, Royal," I said, surprising myself. I would have thought that's exactly what I'd want. I guess it was—before. After seeing that hint of uncertainty in his eyes, I knew he wasn't playing me.

Royal brushed a hand over my hair, his eyes soft. "It's not about proving something to you. You're important, Daisy. I know we're just getting started, but you're not a fling. I don't want to rush."

I didn't know what to say. A joke sprang to my lips about pretending we were a fling or using him for sex. I kept my mouth shut. This wasn't the time. Digging deep for courage, I told him the truth. "You're important, too, Royal. I wouldn't be ready for more if you weren't. But I can wait until you're ready, too."

Royal's chest rumbled in a laugh. "I must be nuts. But I still want to wait."

I only hummed in my throat in response.

We stayed where we were, stretched out on the swing. Royal dropped a foot to the porch and nudged, sending us swaying gently back and forth. In the trees on the other side of the railing a firefly lit, then another.

I rested my head on Royal's chest, listening to the thump of his heart in one ear and the babble of the river in the other as he stroked his hand up and down my spine. With each pass of his hand, I melted into him a little more.

This was heaven. Right here, cradled against Royal, the warm evening shrouding us in calm quiet. I didn't stir until I felt my eyes drooping shut.

Into the dark, Royal said, "I have to get you home before we fall asleep here and we're too stiff to walk tomorrow."

"I'd love to call you an old man for saying that, but I fell asleep on my couch the other day and my back was killing me when I woke up. I've reached the age where I have to sleep in a bed."

"No camping for you?" Royal rubbed the backs of his fingers against my cheek.

"Camping is an exception. I haven't been in forever, but I'll sleep on the ground if I'm in a tent."

"I'll keep that in mind."

Royal insisted on driving me home. He pulled into the parking spot behind the bakery and got out, my hand in his as he walked me upstairs to my door.

"I'd like you to come to dinner at Heartstone on Sunday," he said simply.

"You're inviting me to a family dinner?"

Royal grinned at me. "I need a shield. Ophelia and Bryce are moving into the Manor—thank God—and it's going to be a circus. Can you brave it? For me?"

Despite the frisson of nerves in my gut, I grinned back at him. "I'll protect you. What time should I be there?"

"I'll pick you up at six."

"I'll be ready."

One more sweet, slow kiss and he was gone.

I was exhausted but too wired to sleep. I had to get to bed so I could be up well before dawn. I'd pulled in two last-minute custom cake orders that I'd have to fit in before everything else I had on the schedule.

I straightened my kitchen, put away the dishes I'd left drying on the rack, and turned out the light, hoping that laying down would prompt my brain to stop thinking and fall asleep.

Ten minutes staring at the shadows on my ceiling told me that wasn't going to happen. I wanted to be back on the porch swing, the river in one ear and Royal's heartbeat in the other. I could have stayed there all night.

Missing Royal was enough to propel me out of bed. Not bothering to turn on the lights, the faint moonlight enough to illuminate my small kitchen, I set up the electric kettle and got out the herbal tea Grams had pushed on me the day before, swearing it put her out like a light every night.

I was stirring in a spoonful of honey when headlights flashed below the kitchen window. A door opened and shut, followed by another.

Voices, one of them familiar.

What was my dad doing behind the bakery at this time of night?

In the dark, I was invisible. They probably couldn't even tell the window was open. I didn't resist the urge to eavesdrop. I hitched my hip onto the edge of the sink and looked down to see my father standing beside an unfamiliar car. I couldn't tell the model, but it was shiny and sleek and looked expensive. Not his car.

A woman stood facing him, hands propped on her hips. I couldn't make out all of her words, but her tone was aggravated. I caught enough of her to see shiny dark hair and red lips. She was tall, taller than my dad in her heels, and voluptuous.

I couldn't see my dad cheating on my mom, but what was he doing meeting this woman in the dark? And why here?

She shifted, looking even more annoyed, her voice louder than before. "Don't even think about giving me any of your bullshit, Darren. We're on a timeline here. If you fuck this up I'm not the one you're going to have to deal with. Do you understand?"

"You know I do. You can depend on me."

I imagined I could see the woman's eyes roll as she tossed her hair, but maybe that was projection. Her next words proved me wrong. This woman knew my father. "If I had any other option, I never would have brought you in. You're a weasel and you're lazy."

"Hey, that's uncalled for." I marveled at how genuinely offended my dad sounded.

"I disagree, but you're what I have to work with. Get the job done or I'll let my partner deal with you."

"If it's so important, why don't you do your own dirty work?"

"I'm too well known to pull off this stage of the plan and you know it. Get the job done and I'll get you the cash you need. And if you don't, you'll have a bigger problem than empty pockets."

"Hey, just tell your partner I've got it under control."

"See that you do." The woman got back in the car and pulled out. I watched my father duck out of the parking area behind the bakery and head down the alley to the street. Silently crossing my apartment, I moved to the windows overlooking Main Street, tracking him as he walked back toward the road to Grams' house.

Crap. Now what was I supposed to do?

He was up to something, but I'd known he'd been up to something when he came back to Sawyers Bend. Now I knew he had a partner, but I had no idea who she was. It'd been too dark to see her features clearly, but what I'd seen I didn't recognize, and I don't think I'd ever heard her voice before.

Whatever was between them, I couldn't imagine he was cheating on my mom. I didn't get that vibe. She'd seemed dismissive and pissed, and he hadn't struck me as a guy trying to seduce a woman. More a man putting off his boss over a late assignment.

I didn't even know if what he was up to was illegal. She'd told him to get the job done and her partner would be mad if he didn't, but that didn't necessarily mean they were breaking the law.

West couldn't arrest my dad for secretly meeting a strange woman behind the bakery. People were allowed to have conversations in public. And Grams' heart would break if her son was arrested in Sawyers Bend.

I sipped my tea in the dark and tried to convince myself to forget I'd seen a thing.

I'd keep an eye on my dad, but I was going to do that anyway. For just a second, I thought about telling him to forget the money, to just go and leave us all in peace.

Even if I were willing to forget the money, telling him to go would be a waste of time. Whatever my dad was involved in, it sounded like exactly his kind of trouble.

Darren Hutchins had never walked away from trouble that I could remember. I couldn't imagine him starting now.

Chapter Twenty-One

ROYAL

I DIDN'T THINK I'D BE NERVOUS. THIS WASN'T MY FIRST
rodeo. I'd picked up plenty of women for dates
and usually, my concerns centered around
whether I'd be bored and if I'd get laid at the end. I wasn't
surprised to discover that, like all things with Daisy, this was
different.

Daisy worried about being too complicated, but I wasn't
sure she knew what she was getting into with me. My life had
never been simple. Since my father died it had only grown more
complex.

I thought having Daisy to a family dinner would be like rip-
ping off a bandage. We'd get all the crazy out of the way at once
and hopefully, she'd still want me when it was over. At the time,
it had seemed like the perfect plan.

Now that I was standing in front of her door, a bouquet of daisies clutched in my sweaty fist, I was absolutely questioning my sanity.

Sawyers Bend had no shortage of romantic restaurants. Why wasn't I taking her to one of them? Or I could have driven her into Asheville and taken her someplace really nice, could have arranged to stay in a hotel overnight... Fuck. What the hell had I been thinking?

Her door opened and my gut dove straight to my toes. A man stood there, about the same height as me, with dark hair, broad shoulders, and a lean, rangy build that could have used a few pounds of muscle.

It wasn't his body that was striking, it was his face.

I couldn't quite pin down the mix of ethnicities there. Almond eyes, smooth brown skin a few shades lighter than Daisy's, and dark hair that had a wave to it. His eyes were a startling green framed by thick, black lashes, and his cheekbones could have cut stone. He would have fit right in on a runway.

He could be none other than the famous J.T.

I hadn't been nervous when I ran into Daisy's grandmother, but meeting J.T. had me shaking in my shoes. I bit the bullet and stuck out my hand.

"I'm Royal Sawyer. You must be J.T. It's great to meet you."

J.T.'s fingers closed around mine, his grip strong, but he didn't try to crush my fingers or overpower the handshake. He swung the door wide and stepped back, inviting me in.

"Daze is still getting dressed, but she'll be out in a minute. Taking her to family dinner?" He shook his head, an amused grin on his too-handsome face. "You like to jump right into the deep end, don't you?"

I gave a rueful smile. "I'm starting to wonder what I was thinking. But I guess if she doesn't run screaming, that's a good sign."

The door across the living room opened. Daisy walked out, and all thought fled my mind.

Daisy was always beautiful to me. She had a spark inside her, an inner glow that shone through no matter what. Even after a long day, when she was exhausted, and sweaty, and her hair was all over the place, I still thought she was gorgeous.

I didn't know what gorgeous was.

I'd never seen her like this. She wore a creamy sheath dress that set off her warm skin, curving around her hips and dipping in front enough to show the tiniest hint of cleavage. She'd done something different with her hair, the wild curls strikingly defined, framing her face in shades of auburn, red, and hot pink.

I didn't think she wore much makeup usually, but tonight her eyes were deeper, her lashes longer and her lips pink. Instead of her sneakers, she wore cream spike heels that looked a mile high and made her legs even more unbelievable than they'd been in the first place.

"I don't think I want to share you with my family. You're usually gorgeous, but this is... Wow. All I can say is wow." I shoved the bouquet at her, mouth a little dry. All my smooth compliments had deserted me. All I had was *wow*.

Daisy reached up to tuck a curl behind her ear and J.T. was there, smacking her hand away. "Stop touching your hair, or you'll turn it into a frizz bomb," he ordered.

Daisy scowled at him and hid her hand behind her back. J.T. took the flowers from her other hand. "I need to talk to Royal for a minute. Why don't you run downstairs and get that chocolate cake you baked?"

Daisy raised an eyebrow and glanced between J.T. and me. Her eyes settled on J.T. "Are you going to be nice?"

J.T. turned her toward the door and gave her a gentle shove. "Of course, I'm gonna be nice. I just need to have a chat with Mr.

Sawyer before he takes you off on your date. Indulge me and go get the cake packed up."

Daisy followed orders, stopping at the door to look back at me. "Don't believe anything he says. I'll see you downstairs."

She disappeared, her shoes clicking on the stairs and fading away. I shoved my hand in my pocket and turned back to J.T.

"So?" I asked, wondering if he was going to warn me off.

J.T. shoved his own hands in his pockets and leaned back against the kitchen counter. "I like the suit."

"I don't usually wear one, but it seemed appropriate tonight."

"Since you're taking her to a family dinner, I'm assuming this is serious. All the gossip about you and I've never heard of you bringing any woman home for dinner."

I relaxed. I liked a man who could get straight to the point. And this was J.T.—as Daisy had said, more family than most of her family. Maybe it should have been annoying, but I liked that she had someone looking out for her. Since J.T. was being upfront, I wasn't going to waste time playing games.

"I think it's fair to say this is serious. And you're right, I've never brought a woman home to a family dinner. Hell, we haven't had family dinners since I was a teenager. Daisy isn't like anyone else I've been interested in. I can't make any promises. I don't think we know each other well enough for that. But I want to, and wanting to make promises is a new thing for me."

J.T. considered my answer and nodded gravely. "Since accepting a date at all is a new thing for Daisy, I'd say you two are on the same page. I'm hoping that this is unnecessary, but I sent her ahead because I wanted to tell you this—I've been in your corner since you sent those flowers. Don't make me regret it. Understand?"

"I do. I won't be careless with her. That's one promise I can make."

"Good enough. She's strong. A survivor. But her family is a sore spot and something's up right now—I don't know what because she won't talk to me—so I'm asking you to look out for her."

I nodded. "I already am."

"I can see that. Daisy is the best, you know. And she deserves the best." J.T. tilted his head to the side and scanned me from the top of my head to the tips of my shoes. A smile curved his full lips and he winked. "I think you'll do."

I couldn't help but grin at him. "As long as Daisy thinks so, that's all that matters."

J.T. straightened and raised his chin at the door. "Yeah, I think you'll do. Let's go down before she comes storming up to rescue you. I need to scavenge dinner out of the kitchen anyway."

"Not eating over at Grams'?" I asked. I was curious how J.T. fit in with the rest of Daisy's family.

J.T. rolled his eyes and followed me out of the apartment, closing the door behind us. "If it was just Grams? Definitely. That woman can cook. But I'm gonna take a pass until Daisy's parents skip town again."

"Not their biggest fan?"

J.T.'s eyes went dark and he shook his head as he went through the back door and into the kitchen. In a low voice Daisy wouldn't hear, he said, "It's mutual, but you'll figure them out soon enough if you stick around."

"Gotcha." I dropped the subject as we came into the kitchen. Daisy stood there with an oversized Sweetheart Bakery cake box in her hands. "Wow again," I said. "What's in there?"

"Chocolate cake with a raspberry cream filling. I hope I made enough for everyone."

J.T. grinned. "Daze, that cake is enough for half the town. Now, you two hit the road. I'll lock up here. And Royal?"

I raised an eyebrow and waited.

"I'll be waiting up, so bring her home before she turns into a pumpkin."

Chapter Twenty-Two

DAISY

WHAT DID J.T. SAY?" I HAD TO ASK EVEN THOUGH I doubted Royal would tell me.

Men.

J.T. had been insistent that I give him a few minutes with Royal. I hadn't wanted to, obviously, but J.T. had been oddly stubborn and I hadn't had the heart to shut him down. He was the one person who was always, always in my corner. Just like I was always in his. If he wanted a minute with Royal I had to trust him not to do anything that would embarrass me or screw things up.

Royal shot me an amused grin. "Wouldn't you like to know?" At my glare, he laughed. "Just the normal best-friend-slash-big-brother type stuff. I better watch my step and treat you right, etc. Since I was going to do that anyway, no big deal. I like him."

"Me too," I agreed. "Most of the time."

"He's just looking out for you. I like that you have that. Tenn would probably be grilling you on my behalf by now if he wasn't enslaved to your brownies."

"Just wait till he tries this cake," I said, my nerves easing a little.

"You didn't have to bake a cake, Daisy. Not that I'm complaining. But that's a huge box. It looks like it was a lot of work."

I looked down at the box in my lap. It *was* a huge box and it *had* been a lot of work. Not on the level of a custom cake for two hundred, but still, it had been extra time on what was supposed to be my afternoon off. I didn't mind.

I wasn't always confident in myself, but I was definitely confident in my baking, and I wasn't showing up to dinner at Heartstone Manor empty-handed. I didn't trust myself to pick out wine and I doubted they needed more flowers, but I was sure I could make a good impression with a chocolate cake.

I wasn't just depending on the cake. For the first time in what felt like forever, I'd put serious time into the way I looked. I'd bought the dress a year before after I fell in love with it in a boutique in Asheville. I didn't have anywhere to wear a fancy cocktail dress or the shoes that went with it. J.T. had talked me into getting it anyway. For the first time, I was relieved I'd spent the money.

Tonight, instead of dragging my hair back into a poof or bun like I usually did, I'd loaded it down with product after my shower, carefully separating each curl, and going to work with my diffuser, J.T. helping on the back because—let's face it—I am not a pro with the diffuser.

I looked my best, and I was loaded down with a killer cake, but still, I was nervous.

Royal knew. He reached over and closed his hand around mine, squeezing. "Don't worry about dinner, Daisy. I'm not going to let them scare you off. Anyway, most of my family is pretty cool. And you're bringing cake so it's pretty much guaranteed they'll like you better than they like me."

"I've found cake is a pretty good icebreaker." It was true. Except for those rare people who didn't like sweets, but I pretended those people didn't exist. I'm suspicious of anyone who can't be won over with chocolate.

Royal turned onto the long drive to Heartstone Manor. Oak trees lined the road, their arching branches creating a green tunnel. I could see evidence here and there of landscaping work in progress. In some spots the trees were surrounded by beds of dark mulch, the grass neatly trimmed. In others the forest pressed to the road, weeds chewing at the crumbling asphalt on the edges.

The front courtyard wasn't landscaped, but here every weed had been banished, leaving the grand house bare of adornment and that much more intimidating.

Royal parked at the front. "Stay there," he ordered, getting out. I didn't argue. I was too busy staring up at the front of Heartstone Manor. Three stories tall, the Manor was made of granite, softened by the ivy climbing the walls at the corners. The front door was huge, iron-strapped wood with heavy iron handles I'd bet it took two hands to turn.

My door opened and Royal leaned down to take the cake box from my lap, handling it carefully. We climbed the steps and walked through Heartstone's big wooden door into a whirlwind. Voices carried into the hallway, a man saying something that sounded like, "—too salty," and a woman, irate, "If I hear one more complaint out of you, Finn Sawyer—"

They came into view, the man tall, dark-haired, and undoubtedly one of Royal's siblings. He strode across the entry hall, hand held up as if to fend off the woman who stalked after him.

Her voice raised in a shout. "Finn, don't you walk away from me!" I thought she'd storm after him and out of sight, but she drew to an abrupt halt when she spotted us standing there.

"Please, tell me the cook didn't quit," Royal said.

"Not yet, but if Finn doesn't keep his mouth shut, and she walks out—" She let out a breath, blowing a stray lock of hair out of her eyes. "Well, I was going to say I'd kill him in his sleep, but I think Griffen said something about making him pitch a tent in the woods. Or just kicking him out."

"If only we could figure out a way to make Finn take the cook's place," Royal said. Looking over at me he explained, "Finn is a classically trained chef. Went to the Culinary Institute of America and everything. He even studied in Paris. He's only cooked for us twice but—" Royal rolled his eyes to the ceiling high above. "His food is amazing."

The woman crossed her arms over her chest after flipping a strawberry blonde braid back over her shoulder. She wore a black and white patterned a-line dress and a cute pair of dark-green Mary Janes I recognized as being comfortable enough to stand in all day.

"I wouldn't know," she grumbled, "because he didn't save any for me, but it doesn't matter if his food is delicious considering he thinks he's too good to cook for the rest of us. I wouldn't pay him any attention except he keeps trying to scare away our cook."

She shook her head and held out a hand to me. "I'm sorry, Finn distracted me. You must be Daisy." I took her hand and shook. "I'm Savannah. I'm the housekeeper at Heartstone Manor. If you need anything while you're here just let me know." She turned her alert gray eyes to the cake box in Royal's hands. "What's this?"

"I baked a cake. I wasn't sure what you had planned for dessert, so you can always save it for another night. It will keep for a few days."

Savannah took the box from Royal, hefting it gingerly. With a raised eyebrow at me, she said, "I hope you know you owe me five pounds. I have a thing for your ginger-molasses cookies. A big thing. What kind of cake is this?"

"Chocolate, with double chocolate frosting and raspberry and cream filling." I know I'd baked it, but my mouth watered anyway. It was my favorite cake. I knew exactly how good it was.

"I think tonight's dessert can be saved for tomorrow," Savannah said. "We'll have this instead. So thoughtful of you to bake for this crowd of heathens. I'll bring it down to the kitchen. We don't have an appropriate space for before-dinner cocktails yet, so everyone's just milling around the dining room. Dinner will be served in about ten minutes. Not enough time for a tour," a pointed look at Royal, "but enough to get a glass of wine. I think Hope just came down. She's looking forward to seeing you, Daisy." With that, she turned for the back of the hall, heading, I guessed, to the kitchens.

"Nice to meet you, Savannah," I called out as she strode away.

She raised her chin back in our direction as she walked. "You too, Daisy. Enjoy your visit to the madhouse."

I looked at Royal. "She's not what I expected. I like her."

"I do, too. Her mother, Miss Martha, was the housekeeper here most of my life. I grew up with Savannah running around the house. We got lucky she agreed to take on the job. She's ridiculously efficient, and she doesn't put up with crap from anyone. Especially Finn."

"Is Finn usually difficult?" I asked, taking the arm Royal held out for me.

"No, that's the funny thing. He's pretty chill. I haven't seen him much—he left home after high school, joined the Army, and got out and went to culinary school. He didn't come home often. Didn't get along with Prentice. But he was always laid-back before, and since he's been home it doesn't seem like much has changed except when it comes to the cook and Savannah.

If he drives the cook to quit I really do think Savannah might kill him. She's got her hands full trying to turn this place into a livable home again. She doesn't need to worry about feeding all of us on top of that."

Looking around, I could see what he meant. The front hall was huge, the ceiling arcing two stories above us with a massive chandelier in the center. What I could see of the house was clean and polished, the wood warm and glowing, the crystal chandelier sparkling.

There was very little furniture and no artwork. It looked unfinished. As we passed through the front hall, arching doorways opened on either side into what should have been formal parlors. Both rooms were empty.

A little further, and we turned left through open double doors into a dining room that was twice as big as the building that held my bakery and apartment. The dark-beamed and white plaster ceiling rose a full two stories above us, the great iron chandeliers glowing, the long table shining, set with enough places to feed an army. Or just the Sawyers.

Royal's family was clustered at the far end of the dining room in a smaller area with a wide bay window, set up with its own table and chairs. Maybe a breakfast area. Instead of being set for a meal, the table held a selection of appetizers and several open bottles of wine. My nerves cranked up a notch with so many near-strangers milling around, but Hope spotted us and, hooking her arm through Griffen's, made a beeline straight for us.

"You look amazing!" Hope circled me, checking out my dress and hair before drawing me into a tight hug. From behind her, I heard Griffen say to Royal, "You brought her to family dinner on your first date? Brave man."

"Crazy man," Hope corrected.

"Same difference," Royal said, tugging me back from Hope and winding his arm around my waist. With the heat of his body at my side, I wasn't nervous anymore. "Anyway, if a family dinner doesn't scare her away, nothing will."

"I don't scare that easily." I didn't, usually.

I accepted a glass of wine from Hope and had barely taken a sip before a gong sounded from somewhere in the house. Everyone turned and started for the massive dining room table.

Chapter Twenty-Three

DAISY

ROYAL HELD OUT HIS ARM AND I TOOK IT, FOLLOWING him to our place at the table, surprised to see a beautifully drawn note card in my spot, right beside Royal's. Savannah was good.

As if my thought had conjured her out of thin air, she appeared at my right and gracefully set a steaming bowl of soup in front of me, then Royal, before disappearing through a door at the other end of the room. She managed to serve the entire table full of Sawyers while my soup was still hot.

I dipped in a spoon to taste. Rich, salty, beef broth. Onions—a little overcooked—and too much cheese melted on top. I snuck a glance across the table at Finn Sawyer, not surprised to see his eyes roll to the ceiling above, and not in ecstasy.

The soup was decent, don't get me wrong. I'm the last person to complain, particularly when I'm a guest. I also make it a policy not to complain about food that I didn't have to cook. If someone else is kind enough to feed me, I eat with a smile on my face. A lesson Finn Sawyer apparently hadn't learned.

Royal leaned into my side. "If Finn doesn't eat that soup, Savannah might dump it over his head."

Watching Royal's brother across the table, I whispered back, "No way he eats all of it."

"Is it that bad?" Royal ate another spoonful slowly, maybe trying to taste what Finn found so unsatisfactory.

"It's not *bad*," I assured him. "But if Finn went to CIA he has a more refined palate than the rest of you, and while the soup is okay, it isn't great. "

Across the table, Finn set his soup spoon down with a clatter and leaned back in his chair. Savannah was at his left almost immediately, clearing his soup with a scowl.

"I guess he ate just enough to save himself from a soup bath," Royal said.

I laughed, and looking across the table, I caught the eye of Royal's youngest sister, Sterling. To my surprise, she winked at me, and I found myself winking back. Then she tilted her head at Parker's husband beside her and rolled her eyes. He was going on and on about a polo team he played for up in New York, giving us a play-by-play of an entire match.

To everyone's dismay, someone else picked up the conversational baton and started arguing with Parker's husband about polo. Royal leaned in to whisper, "I should have introduced you to everyone before dinner, but we ran out of time. The one sitting next to Sterling is Tyler, Parker's husband. My cousin Bryce is the one talking right now. His mother Ophelia is sitting next to him."

We listened for another minute as Bryce droned on about his own successes on the polo field. Royal sat back and rolled his eyes, suddenly looking so much like Sterling it was uncanny. Under his breath, he murmured, "Christ, it's like Lifestyles of the Rich and Boring."

This time I laughed out loud. I couldn't help it. Royal had nailed the two of them so perfectly. Rich, good-looking, and god-awful boring. Tyler and Bryce played a game of who's more privileged through the rest of the soup course and the boring-but-edible salad.

I pretended to concentrate on my food but instead studied the table. Griffen was wrapped up in Hope, neither of them paying any attention to Bryce and Tyler. Hope looked like her appetite was giving her trouble and Griffen was trying to find the choicest bites that might tempt her to eat. I liked watching them together. Hope had spent most of her life taking care of other people. It was nice to see someone taking care of her.

Parker was nodding now and then, a vague smile on her face. She looked like a woman who had a lot of practice pretending she was paying attention when she was actually doing anything but.

Royal's Aunt Ophelia beamed at her son as if she couldn't imagine a child more brilliant and wonderful than this one. So far, he didn't seem particularly obnoxious, just full of himself and annoying.

Sterling took a deep sip of wine, both Griffen and Royal watching. Royal's other sisters, Avery and Quinn, were all the way at the other end of the table, seated next to each other, deep in a quiet conversation the rest of us couldn't hear.

Too bad we couldn't stick Tyler and Bryce together, maybe in another room. Then the rest of us could talk about something other than... What were they on about now? Sailing?

Savannah was back, smoothly clearing the salad, joined by a woman dressed in a chef's uniform. They worked as a well-or-chestrated team, Savannah removing the salad plate moments before the cook placed the entrée in front of each diner. She scowled down at Finn as she served him his food. I had to wonder if his meal would be edible.

The rest of the dinner might have gone differently if the chef hadn't chosen that night to serve peas. I never would have believed it, sitting in that elegant dining room with so many well-dressed people, but everything spiraled out of control in the blink of an eye.

At his mother's encouragement, Bryce was droning on about winning some tennis tournament at a club they belonged to. Sterling, sitting opposite him, took another long sip of wine before she slumped back in her chair, her eyes glued to the ceiling as if praying for patience. She wasn't the only one.

Before anyone realized what she was up to, Sterling placed one round, green pea directly in the center of her silver spoon and catapulted it across the table, directly at her cousin Bryce.

I slammed my hand over my mouth before the laugh could escape as Bryce lifted his fingers to brush at his hair, too caught up in his own story to realize he'd been struck by one of Sterling's peas. Undaunted, she shot again. This time she caught him straight between the eyes.

Griffen leaned past Hope—I'm assuming to tell Sterling to knock it off. He was too late. Bryce flung his own peas back across the table, missing Sterling and smacking Tyler in the face. After the way those two had bored us all to death through dinner, I had to resist the urge to clap.

Beside me, Royal was shaking with suppressed laughter. Someone at the other end of the table, maybe Avery or Quinn, pitched a dinner roll at our end. I don't even think they were aiming at someone specific. I think whoever threw it just wanted to throw something. From there, the battle was on.

Projectiles burst from every direction—dinner rolls, bits of mushroom—I'm pretty sure I even spotted a shrimp flying through the air. Torn between amusement and wanting to protect my new dress, I opted to stay out of the fight. Royal mostly did, though he couldn't resist flicking peas at Bryce and Ophelia when they were looking the other way.

Royal caught Griffen's eye. "Aren't you going to put a stop to this?"

Griffen shrugged, a smile teasing his mouth. "Eventually. If I have to. Everyone's having so much fun, I don't have the heart to stop them now."

Griffen didn't want to stop them, but the second I saw Savannah's face, I thought it might have been better if he had. Heartstone Manor's efficient, friendly housekeeper looked like her head was going to explode. Her face flushed a deep pink, she opened her mouth—I thought to yell—then snapped it shut as if she'd thought better of what she wanted to say. I imagined I could hear her teeth grinding from across the room.

Slowly, everyone ceased fire, the heat of battle chilled by the ice in Savannah's eyes.

"I am not cleaning this up. If you all plan to act like children you can clean up your messes. Let me know when you're done, and we'll consider clearing the dinner dishes and serving you chocolate cake, but if there's a single pea on this carpet, you get nothing. Understood?"

The table echoed with a mumbled round of, "Understood." That might have been it, but Finn dared to add, "I wouldn't have thrown the peas if they hadn't been overcooked."

Savannah's face contorted as she let out a sound somewhere between a roar and a growl. She stormed across the space separating them, snatched up Finn's half-full plate, and slammed it down over his head. Rich cream sauce dripped from his dark hair, staining his shirt, peas and mushrooms catching in the dark strands before tumbling to his lap.

Savannah turned on her heel and strode from the dining room, the door swinging shut behind her.

"Someday," Royal said to his younger brother, "you're going to learn when to keep your mouth shut."

"Not likely," Finn said, shaking his head. "If the rest of you don't mind, I'm going to go change clothes and wash this bland sauce out of my hair."

"You're supposed to help us clean up!" Sterling called after him. Finn raised a hand in acknowledgment but didn't stop.

"You started it, you should have to clean it all up," Bryce said, pointing his finger at Sterling.

"Good luck with that," Sterling shouted back, lurching to her feet. She grabbed for her half-full glass of wine. I don't know if she'd been drinking more than we saw or if she just caught the edge of her heel, but she tipped to the side, upending the glass of red wine over Tyler's head.

Parker's husband shot from his seat, glaring at everyone, even his wife. "That is *it*! You people are all insane. I don't know how I lasted so long in this hick town, but I'm out of here. I don't care how much money is in it for us at the end. I'm done."

Parker leveled cool eyes on her husband. "So, you're going back to New York then?"

"I'm sure as hell not staying here for another five years. I thought I could put up with it. For you. But this is a nightmare. The house is a disaster and your family is insane. Every single one of them. I won't have anything to do with it. I'll be on the next plane out. If you care about this marriage, you can get started packing our bags."

As one, we watched Tyler storm out of the dining room, just like Savannah had. Unlike Savannah, I was pretty sure Tyler wasn't coming back. Parker sat in her seat, face blank, her hand shaking only the tiniest bit as she took another sip of wine.

Sterling sank into Tyler's abandoned chair and threw her arms around Parker in an awkward hug. I couldn't catch what she said, but the tone was apologetic, Sterling's face distraught.

Parker said something back that must have been comforting. Sterling straightened, shoving away her own wine glass and reaching for the bottle to top off Parker's.

"Aren't you going to do something?" Bryce demanded. "He's the only decent one of all of you. Probably because he's not a Sawyer."

"No," Parker said. "I'm tired of chasing after him, soothing his hurt feelings and trying to make everything better. If he doesn't want to live in Heartstone Manor with the rest of us, then he can go."

Bryce seemed ready to argue, but Royal stepped in. "Daisy brought a double chocolate cake for dessert. If any of you want some, I suggest you get to cleaning."

I pushed back my chair, ready to pitch in, though I hadn't thrown a single pea. Royal took my arm and tugged me away from the table to where Griffen stood with Hope, neither of them cleaning either.

Fair enough since they also hadn't thrown anything. Griffen was talking quietly with Hope.

"What's wrong? Are you okay?" Royal asked.

"I'm fine," Hope insisted.

"You're not, you're turning green," Griffen said. "I'm taking you up to bed now. I just have to—" he cut off abruptly. "Damn."

"What is it?" Royal asked.

"It's nothing, really. It's just that I told Hawk I'd go check out the watchtower. I was supposed to do it this afternoon and then—" A shared glance with Hope.

"I distracted you," she said with a weak smile. "Can't you do it tomorrow?"

"Yeah, I guess. Except Hawk needed that report to update orders for supplies, and he wanted to send the orders in first thing. I was supposed to do it a few days ago. And we're going into Asheville tomorrow to meet with Brax about that project he wants to invest in."

"We can do it," Royal said, "if Hope has a pair of shoes she can lend Daisy. Just let me know what we should look out for. I'll see if I can talk Savannah into letting us take dessert on the road." Royal turned to me. "It's a short walk past the gardens, but the watchtower is something to see. Definitely more romantic than cleaning peas off the carpet."

"If Hope can hook me up with a pair of shoes, that sounds great."

Chapter Twenty-Four

DAISY

I ONLY FELT A LITTLE GUILTY ABOUT LEAVING WHILE everyone else was still cleaning up. Hope found me a pair of sneakers that fit when we laced them tightly, and Royal met me by the back door with a bag that looked like it held more than two pieces of cake. The sun had only just begun to drop in the sky. Plenty of time for a short hike.

We headed out, taking the gravel path that led us past the bench and tree where we sat on my first visit to Heartstone Manor. The path wound deeper into the gardens, and it didn't take much imagination to see how beautiful they must have been before Royal's father had abandoned them.

Through the scraggly bushes, I caught a flash of water off to my right along with the roofline of another structure. "Do you have a pool?"

I wished the words back as soon as I asked them. This was Heartstone Manor. Of course, they had a pool. Royal sent me a grin, the one that always made my heart speed up. "The pool is one of the first things Griffen fixed. The pool house, on the other hand, might fall down on our heads. As long as we can swim when it gets hot, none of us cares."

"I wouldn't care either. I love splashing in the river when it gets hot in the summer, but it must be sweet to have a pool."

This time, Royal's grin held a flash of heat. "You're welcome to swim anytime. Just for curiosity's sake… Are you a bikini kind of girl?"

I grinned back, knowing my own eyes held that same flash of heat. I couldn't help it. His question made me think about wearing a bikini for Royal. And straight from there, my brain conjured a vision of Royal in board shorts, wet from the water. That hard body and all that smooth skin. I felt the flush hit my cheeks. Too long without sex was turning me into a perv. Then again, if there were ever a man worth perving over, he was definitely Royal.

"So?"

His raised eyebrow was so hot my imagination ditched the board shorts and wallowed in the thought of Royal naked. Naked and wet. Wait, what had he asked? "Um, if it was just the two of us? Maybe a bikini. If anyone else is around, definitely a one piece."

"I'll ban them all from the pool if it gets me you in a bikini." Distracted by thoughts of what Royal and I could do mostly naked, I didn't notice as the gardens transitioned from a formal parterre design into rolling flower beds that welcomed the approaching forest.

In fact, as I paid more attention, I realized that the forest had well overgrown its original boundaries, small saplings and waist-high weeds taking over what I imagined were once gorgeously abundant flower beds.

The path left the gardens and crossed through a stretch of overgrown grass and weeds, the gravel we walked on thinner and spotty as if it hadn't been refreshed or raked in a long time. Before I knew it, we were in the woods. Here the path was narrower with even less gravel but still clear enough to follow.

The woods enveloped us, leaves rustling in the wind, insects chattering. Now and then a branch would break, signaling the presence of a squirrel or maybe a deer. "Do you hike much?" I asked. "Right now, I'm thinking about how long it's been for me. J.T. and I used to hike all the time, but then work got in the way. I can't remember the last time we hit a trail."

Royal reached to take my elbow as I scrambled over a fallen log. "Same here. I pretty much grew up rambling around these woods. Even after I started at The Inn, I hiked the trails there at least once a week, but lately, it seems like I spend all my time behind a desk."

"I'm glad I love my job," I said, "but sometimes I think I like it too much."

"Exactly. Do you want to go for a hike the next time we both have a day off?"

"I'd love to."

Royal took my hand, tugging me closer so that we walked the narrow trail side by side. "What else do you like to do when you aren't working? "

"Oh, not much, really. Watch movies, I like to read. Go out with a friend if we can get our schedules to match up. And—" My shoulder hitched in a sheepish half-shrug. "I like to mess around in the kitchen. Trying new recipes, flavor combinations. Just playing, I guess. It's more fun when I'm not working. Less pressure. I love baking for work, don't get me wrong, but sometimes it's fun to do it for me. Just to see what's going to happen."

"I bet you get your best recipes that way."

"You'd be right. Sometimes what I come up with is inedible, but that's the fun of experimenting. I can't wait until we can add tables at Sweetheart and I can start playing with a lunch menu. I—"

I was going to say something else, but I have no idea what. All words were swept from my mind as we stepped into the clearing surrounding the watchtower.

Now I understood why they called it a watchtower. Set on a thrust of granite that lifted most of the clearing a good fifteen feet above the path, the entire building looked as if it had grown organically from the mountain itself. The watchtower was only one room in size, maybe twenty feet by twenty feet, but it was tall. Really tall.

We climbed steps carved into the granite, wide and deep enough to have withstood well over a century of use. Not that they'd been used recently. Weeds had taken root in every available crack and fissure, leaving the surface slippery.

Royal took my elbow. "Didn't realize the steps would be this bad. I don't want you to slip."

"I'm good," I assured him, but I liked that he was there, just in case. The grass was damp and my borrowed sneakers weren't the best fit.

I was only a little out of breath by the time we reached the door. I tilted my head back and stared up. And up. The entire building was three stories. The first two stories were made of stacked stone with a few narrow windows, every one of them dingy with dust.

From the outside, it looked like each level was taller than normal, putting the third well above the trees. And what a third level it was. Where the first two were solid granite except for those dusty windows, the third was all glass framed in dark wood with barely a roofline to obscure the view. Oddly, while the glass didn't exactly sparkle, it wasn't dull with grime like the first two levels.

"The view from up there must be incredible. I bet you can see all the way to Asheville."

"Not quite that far, but the view is amazing. My great-great-grandfather built this place. His excuse was that we needed to watch out for forest fires. I don't think he ever ended up stationing someone here full time, I think he mostly built it because he wanted to."

"Whatever the reason, it's gorgeous."

Royal looked up, for a moment lost in thought. A drop of water hit my head. Then another. The sky was still clear mostly, but clouds clung to the treetops to the east. The sprinkles didn't alarm me—showers sprang up in the mountains without notice all the time, dropping rain and disappearing as quickly as they'd arrived.

Royal pulled a key from his pocket.

"Do you want to see if this key works before that rain kicks in? I have to check a few things for Griffen, and we can wait out the weather."

"Sure." I thought of my brand-new dress and the dust that was likely everywhere in the watchtower. I'd have to be careful because I really, really wanted to see the inside.

Royal's key turned in the lock with only a little jiggling. The first floor of the watchtower wasn't as dusty as I expected. Maybe because it was bare of furniture except for a few ancient-looking trunks shoved up against the walls. It was dim inside, not a light bulb or lamp to be found.

Answering the question I hadn't asked, Royal said, "No electricity out here. There used to be some oil lamps around. Probably upstairs. Do you want to go up?"

"Absolutely." I followed Royal to the tight spiral staircase in one corner of the room.

"I haven't been out here in years. It was off-limits when I was a teenager. Prentice had it all boarded up so we couldn't sneak in behind his back. Let me get to the second floor before you come up just in case any of these stairs are loose."

The place might have been dusty, but the spiral staircase was solid as a rock. The second floor was almost as empty as the first and equally as dusty. No trunks up here, just a folding card table and some chairs. This room looked like it was used as seldom as the first.

Royal made a few notes on his phone, probably for Griffen. The spiral stairs continued one more flight up to the third floor. That was the one I couldn't wait to see.

I followed Royal again and stopped well before the top, surprised to find a solid ceiling above my head. I was even more surprised to see Royal raise a hand and push, lifting a neat square from the ceiling. A trapdoor.

We climbed through and emerged in what felt like a completely different building. A narrow iron rail surrounded the trapdoor, most likely to prevent an accidental fall through the open hole in the floor. Up here there was a lot less dust, and there was no question what Royal's father had used the watchtower for.

A king-size bed dominated the space, hewn of stripped pine logs polished to a golden shine. There weren't any sheets on the bed, but the mattress looked almost brand-new. I couldn't imagine how they got it up there in the first place. Not through the spiral stairs, that was for sure.

There was another trunk against the wall, and what I thought might be an oversized closet in one corner of the room. Wine glasses sat on a table in another corner, an empty bottle between them.

It wasn't the furnishings that drew my attention. It was the view, even more magnificent than I'd expected. The Blue Ridge Mountains spread around us, a rolling blanket of green in every direction, the slowly setting sun spreading shadows and illuminating the treetops, turning the mountains into a kaleidoscope of green.

"So beautiful," I breathed, mostly to myself.

Royal came up beside me, his arm settling around my shoulder. "It really is. When you see these mountains every day you kind of take them for granted. But seeing them like this, with you..." He turned to face me, his eyes serious. "It reminds me how lucky I am."

His hand came up to cup my face, the side of his thumb stroking my cheek. I leaned into him, his steady, solemn expression filling an empty place in my heart. Filling it so full it hurt.

"I know what you mean," I said, my breath so tight in my chest the words barely squeaked out. "I'm feeling pretty lucky, too, right now."

Royal's eyes crinkled at the edges, chasing off his serious expression. The corner of his mouth quirked up. "Oh, really? Feeling lucky? How lucky?"

"This lucky." I wound my arms around his neck, tilting my head up and tugging him closer. It felt like a million years since I had his lips on mine. As always, Royal didn't disappoint me.

His kiss started out gentle, his lips caressing mine, teasing them open, though I didn't need the tease. So many kisses and so little of anything else. I wanted Royal. Wanted his kiss, his touch. Wanted everything.

I made a little sound in the back of my throat and the kiss turned hungry, Royal's mouth demanding. My fingers curled, gripping his shirt. Our teeth clashed, tongues tangling, but neither of us pulled back. I arched into him, needing to get closer. More. I wanted more.

I was so lost in Royal's kiss, I almost missed it.

A low thump, like metal hitting wood. Then more—a harsh scrape of metal on metal and the muffled thud of footsteps.

Footsteps.

Royal got his head together before I did. He dropped his arms from around me and nudged me behind him, eyes scouring the room.

It didn't take us long to spot the trapdoor, flush with the floor. I thought we'd left it open. Royal must have agreed because he bolted across the room and yanked on the handle. The trapdoor didn't move.

He stared at it for a long moment before straightening and moving to the windows facing the path back to Heartstone. I joined him just in time to see a tall figure with gilded blond hair disappear into the trees.

Chapter Twenty-Five

DAISY

"THAT FUCKING SON OF A BITCH. GODDAMMIT." ROYAL spun around, eyes searching the room once again.

"What? What happened? Who was that?" Watching Royal pace back and forth, I had the distinct feeling he knew a lot more about whatever was going on than I did.

"It was Bryce. And I'm almost positive he just locked us in here." Royal went back to the trapdoor and yanked again with no better luck than the first time. "It's supposed to lock from above, not below," he muttered. "Bastard must have jammed it."

My hands automatically went to my pockets for my phone. Nothing. This dress didn't have pockets, and even if it had, I'd left my phone in Royal's car. I hadn't planned on taking any calls while at dinner, and I'd figured it was close enough if I needed it. Close, maybe, but it might as well have been on the moon for all the good it would do me now.

"What do we do? What about your phone? Can you call the house?"

Royal pulled his phone from his pocket, scowling at the screen. "No service." He tried to dial anyway, but the call didn't go through. "Useless," he grumbled, tossing the phone onto the table.

I watched Royal pace around the room, looking out of the windows as he moved, studying the space for anything he could use to pry open the trapdoor. There wasn't much. And by not much, I mean there wasn't anything. The small room I'd taken for a closet turned out to be a rough bathroom with a composting toilet, a few jugs of water, and some towels. Good to know we had a bathroom since we were locked in here, but I would rather have had a way out.

Royal unearthed several bottles of wine and a few blankets from one of the trunks against the wall. In another, he found three of the oil lamps he'd mentioned, neatly stowed beside a box of matches and a can of oil.

There wasn't a single tool, radio, phone, walkie-talkie, or carrier pigeon. No way to break through the trapdoor and no way to let anyone know we were stuck. It didn't make sense.

"Why would Bryce lock us in the tower? Just to be a jerk?" From everything I'd heard, being a jerk seem to be Bryce's raison d'être, but trapping us in the abandoned watchtower seemed a little extreme.

Royal took a deep breath, staring up at the ceiling and thinking furiously, his hands wrapped behind his head. He exhaled slowly, dropping his hands to his sides.

"Daisy, I'm so sorry this happened. If I'd had any idea he was following us, I never would have brought you here."

"It's not your fault, Royal. I just don't get why he'd do it. Is he that much of an ass?"

"He is, but that's not why he did it." Royal started to pace the room again, checking out the windows.

"What are you looking for? Do you think he'll come back?" Royal stopped and met my eyes, shifting uncomfortably. "What? What's going on that you don't want to tell me?"

"It's not that I don't want to tell you," Royal admitted, "it's that I'm not sure if I'm right, and if I am no one is supposed to know, including me."

"Can we get out of here? On our own, I mean."

Royal leveled a heavy glare on the closed trapdoor. "Unlikely."

"Then you might as well tell me why we're here. I can keep my mouth shut."

"Fair enough. I'll tell you over wine and cake." He glanced up at the beamed ceiling a good ten feet above our heads, then to the increasing rain outside. "At least the roof doesn't leak." Royal cracked one of the smaller windows and a gust of damp, clean air swirled through the watchtower.

I cleared the small table, wiping off the thin layer of dust covering it. Royal set out a plastic container holding two generous slices of cake along with a corked bottle of white wine, two plastic, stemless wine glasses, two forks, and two linen napkins. Before he sat, he lit the oil lamps, and a golden glow spread through the watchtower.

"I like a man who comes prepared." I sat, taking a sip of the crisp, sweet wine.

Royal winked. "Oh, I'm prepared for all sorts of things." I liked the sound of that. He glanced at the trap door again. "Except for that."

"About that..." I prompted.

"Yeah, about that. You've heard about my father's will, right?"

"Hope told me a little. That he put all of your inheritances in trusts with Griffen as trustee, and you have to live at Heartstone for five years before you can get the money."

"That's part of it. We can't sleep away from the house more than a few nights a year. Prentice created a separate trust for the house. That's where the bulk of his assets went. Houses like Heartstone are a bitch to keep running. Impossible without a truckload of cash. If we don't follow his rules, the balance of our trusts is put into the trust for Heartstone, and we're barred from all family property, including our places of employment if we work for the company. Which all of us do."

"That's..." I tried to think of a word for it. On one hand, forcing his children to live in the family mansion wasn't the cruelest thing Prentice could have done, especially if the reward was a big chunk of cash. On the other, threatening to take both their home and their livelihoods for not doing as they were told... "That's weird. Could you contest it?"

Royal let out a laugh tinged with bitterness. "That was the 'stinger', as Prentice called it. If we contest the will, everything goes to Bryce."

I stared back at him in shock. "Everything? Did your father like Bryce?"

Another laugh, this one more than *tinged* with bitterness. "Hell, no. He thought Bryce was as much of an asshole as the rest of us. Prentice knew we wouldn't follow his bullshit rules for his sake, but we'd do almost anything to keep Bryce from getting the Sawyer estate. Bryce would burn through every cent before we could stop him."

"But as long as you don't contest it, everything is safe from Bryce, right?" I was more convinced than ever that Prentice Sawyer had been a major bastard, but I still didn't get why his will would drive Bryce to lock us in the watchtower.

"Based on what the family lawyer told us, yes. But after he was done reading the will to the rest of us, he sent us away and kept Griffen and Hope for a second, private meeting. No one but the three of them knows what was said, but when they were done, Griffen and Hope were married, and they haven't been apart since."

Royal didn't elaborate on what that might mean. He leaned in and took a hefty bite of cake, leaving me to work out the puzzle on my own.

Clearly, there had been further stipulations on Hope and Griffen. Hope had been closed-mouthed about the whole thing with me, at least about what had driven her to marry Griffen so quickly. I hadn't pressed because she'd been so happy, and Griffen clearly doted on her.

Almost as an afterthought, Royal added, "When Griffen got run off the road, West thought it might have been me. Hope spilled that I wasn't in the line of succession anymore. If anything happens to Griffen before he has an heir, Bryce inherits. Though Harvey—our lawyer—swears he hasn't told him anything about that part of the will."

"Good thing Hope is pregnant then," I said, the implications spinning in my brain. Suddenly a puzzle piece clicked into place. "You think there's a stipulation about Griffen and Hope being together. Like with the rest of you and living at the house."

Royal took a slow sip of wine. "I do. They've been joined at the hip, which could be normal for newlyweds, especially with Hope pregnant and not feeling well. I don't think Griffen would willingly leave her side right now, even if he could. But back at the start they weren't exactly head over heels and still, they stuck together. I always thought the will forced them to get married—you know Hope's uncle Edgar was practically Prentice's partner. Their businesses are so intertwined. They're like two feudal kings, bartering an heir to keep the wealth intact."

"Ironic that after so many years treating Hope as no more than an assistant, she's the only one left to help you and Griffen run Sawyer Enterprises."

"She's smart as a whip, too. Which I think they always knew, but they shoved her aside anyway. I hope she stays on, at least part-time, after the baby comes."

Royal looked more comfortable talking about business than the will, but I wasn't ready to let it go. "You think Hope and Griffen aren't allowed to spend a night apart." Another puzzle piece clicked into place. "And Griffen was supposed to come out here tonight. Not you."

We both looked over at the trapdoor, and from there to where we'd stood by the window, kissing. "The bed would have blocked his view. He would have seen your back, but he could have missed me. He wouldn't have been able to see your face without coming all the way up the stairs."

I leaned back in my chair, staring up at the dark beams of the ceiling. Every inch of this place was gorgeous. Nice, considering we were stuck here. "Griffen and Hope went upstairs before we left. I bet they don't come down until morning. Bryce won't know he trapped the wrong Sawyer until tomorrow."

"Was J.T. serious about waiting up for you? Is he going to worry when you don't come home by ten?"

I loved that Royal thought to ask about J.T. My lips curved up at the thought of J.T.'s reaction when I didn't come home. "He'll be thrilled. And everyone else will just assume you swept me off somewhere private to have your way with me. No one's going to miss us until tomorrow."

Royal's eyes were steady on my face, a spark lit deep within the vibrant blue. "Well, they're not wrong. I did sweep you off to have my way with you."

"Hmm." The hum in my throat vibrated through my entire body. Here we were, all alone, with that big, empty bed. "So, when you said you were prepared for all sorts of things…"

Royal reached in his pocket and slapped something down on the table between us. Red foil glinted in the glow of the oil lamp. Two condoms. I picked them up and tapped the edges on the table as if considering what to do with them.

"Two condoms? Ambitious."

Royal laughed, a deep, genuine laugh I felt all the way to my toes. Plucking the condoms from my hand, he said, "Not hardly. With you? Two will barely get me started." He lay the two foil squares on the table the same way he might have laid out a hand of poker. "And I wasn't ambitious so much as hopeful. I've been trying to wait, Daisy. And it's been a hell of a lot harder than I expected. But I don't want to use those unless you're sure. I know I have a repu—"

I cut off the rest of Royal's words. "I'm sure."

His eyebrows shot up. "Just because we're trapped here doesn't mean—"

"I'm sure," I repeated. I had no doubt Royal wanted me. He'd made that clear. And I'd stopped worrying about his reputation. He'd worked hard to make sure I understood this was different. That I was different. Either I trusted he meant what he said, or I might as well forget about this whole thing.

Royal's mouth opened again, and I was done. I knew exactly how to change the subject. I pushed back my chair and stood. His deep blue eyes widened, the flame buried there burning brighter. It was easy to toe-off my borrowed sneakers. Even easier to grab the hem of my dress and whip it over my head.

Chapter Twenty-Six

DAISY

I STOOD BEFORE HIM IN LACE LINGERIE THE EXACT tawny shade of my skin, my breasts already swelling, nipples drawing tight just at the heat of his eyes on me. His throat worked as he swallowed hard. Before he could move, I straddled his lap, facing him, and went to work on his tie.

Color hit his cheeks. He swallowed hard again. He lifted one hand, and I caught it in mine. Getting up, I stepped behind him, pulling one of his arms behind the chair, then the other. Using his tie, I secured his hands to the chair before I moved back in front of him.

Power surged through me, fueled by lust and the hungry look in Royal's eyes. It wasn't just his eyes—his whole body was wound tight. Propping my hands on my hips, thrusting my modest breasts closer to his face, I shot out one hip and gave it to him straight.

"Here's the deal. It's been a long time for me. And it means a lot that you wanted to wait. More than I know how to tell you. But I can show you."

I leaned in and unbuttoned his shirt, my knuckles grazing his chest. "If you'd tried to take me to bed before this I probably would have run scared or lost interest. But you didn't. You waited until I was sure. And now, I think—Lift up."

His fascinated gaze locked to my face, Royal lifted his hips from the chair. I slid his pants down over that perfect ass and pulled them from his legs.

Standing back, I took a good long look.

Yum.

Royal Sawyer, on full display for my pleasure, was the most fascinating, gorgeous, sexy thing I'd ever seen. He was already hard, his cock straining for attention. I wasn't going to make him wait.

I stepped between his legs and stroked one hand up that deliciously thick, very hard cock. "I think," I continued, "that this first time, I'm going to seduce you. That way you can be absolutely sure I want you just as much as you want me." I gave the head of his cock a squeeze, then released him and stepped back as if something had occurred to me.

"Unless you want me to stop." I glanced back over my shoulder at one of the trunks Royal had opened. "I think I saw a book back there. We could read."

Royal's growl had my pussy clenching with impatience. I was having fun playing with him, but my body was ready to get to the main event.

"So, no to stopping?"

Royal's eyes were pure blue flame, his breath coming faster, but he didn't strain against the tie binding him to the chair. So much need and so much patience. It was a heady combination. Irresistible.

"I never guessed you'd be a tease." His voice was a growl, his eyes hungry as they absorbed my body.

"We have a lot to learn about each other," I said, wishing I still wore my heels as I sauntered closer.

Standing between his legs again, I leaned down to press my lips to his. Royal took control of the kiss before my first breath. All that restrained need burst free, his mouth claiming mine. I was caught, tempted to drop into his lap and keep kissing him forever.

No. I had a plan.

Somehow, I tore myself away and dropped to my knees, trading an up-close view of his mouth for one of his cock. He was as gorgeous here as he was everywhere else. Thick, hard, a bead of moisture already gathering at the tip.

It had been a while, but I have a good imagination. And motivation. I couldn't remember ever wanting to get to know a cock quite like I did this one. I started slow, swiping up that bead of moisture with a fingertip before popping my finger in my mouth. I sucked him from my skin, my eyes on his. Salty, musky. My pussy flooded at the taste.

Royal groaned. "Daisy—"

He didn't get another word out. I leaned in and licked slowly, tasting every inch from the base of that gorgeous cock, all the way to the tip. Then back down and back up again. Royal was silent except for his harsh, quick breaths.

When I closed my mouth on the head of his cock and gave a hard suck, he moaned my name again as if it was dragged from him by the pull of my mouth. He was a lot for me to handle, but I didn't stop.

I dropped one hand between my legs, sliding my fingers inside my panties. Wet. I was so wet and I'd barely touched him.

Gathering as much of my own moisture as I could, I slipped my hand back out and wrapped it around the base of his cock, giving an experimental swirl of my grip. Royal's head tipped back, chest vibrating with his moan.

My mouth covered what my hand didn't and between the two I enveloped his cock, sucking and squeezing and stroking, teasing until he was shaking.

"Daisy, God, Daisy, oh, God, you have to stop or I'm gonna—Daisy, Daisy."

That was pretty much all he could say. Good. I didn't want him thinking, I wanted him to feel. Now, I was at a crossroads. I could stay right where I was and suck his beautiful cock until he came in my mouth. I wanted that, which was a bit of a surprise, but more, I wanted to see his face when he came. Wanted him to see mine.

Slowly, I pulled my mouth up, leaving him with one last lick. I stood, snagging one of the condoms off the table. Reaching behind me, I flicked open my bra with two fingers, shaking it down my arms and tossing it to the floor. That done, I hooked my thumbs in my lace panties and shimmied them down to join my bra.

One step closer and I straddled him, keeping my eyes on his aroused face as I dealt with the condom. I hadn't opened one of these babies in a while, and I did not want to tear it. We only had two. Once I had it out and ready to roll on, I looked up to see him watching me intently, flags of red on his cheeks, his eyes pure blue flame.

I rolled the condom down slowly, teasing again just because I could. Looking down, judging the distance between his cock and my very needy pussy, I slowly lowered myself, gasping as the head brushed my entrance.

Even through the condom, he was hot. I was so wet he slid inside easily. I dropped onto him by degrees, the awkward position almost knocking me off my balance and sending us both tumbling to the floor, chair and all.

Full. I was so full of Royal. I rocked my hips, my clit scraping the rough hair at the base of his cock, sending shards of bliss up my spine and down to my toes.

"Fuck, Daisy. Fuck me, Daisy. Please."

It was the please that got me. Oh, who the hell was I kidding? It was everything. Royal inside me, feeling so fucking good. The desperate desire in his eyes, mirroring everything I felt inside.

I ground my hips in a circle and took his mouth with mine, kissing him frantically, everything inside me pouring into him. How much I wanted him, how good he felt, how fucking perfect this was.

Royal surged up, shoulders twisting, and with a shattering crack of wood, he tore his arms free of the tie, his hands coming around to close over the curve of my ass, lifting and dropping me on his cock.

That was all it took to send me flying straight over the edge, the orgasm igniting inside me, turning me to fire. I gasped and cried out his name over and over, "Royal, Royal, Royal."

My orgasm must have been too much for the ancient chair. With a spectacular symphony of cracking wood, the chair crumbled beneath us, sending our bodies crashing to the floor.

Royal's hands on my ass tightened as we fell. He rolled, coming down on his back, protecting me from the splinters of the chair.

"Fuck, are you okay?" Royal's dazed eyes searched mine.

"Uh-huh. You okay?" I could barely string two words together, my body still pulsing from coming so hard.

"I will be," Royal muttered, rolling away from the remains of the chair, taking me to my back and thrusting hard. His mouth settled beside my ear, his breath hot, coming in hard, fast pants.

"Daisy, God, Daisy." Inexplicably, impossibly, I was climbing to another orgasm after only a few hard thrusts. I gripped Royal's hard shoulders in my fingers, his cock filling me so perfectly. With a roar, Royal buried himself even deeper inside me, his body going stiff, the orgasm washing through him until he was limp and gasping for breath.

He rolled again, holding me on top of him, still connected, still caught halfway to a second orgasm. Fingers trailed down my spine to slide over my ass, giving one cheek a squeeze before skimming back up to tangle in my hair. We lay there for a long minute, just breathing, our hearts thundering in rhythm.

Royal moved first, executing an impressive ab crunch that took both of us to a sitting position. Rolling to his feet, he carried me to the bed. "Don't move."

I let my head fall to the side and watched him disappear into the small bathroom. He came out after a minute without the condom, a damp cloth in his hand. Climbing on the bed beside me, he nudged my legs wider and pressed the cloth between them. When I moved to take it, he pushed my hand away.

"Let me." Royal stretched out by my side, his long, hard body hot, his eyes sleepy and sated. His touch gentle, he cleaned me with the cloth and tossed it on the floor. Rolling me into him, he pulled me close, my back to his front, his arm tight around my waist, his lips at my ear.

"You were going to come again, weren't you?"

"Hmm," I let out a little humming breath as I considered that. "History would suggest there's no way, but yeah, I think I was. But it's—"

A squeeze of his arms and I knew he had that wicked grin on his face, even though I couldn't see him. It was in his voice, sending a tingle through me when he spoke. "My apologies. I broke. You came and you were so tight and wet—I couldn't hold out. I'll make it up to you."

A hitching laugh shook me. "Any more and you might give me a heart attack."

"You're young," he said philosophically. "You'll survive."

Just as I was getting used to his heat at my back, Royal's arm lifted and he was gone, rolling to the other side of the bed. His feet hit the floor for a bare second and he was back, hooking his hands under my arms and hauling me up the bed.

He was a lot faster and smoother than me. Before I realized what he was up to, my arms were above my head, his silk tie wrapped firmly around my wrists, anchoring them to the bed frame. With any other man, I would have panicked.

Bondage wasn't my thing. Usually. Or ever before. I'd had a boyfriend suggest it, but I hadn't been able to relax, too freaked out by not being able to move.

Not with Royal. For one thing, I'd started this by tying him to the chair, and look how that had turned out. I couldn't wait to see what Royal had in mind for his turn.

And for another, I trusted him.

I'd never thought I'd reach a point in my life where I trusted any man other than J.T. But here we were, and I wasn't going to waste time lying to myself. I trusted Royal, so much that even after I let him tie me to the bed I felt no fear, only rising anticipation, the tingle of that nascent orgasm sparking back to life.

Royal knelt over me, settling his hands on the sides of my ankles and sliding them up, the tips of his fingers exploring, feeling everything. His hands moved over my legs, my hips, dipping into my waist, his thumbs sliding in to meet over my belly button before cruising up again to graze the outside of my breasts. When he was done, I tingled all over. Then he slid those gentle hands back down and up again, just touching, stroking, setting me on fire with his gentle worship of my body.

Cherished. I'd never felt cherished before. He didn't go for my breasts or my pussy. Not yet. Instead, he kissed the tip of one elbow, my belly button, the side of my hip, touching me with so much focus tears sprang to my eyes.

He had me all mixed up, my heart so full, my body teased almost to the edge of another orgasm. I wanted to beg him to get out that second condom, to ease the growing tension. I kept my mouth shut. Almost as much as I wanted to come, I wanted to see what came next.

Chapter Twenty-Seven

DAISY

"DO YOUR ARMS HURT?" ROYAL BREATHED INTO MY EAR.

I shook my head. "Uh-uh. Not my arms."

"Mmm, then what? Here?" He ran a light finger over my ribs and I flinched at the tickling sensation. I shook my head again.

"Here?" Another stroke, this time over my hip bone.

Another shake of my head followed by a squirm. Teasing bastard. But he'd been so patient when I'd tied him to the chair. I could hold out a little longer. Maybe. I hoped I could. He settled himself between my legs, his upper body weighing me down, his face inches from my breasts.

"What about here?"

It took him a fucking eternity, but finally, his fingertip lightly grazed my tight nipple. I jolted as if touched by a live wire.

"Mmm. I'd better see what I can do about that." Royal leaned his dark head over my breast, closed his mouth over my nipple, and sucked. Hard.

Lightning shot straight from my nipple to my clit. I let out a moan, the primal, needy sound nothing I'd ever heard from my own body.

"I bet this one hurts, too."

Before I could get my brain together to answer, his mouth was on my other breast. He sucked, trading one side for the other, ignoring my moans as he pulled me closer and closer to detonation. Just when I thought I couldn't take it anymore, he lifted his head, his blue eyes pure flame.

"I could do that all day, but there's something else I want before you come again." Rocking from side to side, he eased himself down the bed, using his mouth on me as he went, licking the underside of my breast, tasting my belly button, and finally burying his face between my legs.

My eyes squeezed shut. I practically came off the bed when his mouth closed over my clit. Oh, my God. He sucked, then licked, then sucked again, the pleasure so strong I couldn't move, couldn't breathe. He shifted again and a finger touched my opening, pressing in.

That was all it took. His mouth on my clit, his finger inside me, and I went off again, my back arching so hard I wondered if I'd break the bed. This time I didn't call his name. This time I'm pretty sure I screamed.

He was still down there when I came back to myself, a smug smile on his gorgeous face. With a wink, he slid back up my body to end up exactly where he'd been before, his face even with my breasts.

"Your arms still okay? Not numb or hurting?"

I shook my head automatically.

"You sure?"

Words wouldn't form. I nodded instead.

"Good. I want to try that again."

"Again?" I croaked.

"Unless you want me to stop. I could go get that book you mentioned."

I managed a weak smile and shook my head one more time. "If you really want to try again, I won't talk you out of it."

That wicked grin was so hot, if I hadn't just come I'd be on the edge. But I had, and it was going to take me some time to get there again. I thought. Turns out, when Royal got his mouth on me, it didn't take long at all. He worshiped my breasts, leaving my nipples swollen and hard, each suck drawing whimpers from my throat.

This time he made his way down my body even more slowly, skipping my pussy to nip my inner thigh, to spread my legs wide and explore every inch of me. I was beyond embarrassment, too eager and aroused to think to stop him. Two fingers slid inside, stretching me as they filled me, his mouth sucking my clit again, shooting me straight for the stars.

Out of nowhere, he stopped. I cried out in frustration. Not that I hadn't already had two orgasms, but now I wanted one more. So greedy for him. He was turning me into a monster. Royal disappeared, the bed shifting as he got up and—thank God—grabbed the second condom.

"I need to feel you come on my cock again." He rolled on the condom a lot faster than I'd managed it before, and he was between my legs, his cock pushing inside, my pussy swollen and over-sensitive. My brain short-circuited from the overload. It felt so good, so fucking amazingly good to have him there, filling me, his big body on top of me, eclipsing everything but Royal and the sheer, knife-edge pleasure of fucking him.

I couldn't think, couldn't even moan his name. My knees came up, lifting my body to him, open, inviting everything he could give me and more. With a low growl, he fucked me harder, every thrust slamming the base of his cock right into my clit, his cock claiming every inch of my pussy, my body, for his own.

I don't think 'orgasm' is the right word for it. The pleasure didn't peak this time. No, it detonated, turning me inside out, remaking me into a different woman. Royal's woman. And the idea of that didn't scare me in the least. Not then, with emotion flooding me, filling every cell in my body, every corner of my mind and my heart.

Every lonely dark place in my soul was bright with Royal.

I held him tight with my legs as he came, his face almost bestial in his release. My arms were free before he had a chance to relax, the tie tossed to the floor as he rolled me into his arms. We clung to each other, hearts pounding, sweat gluing us together, breath panting in unison.

Neither of us spoke. I didn't have words. I couldn't tell him what I was feeling, not yet. I wasn't quite ready for that. But I wasn't going to pretend this was just sex. Wasn't going to make a quip and roll off the bed for the bathroom.

Royal stroked my hair, his face buried in my neck, saving me from having to think of what to say. I was drifting off, so warm and wrung out that it took me a minute to realize he was getting up. "Where you going?" I managed to mumble.

"Nowhere, I'll be right back."

I heard sounds, maybe from the bathroom. Royal walking around. At one point, he said, "Here," and lifted my head to slide something underneath. Not a pillow. I cracked one eye. A folded blanket. Much better than the bare mattress.

I cracked my eyes again when the wet cloth stroked down my skin, cleaning off the sweat and leaving me wonderfully cool under the faint breeze from the open window. With a nudge, he rolled me over, treating my backside to the same slow, careful strokes of the cloth. Then the cloth was gone and Royal was there, rolling me into him so my head rested on his chest, a blanket covering us lightly. I drifted off again, one arm flung over Royal's waist, fingers curled into his side, holding on to him even in sleep.

My bladder woke me later. I wasn't wearing a watch, but the sky outside the watchtower was dark, sparkling with stars. The rain was over, the air in the watchtower a little cool when I slipped from the cozy cocoon Royal and I had created beneath the blanket. He'd left one of the oil lamps burning low, making it easy to find my way to the tiny closet of a bathroom. I managed to figure out the composting toilet in the near-dark, pouring water on a towel in lieu of washing my hands.

I paused on the way back to bed to look out the windows, squinting into the dark to catch the sparkle of stars above the dark shadows of the mountains. We'd have to try this again when the moon was full. I'd bet the view would be almost as gorgeous as it had been in daylight.

"Okay?" Royal's sleepy voice came from behind me. I turned to see him propped up on one elbow, his hair falling into one eye, a sleepy smile on that irresistible mouth.

I didn't answer with words. Turning, I crawled back into bed, sliding my body against his, and pressed my mouth to his lips. Our kisses earlier had been so desperate, so hungry, they'd almost been a fight, albeit a fight with both of us on the same side. This kiss was different. Lazy. Sweet. Possessive.

I wasn't giving this man back. He was mine now. And I was his.

I was seriously regretting the lack of just one more condom when Royal turned me on my side and started to inch down the bed. Hmmm, okay, not going to argue about that. But... Maybe I was.

I wanted his mouth on me again, no question, but the idea of it had me thinking about earlier and wishing he'd come when I'd had my mouth on him. I rolled back and managed to flip around without rolling off the bed or kicking Royal in the face.

Settling back on my side, his already hard cock exactly where I wanted it, I glanced down our bodies to find Royal grinning up at me. He slung my top leg over his shoulder, spreading me open, and licked. I smothered my gasp with his cock, taking him as deep as I could. We were lazy, slow, all our frantic need assuaged earlier in the night. I wanted to come, wanted to feel him come, but I wasn't in a hurry to get there.

What I really wanted was to take my time, to explore what made him feel good, what he liked. To absorb the way he tasted, the scent of him, the sounds he made, even while he was doing the same for me. We came together, drawing the pleasure from each other and sending it back. Royal pulled me close for a slow, deep kiss before we settled back under the blanket, arms and legs entwined.

I can't remember the last time I slept through dawn. It never happened. Even on my day off my eyes flicked open well before five am. Not that day. It must have been all the orgasms because I slept like the dead, waking with a jolt to blink furiously at the sting of bright sunlight, heart thudding so loud that at first I didn't understand that the pounding sound in my ears wasn't my heart.

Wood. It was a fist on wood. And a voice. "Royal! Royal! You guys in there?"

"Fuck." Royal sat up, pulling the blanket to cover me. "Griffen? Is that you?"

A muffled, "Thank God." Then, "You guys alright?"

Royal shot an amused glance at me. I grinned back. "We're alright, but could you give us a minute before you open the—"

Too late. The trapdoor flipped up and Griffen's head popped through, a smirk on his face. All at once, my amusement fled and heat burned in my cheeks. I was naked, probably reeked of sex, and all that stood between me and my friend's husband was a thin blanket. I dove beneath, my only thought to hide. Royal's hand came down on my back, holding the blanket in place.

"Can you give us a sec? We're not exactly decent."

A female laugh drifted up from below along with what I thought was a faint, "Told you so." Something thumped on the floor.

"We were hoping you were here. Hope put that together for Daisy. I'll let the others know you're okay."

"The others?" I asked from beneath the blanket.

Royal relayed my question. "Uh, who else is there?"

"Just me, Hope, West, and Sterling."

"Did you need to bring a crowd?" Royal rubbed my back, trying to soothe my sudden tension.

"West wouldn't take no for an answer. Apparently, Ms. Hutchins called him when Daisy didn't show up to open the bakery. Sterling and Hope are just nosy."

"Worried! I was worried!" Hope. I thought about giving her a hard time. Then I remembered that thump on the floor and that Hope had brought me something. Please, let it be clean clothes. I peeled back the blanket and looked up at Royal, who was grinning down at me.

"I'll get rid of them," he promised in a whisper. "Shut the door for a sec," he called down to Griffen. The door thudded shut. "I'm going to hit the bathroom and pull on some clothes, go down there and send them all back to the house so you can get dressed in peace."

"K," I squeaked, mortified by the idea of Weston Garfield busting up my morning-after at the behest of my worried grandmother.

Ignoring the crowd waiting below, Royal pressed a kiss to my forehead, then my lips. "Last night was magic, Daisy. Not quite what I had planned but magic all the same."

I reached up and curved my hand over the nape of his neck, bringing him down for another kiss. "Magic," I whispered against his lips.

At that moment in time, it was the truest thing I knew, all the way to the depths of my soul. Together we made magic, and all I wanted was more.

Chapter Twenty-Eight

ROYAL

I STRODE THROUGH THE LOBBY OF THE INN, WHIS-
tling under my breath. Everything was on track for
the day. Construction on the first few cottages was
moving along, I'd managed the latest guest crisis, and Daisy was
on her way to meet me in my office for lunch.

It was hard to believe that almost a month had passed since
the night Daisy and I were trapped in the watchtower. Some
things had stayed the same, but the framework of my life had
turned upside down, and I had no intention of letting it go back
to normal. Not ever.

Daisy and I had barely slept apart since that night. I couldn't
bear the idea of being alone in my bed, the sheets cold, Daisy's soft body out of reach. She hadn't argued, only interested
in sleeping apart from me the one weekend J.T. came home.

Whatever was off-kilter between them, I wanted it set right for Daisy's sake, so I sucked it up and encouraged her to spend time with him when she could. The rest of the nights she was mine.

Together we ignored the rest of the world. I hadn't yet met her parents. She was hesitant to introduce us, and I didn't push. I knew she had issues with her father and she'd mentioned they didn't approve of her dating me, but she didn't want to talk about it.

It went against the grain to let a problem fester—if it had been up to me we would have set things straight and gone on with our lives—but Daisy was stubborn and we were talking about her family, not mine, so I let it go for now. We'd deal with them eventually. For the moment, everything was so good I didn't have much trouble convincing myself to focus on Daisy and ignore her family.

My family wasn't as easy to dismiss. Partly because I worked with three of them, but mostly because we had to spend every night at Heartstone Manor. Savannah was more than our housekeeper, she was our prison guard, reporting to the family attorney if one of us missed a night spent in the house.

Savannah was subtle in her duty, keeping an eye on our comings and goings with the help of the security team but never making a big deal of it. We were all well aware of what would happen if we missed too many nights at home. So far, no one was pushing the limits.

I couldn't complain. I had a luxurious suite in Heartstone Manor and a short commute unlike my youngest brother, Brax, who worked out of his office in Asheville and had an hour-long drive both ways, his new condo in town already sublet to strangers.

Having Daisy in my life had changed more than my sleeping habits. Lucky for me, she understood the situation with the will and never complained about having to stay at Heartstone.

My siblings liked her, and Parker's husband was long gone, but Bryce went out of his way to be an ass on a regular basis, just because he could. We both avoided him as much as possible.

It was barely a month, and we were pretty much living together.

It should have felt too fast.

I should have felt trapped.

I should be itching for a new diversion.

I wasn't.

I woke up by four every morning to make love to Daisy before pulling her into a quick shower and driving us both into town. Well before dawn, I left her in her kitchen with a kiss, though some mornings she made me wait until she'd cooked us both breakfast.

I hit my desk hours before the rest of the management staff, at first surprising the night-shift desk clerks. By now, they were used to me coming in while the rest of the town was sleeping. Tenn showed up each morning to find me almost finished with my paperwork, ready to work with Forrest or jump on whatever fire had to be put out next.

Most days I headed to Heartstone for lunch unless Daisy could get away to meet me. She was oddly reluctant to talk details on the bakery expansion, but she was eager to test new recipes for the planned lunch menu, and I loved being her guinea pig.

Evenings, when I was done working with Griffen and Hope, I'd drive back into town for Daisy. Sometimes we'd cook dinner together and eat in her little apartment above the bakery.

Other nights we'd order dinner up to my office and eat at The Inn. One memorable night I brought her back to the watchtower, this time armed with more supplies, and Bryce safely secured at the big house. We didn't get much sleep, but it was worth it.

Every once in a while, we ate with everyone else at Heartstone Manor. My family was a lot to handle on a good day, and while Daisy didn't seem to mind them, I didn't want to scare her off. I couldn't. I'd only been seeing her for a short time, and I already knew I couldn't live without her.

Everything in my life was better with Daisy. Everything. Being with Daisy somehow gave me more patience with the little things. Not that my family and the problems at The Inn were little things.

Bryce and Ophelia had moved into Heartstone, but the sabotage hadn't stopped. Deliberately broken plumbing in a vacant room that caused thousands in damage and lost room charges. An attempt to switch supplies in the kitchen that might have spoiled dozens of meals if the sous-chef hadn't tasted the salt before seasoning her sauce.

As much as I wanted to blame Bryce for the problems at The Inn, we had to acknowledge that he wasn't the culprit. He'd admitted he locked us in the watchtower, sneering that it was just a prank, and we should learn to take a joke.

Ah, the refrain of petty bullies everywhere. *I was only joking*. Bryce was more of an asshole every day, but he wasn't the one fucking with my Inn, so I mostly ignored him.

My cheerful whistle died as I passed through the back of the lobby and spotted Sterling talking to Forrest in the restaurant. An early lunch? She was wearing a suit, a file folder on the table beside her, looking as professional and composed as I'd ever seen her, but something about the way she leaned in and smiled at Forrest struck me as off. His returning smile was the same. A little too friendly. A little too personal.

So far, he seemed like a good enough guy. He was a great fit for The Inn and got along well with Tenn and me. But being a decent guy didn't mean he was right for my baby sister. She was vulnerable, trying to start a whole new life, drinking less, and working full time. So far, so good. I didn't want some guy to fuck it up for her.

Not your business, I tried to tell myself as I walked past the restaurant and opened the door to the stairwell. A man in an Inn uniform brushed by me, his shoulder knocking me back a step. I turned to say something, and he disappeared around the corner, leaving me with the impression that I knew him from somewhere, and not The Inn.

I might have thought about it longer, but one of my desk clerks caught me, asking me to take a look at a problem before I headed upstairs.

I had a few minutes before Daisy would be here, so I followed the clerk back to the front desk, sending Daisy a quick text to let her know where I was. Good thing, because the small problem turned out to be a major IT snafu. By the time we figured out what had happened and our IT guy was on the case, Daisy had arrived.

She stood across the desk, dressed in khaki shorts and her pink Sweetheart Bakery polo shirt, carrying a big, twine-handled paper bag with the bakery logo on the side.

I shouldn't kiss her in the lobby. That would be inappropriate.

That's what the stairwell was for.

"Ready?" she asked.

I knew she only had an hour for lunch, her afternoon packed with custom projects she had to finish. Fortunately, the IT guy was on top of the problem and the reservations system would be back up soon. How someone got in the system to mess with the settings was a whole other issue. One I'd deal with later. *After* lunch with Daisy. I had my priorities straight.

"I'm ready. Picnic or my office?"

"You haven't been outside lately?" she asked. I shook my head. I'd had my face buried in a monitor for the last half hour and hadn't bothered to look out the window. "It's pouring. I'm voting for your office."

"Works for me."

I took the bag from her, sliding my arm around her shoulder. She fit into my side perfectly, keeping pace as we crossed the lobby to the stairwell. Sterling and Forrest were gone from the restaurant.

I reminded myself to mention their lunch to Daisy. She wasn't close to Sterling like she was with Hope, but they were friendly and getting closer since Daisy was around Heartstone so much. Maybe she'd have a perspective more evolved than, *'Get your hands off my sister!'*

Scratch that, there was no *maybe* about it. Daisy was intelligent and she was a good listener. I was already in the habit of running things by her. She was good at reading people and seeing to the heart of a problem.

Just before we got to the door on the office level, I stopped, turning Daisy to back her against the wall.

She blinked up at me, feigning confusion. "Did you forget something?"

"I did. This." It had been hours since I'd last kissed her. I didn't want to wait another minute. Sure, I could have kissed her in my office. I had before, spending hours with her settled in my lap in my desk chair or stretched out on the couch after dinner. But Penny was at her desk and I didn't want to scandalize Daisy. No kissing in the office during work hours. The stairwell, on the other hand...

Daisy melted into me with a low moan, her lips parting, tongue sneaking out to stroke mine. I'd never get tired of kissing her, of the way she gave herself over to me without hesitation. I could have kissed her for the rest of the afternoon, but I had a meeting at Heartstone in a few hours, and she had to be back at the bakery long before that.

Lifting my head, I absorbed her dazed expression. "Ready for lunch?" I asked, stroking a spiraling curl that had sprung free from her barrette.

"Mmmhmm." She nodded but stood there, staring up at me.

"Do you want me to kiss you again first?"

"Mmmhmm."

Lunch could wait. Kissing Daisy came first. See, didn't I say I had my priorities straight?

I don't know how long we might have lingered in the stairwell, kissing and letting our lunch go cold. With Daisy in my arms, her lips soft and giving under mine, I wasn't in any rush for food. I was thinking about sneaking her into an empty room—something that occurred to me pretty much every time we had lunch in my office—when the heavy stairwell door flew open and a tall figure in sneakers and an Inn uniform came barreling past us, long blond hair sticking out from beneath her Inn cap.

I knew in an instant that this was not one of my people. Like the man who'd bumped me earlier, something about her was familiar but not as one of my employees. The Inn had a big staff, and Tenn and I knew every single one of them. Not just their names, but who they were—hobbies, families, pets.

The problem was I couldn't place either the man in the stairwell earlier or the woman flying down the stairs. They seemed familiar, but that was as far as I got. The only thing I knew for certain was that neither of them should have been wearing an Inn uniform, and there was no reason for anyone to be in the admin suite who didn't work there.

I stepped in front of Daisy, shielding her with my body as I pushed open the door. At first, everything looked normal. Penny's desk was vacant, not unusual since Daisy and I had been delayed in the stairwell long enough to push into Penny's lunch break. Ditto for Tenn, who'd planned to head out for a run during his lunch break.

The reception area was quiet. Tenn's office door was shut, but mine was open. The faint sound of a moan drifted to us, low and undeniably male. A thump followed, and another moan. Pain. Keeping Daisy behind me, I started for my office.

Chapter Twenty-Nine

ROYAL

*D*AISY, CALL WEST," I ORDERED, DROPPING TO MY KNEES beside Forrest's prone body.

"I'm fine, I'm fine," he tried to say, the words cut off as he braced his arm under him to sit up and ended up falling on his face. Another thump and moan.

"Fuck, stay still you idiot, you're not fine. What the fuck happened? You're bleeding all over the place."

Not waiting for an answer, I yanked at his shirt, pulling it up on one side to reveal a thin slash along his ribs bleeding profusely. "I need something to put pressure on this," I shouted to Daisy, somewhere behind me, still talking to West.

Before I could ask again, a bundle of fabric was shoved in my face. Clean napkins. I pressed them to the slice on Forrest's side, trying not to feel bad about his groan of pain.

"Just lay there and stop trying to get up."

Forrest subsided, his forehead knit in a scowl. With one arm he reached over to hold the napkins to his side. I shoved his hand away. "Fucking chill or you're going to make it worse. Who did this?"

"Did you see her?" Forrest craned his neck as if he could spot his assailant still hanging around the office.

"The blond woman in The Inn uniform who raced past us down the stairs?" At his nod of confirmation, I pulled up my phone and called our head of security, alerting him to the possible suspect. I had a feeling she was long gone, but if she was still hanging around I didn't want to wait for West to get someone looking for her.

"She's not one of ours," I said, and Forrest nodded, his green eyes dark with pain and frustration.

"I didn't recognize her. I would have remembered a blond that tall. And the uniform didn't fit her right. I was just processing all of that when she whipped out a knife and went for me. I think she was planning to stab me in the back, but I turned at the last second and my ribs blocked the knife." He winced at the memory, reaching for his ribs again.

"And you have no idea who it was? Or why she'd want to stab you?"

Forrest's face was drawn with pain, but his eyes were clear. "Royal, I don't think she wanted to stab *me*."

I was still processing his words when Daisy leaned over us, scanning Forrest, assessing his wounds. With a nod, she narrowed her eyes on me. "He's in *your* office, Royal. And if she came up behind him, she probably thought he was you."

Fuck. They were right. Forrest and I are about the same height and build. Both with dark hair, a little longer than it should be and in need of a cut. Someone who was in a rush could easily have seen Forrest leaning over my desk and assumed he was me.

"What were you doing in my office?" I had to ask. We had an open-door policy at The Inn for the most part, but Forest had his own office. Why was he in mine, going through my desk?

"Looking for the Williamson contract. I wanted to double-check the time frame."

"West is on his way up," Daisy said, setting the bag with our lunch on Penny's desk and coming back into my office to stand over us.

Forrest shoved my hands away from the make-shift bandage on his side and lurched into a sitting position, leaning back against the side of my desk as another wave of pain hit him.

"Let me see," I demanded, pulling his hands away from the napkins to check the wound. It was still bleeding but sluggishly. I pressed the napkins back into place and let him take over holding them. "You might not need stitches, but you definitely need to see a doctor."

"Figured that," Forrest grunted. His eyes lit as the elevator door opened. Sterling flew across the reception area into my office, dropping to her knees beside Forrest. "I'm okay—" he started.

"Oh, my God, you're bleeding! Forrest! What the hell happened?" Sterling turned to look at me accusingly as if *I'd* stabbed her new boyfriend. And when had that happened? There was no hiding the fact that these two were more than casual work acquaintances.

"We're trying to figure that out," Daisy soothed, shooting me a look that simultaneously said *What the fuck?* and *Not now.* I was right there with her on the *WTF?* and could grudgingly admit that this moment was not the one to confront my sister over her office romance. Especially not while she was cooing all over my new CFO.

West had followed Sterling in and stood over us, shaking his head. "Can't stay out of trouble, can you?"

"Hey, I was just coming to my office for lunch." I explained what we knew so far, ignoring Forrest and Sterling's whispers.

Narrowing his eyes on the bloody napkins pressed to Forrest's side, West took over. "Royal, walk Daisy back to the bakery. You'll have to reschedule lunch. I'm going to get Forrest to the ER and take his statement. After you drop Daisy, come straight back here, grab Tenn, and we'll go over the whole thing with your security team, see if they found anything."

Sterling glared up at both of us, her hand gripping Forrest's with white knuckles. "I'm coming to the hospital with Forrest."

I thought about arguing and decided that Daisy's look earlier had been right. Now was not the time. Instead, I gave a sharp nod and stood. I took Daisy's hand in mine, only remembering lunch when we were halfway down the block. "I'm sorry about lunch," I said, my voice sounding distant in my own ears. I was still dazed from walking into my office to find Forrest bleeding all over the place. "I should have remembered the bag. Now you don't have anything to eat."

"It's fine," Daisy said absently. "I'm not hungry anymore."

"Yeah, me either."

That was all either of us said until we reached the alley door to Sweetheart's kitchen. Once inside, Daisy stopped and looked up at me, her expression fierce. "Be careful. If that had been you—" She shuddered.

I pulled her into my arms, burying my face in her hair and taking a deep, soothing breath. Rocking her from side to side, I murmured, "I'll be careful. I promise. Nothing is going to happen to me."

"It had better not," Daisy threatened, her eyes worried beneath the false bravado. "I just found you. You aren't allowed to get stabbed."

"I won't," I promised again. Lifting my head, I opened the door to leave. I needed to get to the office and catch Tenn before he came back and saw the blood on the carpet.

Turning the doorknob in my hand, I said, "Lock this behind me. When things are settled, I'll come back to let you know what's going on. But don't let anyone in if you're alone."

"Do you think I'm in danger?" she asked as if that thought hadn't occurred to her. I hated that it had occurred to me.

"I hope not. Sabotage is one thing. If this is escalating to physical attacks, I don't want to take the chance it's going to spill over onto you. It's pretty obvious to anyone watching me that you're an important part of my life. I won't let anything happen to you."

Daisy went to her toes, reaching up to press her lips to mine. "Okay, I'll be careful, too."

I left her with one more kiss, pausing on the other side of the door to wait for the snick of the deadbolt flipping so I knew she was safely locked inside. It came, and I left, my mind racing with possibilities, eyes scanning the street for threats.

This was absurd. Griffen had a guy come after him not long after he'd moved back to Sawyers Bend, but that guy was in jail now, and he'd had a grudge against our father. The list of people who'd hated Prentice was long, but I couldn't think of anyone who'd come after me specifically.

You can't expect logic from a person who'd walk into your office and stab someone, I reminded myself.

We were dealing with someone who was capable of murder. Who the hell knew what they were thinking? I hoped West had some idea of where to go with this because I had nothing.

When I got back, the offices were crowded with evidence techs, my office blocked off by yellow caution tape. Tenn sat at Penny's desk, talking to West and digging into one of the quiches Daisy brought for our lunch. I thought about complaining and then, much like the thing with Sterling and Forrest, decided now was not the time. It wasn't like Daisy was going to eat it anyway.

Two hours later, Forrest was back from the ER, bandaged but not stitched, and we were no closer to figuring out who had attacked him. He was giving me cautious looks when he thought I wasn't paying attention, but I wasn't sure if they were about Sterling or getting stabbed in my place. I didn't ask.

Forrest and I agreed that the woman we'd seen was both tall and blond, but neither of us had recognized her. Something about her struck me as familiar, but when I tried to break it down—was it her face? her build?—I came up empty. I couldn't remember a tall blond. I knew tall women and blond women, but not both together. Of course, she could have been wearing lifts or a wig.

There was definitely premeditation involved. Not just stealing an Inn uniform or the possibility of a disguise, but the security team reported that the system was shut down in the stairwell, elevators, and admin suite on that floor of The Inn. They'd gone offline right around the time I was called back to the front desk to deal with the reservations snafu.

Lucky for me, or I would have been in my office when the mystery woman went after Forrest in my place. Or unlucky because if I'd been in the office with Forrest, it was likely no one would have been stabbed, and she would have tried again another day.

Either way, it was late afternoon by the time West went back to the police department with a plan to question Forrest again the next day in the hopes that he'd remember something useful. Forrest had tried to work the rest of the afternoon, but Tenn and I sent him home to sleep off the worst of the pain. I did not ask if Sterling went with him.

I bailed on Tenn after West left, packing up Daisy's used storage containers to take back to the bakery. I knew she must be dying to know what had happened after she left, and I needed to see her face, to assure myself she was well and safe, insulated from all this craziness. I wasn't keen on the idea that someone had tried to stab me. I was even less keen on the idea that they might come after Daisy.

I can't remember the last time I'd entered Sweetheart Bakery from the front door. Ever since I'd been seeing Daisy I'd used the alley door to the kitchens, bypassing the customers in the front. More to the point, bypassing Grams and Daisy's mother. Grams was all too happy to see me, but the few times I'd crossed paths with Daisy's mom she'd glared at me, prompting Daisy to usher me away before we could be properly introduced.

I let her do it, proving I was a coward when it came to meeting the parents. I'd never bothered to meet a woman's parents before. Maybe it was karma built up from all those casual relationships. My first attempt at a real relationship and her parents hated me. Crossing my fingers that Grams would be alone at the counter, I pushed open the door to Sweetheart Bakery.

Should have texted Daisy and asked her to open the back door, I thought as I was hit with the sweet scent of sugar and the bitter glares of both of Daisy's parents. Great. Just what my day needed.

"Can I help you, sir?" Daisy's mother asked, her voice dripping with saccharine sweetness, her eyes shooting daggers. If I hadn't been sure Forrest's attacker had been white, I might have suspected Sheree Hutchins. I couldn't remember any woman looking at me with so much dislike. It was intense, especially considering we'd never formally met.

Biting the bullet, I stuck out my hand. "No, thank you. I'm Royal, Daisy's boyfriend. I'm sorry we haven't officially met. She asked me to stop by—"

"We know who you are," Daisy's father cut in. He was handsome, with dark hair and chiseled features. He probably had a very charming smile when he used it. I doubted I'd get to see. He glared at me with even more animosity than his wife.

I dropped my hand, shoving it in my back pocket. Well, okay, what now? I was here to see Daisy, not start an argument with her parents, but shoving past them to the kitchen door was too rude despite the way they were acting. I was considering leaving and going to the back door when Sheree spoke up again.

"Look, Daisy isn't here. And from the things she's said, even if she were here, she doesn't want to see you. You need to break it off with her. She wants you to stay away."

I stared at Daisy's parents, dumbfounded. I knew that wasn't true. It couldn't be. I'd only left her side a few hours before. Even if she was freaking out over what had happened to Forrest, she would have called. She absolutely would not have asked her parents to break up with me. No way. Not Daisy.

A niggling doubt ate at me. But what if she had? It didn't bear thinking about. If Daisy had decided she was done with me, I wasn't going away quietly. What we had was too good to give up. Not without a fight.

"I just talked to her a few hours ago, and she asked me to stop by. If she wants to break up with me, I'd like to hear it from her."

Her father's eyes went white-hot with fury. "You don't need to talk to her. You think I don't know all about you? The way you fuck your way through the women in this town? The way you think everyone should bow down to you, one of the mighty Sawyers? Well, fuck you and fuck your family. You can't have my daughter. She's done with you."

Chapter Thirty

DAISY

I COULDN'T BELIEVE WHAT I'D JUST HEARD. WHY? WHY would my dad tell Royal I was done with him?

Rage and humiliation burning through me, I shoved the door wide. Three faces turned to me, Royal's relieved and my parents' defiant.

Of course, they'd be defiant. Why would they feel shame for lying to my boyfriend and humiliating me? My heart ached as I realized I'd been hoping for more. Support maybe? For them to think about me instead of their own agenda?

Whatever I wanted from them, it was clear I wasn't going to get it.

"Dad! Why would you say something like that?" I pushed past them, needing to get to Royal. I reached for his hand, hoping he wasn't too angry to listen. "He's lying. I'm not done with you." More quietly, the truth whispered from my heart. "I'm never going to be done with you, Royal."

His arms went around me before I was done speaking, pulling me tight to his side. "I'm so sorry," I whispered, my cheeks burning with mortification.

"Don't apologize for them," he whispered back. "You didn't do anything wrong. It's not your fault they're—" He ran out of words, probably not ready to call my parents assholes, even if they deserved the title.

Typical Royal, being a good guy even when he was in his rights to say what was on his mind. I spun in his arms, shielding him from Sheree and Darren. They were my problem, not his.

"Why would you treat Royal like this? You know we're together. How could you be so rude?"

"Because he doesn't deserve any better," my father said. "You know who he is. Who his father was. He's just using you."

"You're making a fool of yourself, honey," my mother said, pity in her soft eyes.

I stared at both of them, speechless. "You know that isn't true. And you don't know Royal. I do, and you're wrong."

I wasn't stupid enough to believe them. Maybe Royal and I hadn't talked a lot about what our relationship meant or where it was going, but considering we were practically living together and I'd never been happier in my life, I didn't need the talk. I knew how I felt. I hadn't told him I loved him, but I would as soon as I worked up the nerve.

My father dismissed me with a roll of his eyes. At that moment, I thought I'd never hated him so much in my entire life.

He was about to prove me wrong.

"We've let this go so far, but it needs to stop," he said, ignoring Royal to focus on me. "He's nothing more than a spoiled man-whore and you're acting like a stupid slut. Keep your legs together and get back to work. I don't want to discuss this again."

"*You've let this go?*" I repeated, incredulous. Had he just called Royal a man-whore and me a slut? What the hell? All of a sudden, I was done. "You owe us an apology."

"I'm not apologizing for speaking my truth," my dad said, his chin sticking out in defiance. Hell, he looked just like a sullen little boy when he did that. Why couldn't my parents act like adults?

I crossed my arms over my chest to hide my shaking hands. "Either you apologize, or you can get out of my bakery. I wish you'd never come back here. You say Royal is using me, that he's making a fool of me, but what about you? Are you ever going to pay me back? Or was that just a lie to placate me?"

My father's eyes skipped to Royal at the mention of payment. Just as quickly, he shrugged off his concern. "I told you, I'm working on it. I just need a little more time. And it wasn't your money in the first place."

"It was half my money, which only makes it worse." My voice was shaking, but I kept going. "And you know what? Keep it. Consider us even, pack your things, and leave Sawyers Bend. How about that? If you go, I'll forgive the debt."

I thought that was a pretty good offer, all things considered. I wasn't expecting the rush of relief as I gave up on him repaying me. It didn't last long.

A silky smile spread across my father's face. I braced. Royal must have sensed something coming, because his hand closed over my shoulder, steadying me. I needed it.

"I don't have to pay you back anyway. You took the money from the business, right?"

I gave a stiff nod, so angry at my father I couldn't process the embarrassment of having my stupidity exposed to Royal.

"Then it's my money, too. Didn't Grams tell you?" He cocked his head to the side, innocent concern all over his face.

He was neither innocent nor concerned, he just wanted to set the stage. I couldn't even bring myself to shake my head. Instead, I leaned into Royal, needing his strength at my back.

"Your Grandmother changed her will. Sweetheart Bakery is in her name only, and when she dies, the whole thing comes to me. You're just an employee. So, technically, we could have you charged with felony theft." He gave me a beatific smile, a cat with his paw on the mouse's tail, willing to be generous now that he had all the power.

There was a very good chance I was going to throw up. Just an employee? Grams and I had talked about changing the ownership structure of the business. I thought we just hadn't gotten around to it, and I hadn't pushed because... Because I trusted my grandmother.

My chest was caving in, oxygen strangling in my lungs. Everything I'd worked for was gone. I'd given up on school, thinking I wouldn't need it with Sweetheart in my future. Thinking I was part of a team, that I'd found my place.

It was all a lie.

My father waited for me to say something. I scrabbled for words, mind spinning, stomach slowly turning inside out. Maybe he was lying. It wouldn't be the first time. And Grams wouldn't just give him the bakery. No way.

I tried to imagine him waking up hours before dawn to work his ass off in a hot kitchen.

Not going to happen.

Before I let that realization calm me, I understood.

He wouldn't have to wake up early to bust his ass in the kitchen. That's what I was for.

I refused to cry. Or throw up. My father's smile was kind as he said to Royal, "This is family business, Sawyer. Why don't you give Daisy some space to work this out on her own? She doesn't have time to entertain you. She has special orders to finish."

To me, he added, "Go work out that mood on some dough. We're low on bread up here."

I didn't move. Royal waited, not bothering to acknowledge my father's words. After a few seconds of furious thought, I realized I only had one question. "When did Grams talk to you about her will?" Fists clenched at my sides, I hoped he'd say *'Last year,'* or, *'A while ago.'*

Another of those feline smiles from my father. "We were just talking about it last night, honey."

I was standing in the middle of the bakery, but in reality, my back was against the wall. I could hardly believe what I was doing as I untied my apron with the big pink Sweetheart logo on the front. Tossing it over the counter, I spoke words I'd never imagined would come from my mouth.

"I quit."

I closed my ears to my mother's protests, refused to see my father's angry glare. My brain went straight to the practicalities. I needed my purse and my keys from the kitchen. Just as I started to move, Royal took the lead, blocking my parents in behind the register and clearing my path to the kitchen door.

We were through and in the kitchen before my parents could stop us. They followed, my mother pleading for me to calm down and talk this out.

My father shouted, "You'll be back! No one else in this town will give you a job!"

His words chased me out the door.

Chapter Thirty-One

DAISY

WE SAT IN MY LITTLE BEATER OF A CAR BEHIND THE bakery, Royal waiting patiently for me to say something and me silent with shock.

Had I just quit the bakery? What was I going to do? I didn't have much saved and no formal education past high school. My apartment came with the job. I would have said Grams would never kick me out, but she'd cut me out of the bakery, so who knew what she'd do?

Royal reached over and took my hand. "You and I need to switch seats."

I gave him a blank look. Switch seats?

"You're not in any shape to drive. Switch seats with me." Numb, I did as I was told. When he was settled in the driver's seat, he asked, "Where to? I can take you home to Heartstone.

Or we can track down your grandmother and find out how much of your father's bullshit was true."

I wanted to crawl under the covers of Royal's bed and pretend the entire day hadn't happened. Since the same problems would be waiting for me when I crawled back out, I chose option number two. "Let's find Grams and see what's going on."

We found her at home, folding laundry in front of a daytime game show. Seeing both of us, a brilliant smile spread across her face. As she took in my grim expression and Royal's lack of a greeting, the smile faded away.

"What's wrong, baby? Is everything alright?"

She started to set down the shirt in her hands, worry clouding her familiar features. Maybe this was just a misunderstanding. Maybe he'd been lying to make a point. Maybe— "Did you tell Dad that he was going to inherit the bakery? That I was just an employee?"

Grams's face fell in dismay. "No, Daisy! Of course not!" Relief coursed through me for a moment until I noticed the way she was twisting the shirt in her hands, her eyes looking past me but not at me.

"Grams?" I prompted.

"It will all work out right in the end. I'm leaving the bakery to Darren, but he has to leave it to you. So, it's yours in the long run..."

It was a hammer blow right to my heart. I must have made a sound, because Grams flinched and Royal was right there, his arm coming around my shoulders. I could barely force my mouth to form words.

"Why would you do that? When did you decide? Just a few months ago we were talking about partnership papers and— Why didn't you tell me you'd changed your mind?"

"Because I didn't. Not really. This just delays things. Your father thought—"

Of course, it was his idea. "I'm not going to be a partner?"

Grams stood, setting the laundry on the couch. "Let me make some coffee, and we'll talk this out."

"I don't want coffee, Grams. I just want to get this straight. Were you ever going to make me a partner? Was that ever the plan or did you just tell me that to placate me?"

"No, Daisy, baby, I never lied to you. It's just that your father and Sheree—they need stability. I thought—Darren thought— that if they had something to come home to—"

I sucked in a deep breath. "Since you two are so cozy all of a sudden, did you know he just told Royal I didn't want to see him anymore? And then when I interrupted to correct him, he called Royal a man-whore and me a slut. Is that what you think, too?"

Grams went pale. Her eyes turned to Royal, beseeching. "No, Royal, no. Not at all. I'm so sorry Darren was so rude. I've been thrilled you two are together. Daisy's been so happy—" Her voice faded away, and she looked at the floor. When she raised her head, her eyes were wet. "He's my baby."

"I thought *I* was your baby." The plaintive tone of my voice brought tears of humiliation to my eyes. All my life my parents had ignored me, but it was okay because I had Grams. Except now, it seemed that, in the end, I didn't have her either.

Grams reached for me. I stepped back. I got it now. My dad needed more, so he got more. All my hard work wasn't worth anything. Taking another deep breath to steady myself, I reached for Royal's hand. His fingers closed around mine, holding tight.

"Just so you know," I began, "I lent Dad the twenty thousand dollars we had saved for the renovations. He had a business plan and spreadsheets and I truly thought he was going to pay us back. You've probably figured out that he changed his mind. That's why I keep putting you off on the renovations. Because the money is gone."

"Oh, Daisy, it's okay, baby, I understand."

"Do you? Because I don't. I asked him about it before we came here, and he said he wasn't going to pay us back and technically he could press charges against me for stealing from the bakery."

"Well, that's absurd! Of course, I'd never—"

"I'm telling you because keeping the secret has been making me miserable. And also because when you take over the accounting, you'll see what I did. I'm sorry. I screwed up and now you won't get your deck or outside seating. Not for a while. Probably not ever since Dad won't let you save up that much without talking you into giving it to him instead."

"Daisy, your father—" She stopped and stared at me in confusion. "Why would I take over the accounting?"

"You can't let Mom or Dad do it," I said slowly. I thought that was obvious. "Whatever you do, don't give them access to your banking or the checkbook."

"They wouldn't—" Grams cut off again.

I ignored her. Of course, they would. They'd already gotten away with stealing from her once, though that was mostly my fault. Now that we were talking about accounting, I remembered our clients and the schedule.

"I'll come in tomorrow to finish the event cakes for this weekend."

Grams just stared at me, mouth open, stunned silent. Royal took pity on her. "Eleanor," he said gently, "Daisy quit the bakery."

Another thing I thought would be obvious. A tear spilled down Grams' cheek, and I felt like absolute dog shit for making my grandmother cry.

"Grams," I said, my voice hitching, "I can't stay. I thought it was ours, that we were a team. I won't work with Dad. Not after what he did and the things he said. I don't think you should either, but it's been made very clear that it isn't my business."

"Daisy. I can't choose—"

Horror engulfed me. That wasn't what I meant. "I'm not trying to make you choose. I understand that he's your son. I get it. I know how much you love him, how happy you are when he's home. If this makes them stay—"

My throat locked up, tears flooding my eyes until I couldn't see. I wanted Grams to be happy. I loved her too much to want anything else. I just couldn't be a part of her happiness if it came at this cost. Dad would ruin her. I wasn't sticking around to watch.

At that thought, I reached my limit. "I love you," I forced out, darting forward to catch her in a brief hug before I bolted out the front door. Royal followed after a moment, taking my arm and helping me into the car.

"What did you say to her?" I asked when I thought I could get a word out.

"That I'd look out for you."

I wanted to be strong, to tell him I didn't need him to look out for me, but right then, I very much did. I couldn't really see where he was driving. Grams' face kept popping into my head, that look of confusion and pain. Hurting her left my chest hollow and aching, my stomach sick. I almost told Royal to turn the car around and go back, but then I thought of my father, that smug smile and the sound of him calling me a slut for falling in love with a good man.

No, there was no going back. I loved Grams so much, but Dad was her problem. I'd never been able to get him to be a good father or a good son, and he sure as hell didn't fit my definition of a good husband. I'd never understand why my mother put up with him. How could she choose him over her own child? That question pulled a hitching sob from my throat.

"Daisy." Royal reached over and squeezed my hand. I looked up to see that we were pulling to a stop in The Inn's parking lot.

"I'm going to bring you home to Heartstone. We'll go straight up to my rooms and you won't have to see anyone. We can leave your car here. Do you need anything?"

A decent set of parents? My life back the way I thought it was?

I shook my head. Royal couldn't fix this for me. I managed to whisper, "Thanks," my voice thick. His lips pressed to my forehead and a fresh wave of tears cascaded from my eyes. What had I done to deserve this man? My life was a mess, my father had insulted him, and here he was, taking care of me.

"Thank you," I said again, this time clearer, the blue of his gaze burning away the moisture in my eyes.

He dropped another kiss, this time on my lips. "Anything for you, Daisy. You should know that by now."

Anything for me.

He was the first person to say those words to me. That should have scared me. It didn't. I knew I'd do anything for Royal, too.

I had no idea how soon I'd understand what that really meant, and how much it would cost me.

Chapter Thirty-Two

ROYAL

*D*AISY WAS A SHELL OF HERSELF.

I'm not a violent kind of guy. I usually figure problems can be better solved with a smile and words than throwing a punch. All of that went out the window when it came to Daisy's father. I didn't give a shit what he called me, but calling her a slut?

I hate that word on a good day. Why should anyone be called names for liking sex? It was stupid and narrow-minded. But to say that to Daisy? Daisy, who hadn't even dated in over a year? Daisy, who was so sweet, and funny, and everything I'd ever wanted in a woman—everything I never knew I needed.

I white-knuckled the steering wheel all the way to Heart-stone so I wouldn't swing the car around and head straight back to Sweetheart to put Darren Hutchins on his ass.

Now I knew what she'd been hiding about the bakery and the stalled renovations.

Again, I repressed the urge to pulverize her father. What kind of asshole steals from both his daughter and his mother at the same time? And then says he'll have her arrested when she asks for the money back?

I heard a grinding noise, and for a second, I thought it was my car. I realized it was my teeth and that a headache was throbbing behind my eyes.

Fuck. I had to get it together for Daisy. She needed me to support her, not trample in, fists swinging.

At Heartstone, I parked beside the garage and ushered Daisy in through the side door, straight to the family wing on the second floor. We didn't run into anyone on the way. Daisy's shoulders sagged in relief when we closed the door to my suite behind us.

I texted Savannah to let her know Daisy'd had a bad day, and we'd be skipping dinner in favor of the privacy of my suite. I knew better than to ask for the meal to be served up here—Savannah didn't do room service—but she surprised me by offering to have our food delivered.

Daisy was loved, she just didn't know by how many people. Not yet. Her family might have let her down, but mine was jumping in to pick up the slack.

Daisy paced the living room of my suite, wiping her eyes now and then as I tried to think of what to say.

"I'll have to move," she muttered to herself, dashing away a fresh wave of tears. I struggled to push back the need to kick her father's ass.

"You can move in with me," I said with a shrug.

She might as well be living here already. I'd cleared space for her in the closet weeks ago, ditto for the bathroom. I had one of the bigger suites in Heartstone Manor, with a spacious bedroom and bathroom, huge walk-in closet, and a sitting room-slash-office. The only suite bigger was the one Griffen shared with Hope.

Daisy followed my eyes around the room. It was easily several times the size of her small apartment over the bakery, and far more luxurious. Prentice had let whole wings of Heartstone fall into disrepair, but the family wing had remained intact if a little dusty.

She gave me a look that had me doubting my sanity.

"You don't want to move in with me?" I asked.

A heavy sigh gusted out. "It's not that, Royal. I love being here with you, but we've only been seeing each other for a month. It's way too soon to move in together."

"Maybe, but—" A knock fell on the door.

Annoyed at the interruption, I strode across the room to find Hope standing there, a small white bag in one hand. She leaned around me, looking for Daisy. When their eyes met, Hope brushed past me, holding the bag out to Daisy.

"I don't want to interrupt, but I was with Savannah when Royal texted and I thought these might help."

Daisy took the bag, read the logo on the front, and shoved them back at Hope. "I can't take them."

I checked the logo and understood. *The Chocolate Obsession*, a well-known, award-winning chocolatier based out of Asheville. Their chocolates were both amazing and very expensive. Also precious, since the shop was an hour away.

Hope refused the bag, shaking her head at Daisy. "You look miserable. What happened?" Hope's warm brown eyes shot to me, accusation hovering. I shook my head back.

"I quit the bakery," Daisy said.

Hope gasped and sank into the armchair beside the sofa. "Daisy, why? What happened? Is Grams okay?"

"She's fine, I guess. It's my dad—"

Daisy filled Hope in on the details. I took the bag from her hand before she could crush it and removed the box inside. Hope had the right idea. Daisy needed something sweet. Just as she finished retelling the saga of the day, I handed her a chocolate-covered caramel sprinkled with rough sea salt.

"Eat it," I ordered. I expected her glare. I didn't expect Hope to back me up.

"You need them more than I do, Daisy." She stood over Daisy with her hands on her hips until Daisy took a tentative bite of the caramel. Her eyes sank shut as the sharp salt and sweet caramel hit her taste buds, and suddenly I wanted to push Hope from the room and feed Daisy in private.

"Do you know what you're going to do?" Hope asked.

Before Daisy could answer, I said, "I'm trying to convince her to move in here." At Hope's surprised look, I added, "With me. Because she doesn't want to live in the bakery apartment."

"It's too soon," Daisy put in and took another nibble of the caramel.

"It's only too soon if you feel like it's too soon." Hope waited for Daisy to look up at her. "Does it feel like it's too soon?"

Daisy glanced at me, then at Hope. Finally, she said, "It feels like I'm in the middle of a tornado. I don't know if it's too soon or how long I'm supposed to wait. My whole life is turned around and I don't know anything." That last part came out as a wail, a new flood of tears falling down Daisy's cheeks. Hell.

I pulled her into my arms, bringing her head to my shoulder. With a hard exhale, Daisy pressed her face into my neck, her body shuddering under my hands. Hope watched us, her face soft.

"I'll give you two some privacy. Daisy, if you need me, I'm here." She let herself out of the room, closing the door softly behind her.

"I'm sorry," Daisy murmured, her lips warm against my neck. "I can't seem to get it together. I know I need to plan, to figure this out, but I can't. I feel like someone died."

Rubbing my hand up and down her back, I searched for the right words. "You don't have to plan. And you don't have to know what you want. Not yet. For now, let's just take this one day at a time. Maybe one hour at a time. And give yourself a break. You feel like someone died because you're grieving. Your parents let you down, which wasn't the biggest surprise, but I know what happened with Grams was way out of left field—it's too much to take in all at once."

Daisy let out another gusty sigh and sat up. I reached to wipe the tears from her cheek with the side of my thumb. "How about we say you're welcome to stay here until you find something you like better? It's not moving in. You're just crashing here for now. Does that work?"

She nodded. "I'm too inside-out to make any big decisions yet." She let out a hitching laugh. "Other than quitting my job. I must be crazy."

I took her hands in mine, shaking them lightly to get her attention. "You're not crazy. You're an excellent baker and a great businesswoman. You deserve to have an ownership stake in the bakery. You do not deserve for your father to take advantage of your hard work so he can live the easy life."

"Where am I going to find a job? It's not like there's another bakery in town."

"I don't know, Daze." I cupped her face in my hands and drew her close, pressing a kiss to her lips. "I just know we'll figure this out, and right after a huge family fight is not the time to expect yourself to have all the answers. You need rest and a good meal. And time. I know you feel like you're all alone, but you're not."

As if to punctuate my words, a knock sounded on the door. I rose, grumbling, "Definitely not alone. Maybe we should move to the watchtower. No indoor plumbing, but plenty of privacy."

That earned me a weak laugh. I swung open the door. "What—" I demanded, stopping when I saw Sterling standing there, a bottle of wine in her hand.

She pushed the wine at me and headed straight for Daisy. "Daisy needs a glass of that. It's her favorite."

I grabbed the opener from the mini-kitchenette Savannah had set up in the corner of my suite. It wasn't much, but it covered the basics—a tiny fridge, single-serve coffee maker, basket of snacks, and two wine glasses with an opener.

Sterling dropped onto the sofa beside Daisy and pulled her into an extravagant hug. "I heard what happened from Hope. I always thought your Grams was cool, but—" Sterling shook her head. "She must have lost her mind. And your dad sucks. And speaking of people who suck—"

Sterling looked to me. "I stole that bottle from Bryce's room after he stole it from the wine cellar. I told Savannah she's going to have to lock the wine cellar or the best bottles are going to end up on some auction site. Forrest is okay, by the way," she added with a half-glare in my direction. "Not that you asked."

"I didn't ask because I don't want to know why you care. Or why you were having lunch with him. Stay away from my CFO, Sterling."

Sterling tossed her golden hair over her shoulder and gave Daisy a look that clearly said older brothers were annoying and not to be obeyed. I rolled my eyes and Daisy let out another weak laugh.

Just as I was wondering how to eject Sterling without being a dick, she rose after giving Daisy a long, tight hug. "Everything will be okay. Have a glass of wine. Or three. Eat those caramels

Hope brought you, and get some sleep. Things will work out. I promise."

Sterling was gone in a wave of sweet, floral perfume, closing the door quietly behind her. Daisy took the wine glass I handed her and sipped. "How did she know this is my favorite wine?"

"Sterling pays attention when she wants to. And she likes you."

Daisy sniffed back a tear and sipped her wine again. "I'm so tired," she said, the words slipping out on a sigh of exhaustion. "I want to go to sleep and find out tomorrow that this was all a dream."

Another knock interrupted before I could answer. All this moral support was nice, but it wouldn't kill the rest of them to give us a few minutes of quiet. Savannah was at the door, a rolling cart in front of her laden with covered dishes.

"Did that cart come from The Inn?" I asked, stepping back to let her pass me.

Savannah looked over her shoulder. "Maybe. You'd have to ask Mom. It was in the storage rooms when I got here. But don't get used to room service. I don't have enough staff for that."

Daisy glanced up, her eyes wet again. "Thanks, Savannah. I'm just feeling a little raw. I didn't want to see everyone else."

Savannah gave her a brief hug before setting up the table. "Don't worry about it. Have a good dinner and get some sleep. Things will look better in the morning. No one else will bother you tonight."

No one else did. Daisy ate every bite of her dinner, only wincing a little over the limp salad. At least dessert was good— to be expected considering it was one of hers. Savannah must have picked it up in town since I knew Daisy hadn't brought it herself.

Her stomach full, Daisy's eyes were drooping. It was still early, even for Daisy, but bed was the best place for both of us.

I closed my fingers around hers and pulled her up, my hands going straight to the hem of her shirt.

"We can just go to sleep," I murmured against her neck, meaning every word. I could live without sex if she just wasn't in the mood. And after the day she'd had, I wasn't expecting her to want anything but rest.

I was wrong.

Daisy's hands went to my shirt, pulling it free of my pants, her busy hands sliding over my back before going to work on the buttons.

"I want to go to sleep." She licked across my collarbone, her mouth pausing against my neck to give a sharp little suck. "After."

"After works for me," I agreed. I had her naked in a blink, every inch of her soft skin bared for me to worship. I kissed, stroked, touched until she'd forgotten her miserable day and was writhing on the bed, begging me for more.

She could have more. Daisy could have everything I had to give and beyond. I'd do anything to make her happy. Anything. As Daisy came apart in my arms, I followed her, the brilliant flash of pleasure blanking out my mind.

I had no idea what was coming. No clue that while I thought I had everything under control, things were about to get a whole lot worse.

Chapter Thirty-Three

DAISY

WHAT THE FUCK HAPPENED HERE?" ROYAL STOOD IN THE open doorway of my apartment, his body blocking the view. I edged closer, jabbing him with an elbow until he made room for me.

Holy crap. My place was a disaster. As small as it was, I could see pretty much everything from the door, and everything was a mess.

Drawers turned upside down, the contents of my kitchen scattered over the floor, cushions from the sofa were all over the place, stuffing spilling out.

"Did someone stab my sofa?" My voice sounded high and thin in my ears. Had someone broken in? Why? "Why would someone break into my apartment?" I asked, echoing my inner thoughts. "I don't have anything worth stealing."

"I'm calling West." Royal pulled out his phone, his arm shooting out to stop me as I ventured further into my destroyed apartment.

"I won't touch anything," I promised as Royal started to talk to whoever had answered at the police station.

The destruction was worse in my bedroom. The mattress had stab wounds like my sofa cushions, and my dresser drawers were in the same state as those in my kitchen. It was like someone was searching for something.

At least my recipes were safe, stored in the cloud in a file only I could access. I didn't think they'd be worth much to anyone else—certainly not enough to justify destroying my apartment—but they meant the world to me. They were the only thing I owned that I truly cared about.

I didn't have anything else of value. My TV was ancient, and my laptop was in the bakery office. I guess technically it wasn't my laptop since the bakery had purchased it. Hell, I'd have to add buying a new laptop I couldn't afford to my list of things to do, right after finding a job and a new place to live.

Royal will let you live with him, I reminded myself.

No, I couldn't depend on Royal to solve my problems. I had to handle this myself.

"West will be here soon," Royal said. "We can't touch anything. He asked us to wait downstairs."

Great. I couldn't remember if I'd seen the lights on down there when I came in. As we descended the stairs to the back door of the bakery kitchen, I hoped for a smidge of good luck to offset all the bad. If I had to deal with my family right now, I might just lose it for good.

No one was there. Perversely, the dark, empty kitchen annoyed me. Hadn't anyone heard that I'd quit? Who was going to prep for the day? Grams wasn't used to running the place by herself. Would Mom and Dad pitch in?

Not your problem, I told myself. Maybe it wasn't. But still, I might have been mad at Grams, but I didn't love her any less. Ugh, I had to learn to compartmentalize. I'd worry about Grams later. I had my fill of problems right now.

By the time I'd made a pot of coffee and scrounged up a muffin for Royal, West was at the back door, his hair ruffled, eyes heavy but alert. I handed him coffee and a muffin, and we followed him back up the stairs.

West stood in my doorway, scanning the mess. "Any idea who might have done this?"

I shook my head. "No clue. It doesn't make any sense. I don't have anything worth stealing. Why wouldn't they try for the register downstairs?"

"And there's nothing you can think of that might have to do with this? Nothing you know that maybe you don't want to tell me?"

West's eyes drilled into me. It hit me all of a sudden.

He knew who might have done this, and he expected me to know. I didn't. I racked my brain for anything, anyone who might have broken into my place. I came up blank. Again.

"I really don't, West. If I did, I'd tell you. I swear."

His eyes stayed on me for a long moment. Apparently satisfied that I was telling the truth or figuring he'd get that truth out of me later, West nodded. "Why don't you go down to work and I'll get a few of my people in to dust for prints and check for any other evidence. I'll let you know when you're clear to come back in."

"Okay, thanks." That was all I could say. I wished I knew what was going on or why someone would have broken in, but I didn't.

Compartmentalize.

What did I have to do next?

Go downstairs and finish the custom cake orders I'd promised. Then I could pack up my stuff in the office and figure out the next step.

One thing at a time. That's how I was going to get through this. One thing at a time.

Royal left me at the door with a kiss, turning down my offer of breakfast. "I'll call you later," he promised. "Don't let them guilt you into coming back."

"No chance of that," I said, not sure that was true. At the thought of my parents, I had enough righteous anger to fend off any attempt at guilt. But when I thought of Grams...

An hour later, Grams poked her head through the door. A pang of remorse stabbed my heart. If my mother hadn't followed her, things might have turned out differently.

Instead, my mom raised an eyebrow at me and said, "You owe all of us an apology. Storming out yesterday and going over to stir up your grandmother was just too much. After all she's done for you."

Sheree shook her head slowly at me, her gaze heavy. I tried not to care that she was so disappointed in me. I wasn't the one who was wrong here. Right?

"I'm not going to apologize to anyone," I said, smoothing the edge of frosting at the base of the cake so I could avoid looking at her. "And I don't want to have this conversation again. I meant what I said. I quit. I'm only here because I specifically promised these two cakes, and I don't want to let the clients down."

"You think I can't bake a cake as well as you?" Sheree challenged, her eyes hot.

Someone save me from my mother in a temper. I started to bite my tongue and then decided—what the hell? Why not just say what I was thinking?

"No, you can't," I said flatly. "I've spent years learning to design and decorate cakes. Years. And I've worked with these two clients almost as long. I want to make sure they get exactly what they paid for, and I know you can't pull it off. Maybe Grams, but she's out of practice, and she didn't meet with the

248

clients on the design. When I'm done, you can find out how good you are, because I won't be here to pick up the slack. I hope you like being at work before five am and being on your feet all day."

"Daisy, stop this right now!" My mom's burnished skin went a little gray. "I don't want to hear another word about you quitting."

"Fine, I won't say a word. I'll say this: if you don't get out of this kitchen and leave me in peace, I'll walk out right now and you can finish the cakes yourself. Hopefully, there's still enough cash around to offer a refund."

If possible, my mother's face went a shade or two grayer. She left, Grams on her heels. I got back to work, more than ready to get away from the bakery.

West came by an hour later. "Techs are done at your place. The lock wasn't tampered with. Are you sure you don't know what this was about? You can talk to me, Daisy."

Again, he was looking at me like he knew that I knew what was going on. All I had was the truth. "I really have no idea, West. But I promise that if I figure it out, I'll tell you. I will."

West gave me the same solemn nod he had at my earlier protest and left. I was washing my hands in preparation for more frosting when my father pushed open the door from the front of the bakery.

"Why was Garfield here?" he demanded. "What does the police chief want with you?"

"My place was broken into, and he was letting me know what's going on," I said flatly, unable to meet his eyes. I was too angry to deal with him. Too angry to pretend I had my emotions under control.

"If you're quitting, you'll need to move out."

I nodded sharply, not trusting my voice. He didn't care about the apartment. He was just trying to get a reaction out of me. I knew that, and it didn't matter. My throat was still choked up.

"I don't like you talking to Garfield. Just remember, we're family. If you bring trouble down on one of us, you hurt all of us. Including your grandmother."

His words spun in my head long after the door swung shut behind him. Why did my dad care what I said to West? I didn't know anything about anything.

Unless I did. What did they think I knew? I remembered my dad and the mystery woman talking in the dark behind the bakery all those weeks ago. But he didn't know I'd seen them, and I still had no idea what they'd been talking about. There wasn't anything else.

Not until this morning and my apartment, but I didn't even know why... And wasn't it weird that my dad didn't even ask about the apartment? I told him my place was broken into and his only comment was that he didn't want me talking to the police?

An uneasy suspicion planted itself in my brain. But why? He had the keys, why break in?

The lock wasn't tampered with.

The lock wasn't tampered with because the person who broke in had the keys.

No.

My phone rang. Royal's ringtone. I should answer, but my hands were covered in frosting, and if I answered the phone I'd have to take the gloves off, find a place to put this spatula...

I was avoiding him. My head was too messed up to talk to Royal. I'd call him later.

The phone fell silent, then started ringing again ten seconds later. Royal again. I looked down at the cake and decided I'd finish this up and call him back. Only a few more minutes. Then I'd be at a good stopping point. The phone fell silent, the kitchen quiet for a few too-short minutes.

I braced as the door to the front swung open. Grams walked in, the phone to her ear and a smile on her face. When she reached me, she said, "Here she is," and held the phone to my ear.

"Hello?"

Royal's voice answered. "Hey, I tried your cell, but you didn't pick up."

"Sorry, my hands are covered with frosting. Is everything okay?"

"I didn't mean to worry you. West stopped by with an update on the Forrest thing and said your place was cleared. I have a few staff in housekeeping who're coming off shift and wouldn't mind earning a few bucks to clean up a mess. Can I send them over to your place?"

My heart pinched in my chest, his sweetness almost painful. Tears sprung to my eyes. I was done with crying, but Royal was too much. "I can't afford—"

"Daisy. Let me help."

What else could I say? Nothing, except, "Thank you. That would be great. I'll make it up to you."

"Make me a mixed berry pie one of these days, and we'll call it even."

"It's a deal," I said and sniffed.

"You okay?" His voice was gentle, soothing the ragged tears in my soul.

Aware my grandmother was close enough to hear considering she was holding the phone to my ear, I said, "Sure. I'm fine. I'll go unlock the door upstairs as soon as I finish this frosting."

"Come see me when you're done there. I'll be at The Inn all day. Griffen and Hope took the day off, and I have a pile of stuff to do here. I'll probably be late, but I want to see you."

"Okay. As soon as I'm done."

Grams pulled the phone away at my nod and clicked the button to end the call. "What's going on? Why did Royal need to talk to you so badly he couldn't wait for you to call back?"

"Someone broke into my place last night and made a huge mess. He's sending someone to clean it up for me."

"Is that why Weston was here?" Grams narrowed her eyes at me, knowing I wasn't telling her everything.

"Yes. It's not a big deal."

I couldn't remember ever feeling this awkward tension with Grams. Even when I was a teenager and we'd fight I never felt like this. There was a wall between us, and I didn't know how to tear it down. Didn't know if I wanted to.

Grams nodded, then hesitated. I braced. "Daisy," she said slowly, "I talked to your father about the money you said you gave him. He said he didn't know what I was talking about. When I checked the account, it showed a transfer to you, but that was it."

I just stared at her, puzzle pieces clicking into place inside my brain. "We had a contract. Of course, we had a contract. It's up in my apartment."

My apartment that had been broken into. I went straight to the sink to strip off my gloves and wash my hands. Grams followed behind. I didn't want her to see the mess upstairs and worry more.

"I'll go get it and bring it back down," I said, heading for the stairs.

Grams didn't follow, just watched me leave, her eyes sad.

Chapter Thirty-Four

DAISY

I WAS PRETTY SURE WHAT I WOULD FIND WHEN I opened my closet. I hadn't thought to check my file box earlier that morning. For the most part, it was full of bills, the paperwork on my car, and not much else. I'd forgotten about the contract.

The file box was shoved in the back of my closet since I didn't use it much. It was tipped on its side, papers strewn over the floor mixed with my shoes and the clothes that had been pulled off the hangers.

Everything else looked like it was there, but the contract was missing. Damn.

My mind raced. Now I had a suspect for the break-in. What was I supposed to do?

Call Royal. That was my first instinct.

Call West. Not something I wanted to do, but probably something I *should* do.

Think it over while you finish the cakes. That I could do.

I was mid-process on both and only an hour or two from finishing them. If my hunch was right and my dad had broken in to steal the contract, another hour or two wouldn't make a big difference. I wanted to go to Grams' house and check his room to see if the contract was there, but if I went rushing out my parents would be suspicious. Especially after I'd made such a big deal about finishing the cakes.

The last stages on my custom cakes felt like they took a million years. No one came back into the kitchen, leaving me to work in peace. I heard the two housekeepers from The Inn climb the stairs not long before I finished.

When I was done with the cakes, I stored them in the cooler, stopped at the laptop on the desk to sign out of my personal email and cloud account, and packed my favorite coffee mug and the rest of my things from the desk.

That done, I was ready to leave. I didn't bother going to the front to let them know. Better if they thought I was still back in the kitchen, working on the cakes. Before I headed to Grams' house, I went upstairs one more time.

The two housekeepers were young, just out of high school, fresh-faced, and not at all daunted by the disaster that was my apartment.

I recognized one of them. Chocolate silk pie and black coffee. She looked up and grinned. "Hey, Daisy! Sorry about this. Are you okay?"

"I'm good." I faked a smile back. "Thanks for doing this. I really appreciate it."

"No problem!" She grinned again. "I'm saving up for a new car, and Kristi wants to go to Cancun with her boyfriend, so we could both use the extra cash."

A thought occurred to me. "Hey, when you do the bedroom and the bathroom, instead of putting my stuff away, could you pack it? I'm going to be moving, so it doesn't make sense to put it all back in the closet when I'm just going to take it back out again."

"Sure, no problem! Moving in with Royal?" She shot me a wink. I tried to smile back.

"Maybe. I'm still deciding."

I got out my suitcases and said a quick hello to Kristi, who'd already started in the bedroom. She was as enthusiastic and perky as the first girl, whose name I didn't remember. Promising she was on top of it, Kristi ushered me out and on my way. I was more than happy to go. I owed Royal big time for this.

I speed-walked to Grams' house. Now that I was on the move, I wanted this done. If he had taken the contract, he'd probably destroyed it. Unless he hadn't had a chance. Looking for it was the longest of long shots, but it was worth a try.

I felt like a thief as I let myself into the empty house. Everything looked normal. Almost. Grams wasn't crazy tidy—we never would have survived my adolescence if she had been—but she was neater than my parents, who'd left their things strewn all over the place. I resisted the urge to pick it all up. Grams had trained me well, but I didn't have time to deal with their mess. I had one of my own.

Their room was worse than the rest of the house—drawers hanging open, dirty clothes slung across the unmade bed. Not my problem, though it would be easier to search if things were where they belonged. Ignoring my annoyance, I began to look for the contract. It wasn't much, only two sheets stapled together, signed and dated by both of us.

They didn't have many papers lying around, and none of them were the contract. After a cursory search, I found a half-eaten sandwich on a plate on the dresser, a huge wad of cash in the sock drawer, and a small pile of unpaid bills. No contract.

I stood in the middle of the bedroom, hands on my hips, and turned a slow circle, studying the room for the best hiding place. I'd checked behind the mirror and under the bed.

Under the bed.

I looked again and pulled out the suitcases I'd seen there. They kept theirs in the same place I'd stored mine. Both were empty. I checked the liners, looking for a gap or place he could have secreted away the contract.

My heart raced when my fingers found a gap in the lining. The papery rustle wasn't the contract—it was a wad of cash, this one bigger than the one I'd found in his sock drawer. I didn't count it, but it was more than I would have expected. What was my dad up to that he had so much cash lying around? Those poker games he'd bragged about or something else?

That was it for the suitcases. The closet? I'd checked the shelves already, but I dragged a chair over for a better look. On the top shelf, my groping hand encountered another rustle. Fabric on top of something else. Paper. Bingo. This had to be it.

I tugged, pulling it all towards me until fabric and paper fell in a heap on my head. I didn't recognize the paper except to see that it wasn't the contract. Torn from a notebook, it had a series of numbers scribbled haphazardly across the otherwise blank page. Creased and worn, it looked like it had been folded and re-folded more than once.

I folded it one more time and left it on the bed. I'd worry about the paper later. I was more concerned about the pile of fabric at my feet.

Even in a crumpled pile on the floor, I recognized it instantly. An Inn uniform, the kind the bellhops and front desk employees wore.

What the hell? Why would my dad have an Inn uniform? My heart sped up, leaving me dizzy.

There was no good reason for him to have an Inn uniform. None. He didn't work there, and the uniforms were expensive.

No one on the staff would have left this lying around. He had to have stolen it. My knees weak, I sank to the edge of the bed, mind reeling with the implications.

Not exactly sure why I was doing it, I pulled out my phone and took a picture of the closet shelf where the cap that matched the rest of the uniform sat, hanging over the edge. I photographed the uniform in its pile on the floor, then lay it across the unmade bed and took one more picture. Then another of the paper I'd found, front and back.

Was I going to tell West?

Hadn't I just promised him that if I knew anything I'd tell him right away? I had.

And I'd meant it when I said it. I did. But the implications of my discovery were so much bigger than I'd imagined.

Mostly because I hadn't imagined I'd learn anything at all. I hadn't let myself think that my dad was behind the break-in, much less that he was the one who'd been trying to destroy Royal's Inn.

I sank on the edge of the bed, staring down at the carpet between my feet, heart racing, chest too tight for a deep breath. Was there any other reason my dad would have an Inn uniform? Anything at all? I could explain away the cash as leftover poker winnings, but not the uniform.

I had to tell West. And Royal.

Royal. My heart ached at the thought of Royal. How could I explain this? He would hate me. How could he not?

You can't keep this a secret.

I couldn't. I wouldn't lie to him. He deserved better. Did that mean I was going to turn my dad in to West?

"I thought I'd find you here. Just can't do what you're told, can you?" my father asked, his voice hard.

I looked up to see him leaning on the door frame, his dark hair falling into his eyes in a rakish wave, his blue eyes sharp. How could I have thought Royal was anything like this man?

Darren might have been my father, but he was a liar and a thief. An opportunist and a con man. Nothing about him was like Royal.

"Why do you have an Inn uniform, Dad?" I asked. I glanced down at my phone, half-hidden by my hip. The camera app was still open. I flicked a thumb to swipe to the video setting and hit the record button. I couldn't get my head around turning my dad in to West, but after the way he'd lied about the contract to Grams, I wanted proof.

"None of your business. What are you doing in my room going through my things, Daisy?"

I thought about coming up with a cover story, but I was tired of all the lying. "Grams said you denied borrowing any money, so I went up to show her the contract you signed, but it was gone. Did you break into my apartment?"

The sly grin that spread across his face was all the answer I needed. Of course, his words were more lies, but the truth was all over him.

"Don't be ridiculous. Why did you have to tell her about the money? I told you I was going to take care of both of you. Bringing my mother into this was a mistake."

"Your mother, my grandmother. And the last time we talked about this, you threatened to have me charged with theft."

"Daisy, girl, you take everything so seriously. Break things off with your boyfriend. He's too cozy with the police chief. Then all you have to do is forget about the money, come back to work where you belong, and everything will go back to normal. You can live over the bakery and do whatever you do with your little fairy friend, and we'll pretend none of this ever happened."

I stared up at him in shocked amazement. Was he insane? He wanted me to break up with Royal, had called J.T. a fairy, and thought after that—and everything else—there was any chance I was going to come back to work for him? *For him?*

No fucking way. Not ever. I wanted to storm out and never see him again. I stayed where I was. I still needed answers, not that it was likely my father would admit to anything.

"Why do you have an Inn uniform, Dad?" I asked again, my voice just as hard and unyielding as his. I was tired of being pushed around. Tired of being disregarded.

"None of your fucking business, Daisy. I'm your father. I don't owe you any explanations. I don't owe you anything."

"You owe me twenty fucking grand. That's what you owe me."

My father smirked, one eyebrow raised. "Prove it."

"You know damn well I can't since you broke into my home and stole the contract."

"You can't prove that either. The only one who has evidence of theft is me. All I have to do is talk my mother into filing charges and you'll be headed to jail. Is that what you want?"

"Grams would never do that to me," I whispered, shock stealing my breath. She wouldn't. No way. Except...

My father cocked his head to the side, his smirk growing deeper. "I bet she would, though. If your mother and I work on her. Tell her you need to learn a lesson, that she can always drop the charges, but we need to scare you straight. And there's the matter of her missing jewelry."

"I didn't take Grams' jewelry!" I shot to my feet, knocking my phone to the floor.

"Are you sure about that?" he asked, and I knew I'd lost.

I knelt to pick up my phone, locking the screen so it wouldn't stop recording when I shoved it in my pocket. I didn't have much, just threats, but it was something. At the very least, it was proof that my father was the manipulative bastard I'd always suspected he was. I tried to pick up The Inn uniform.

"Don't even fucking think about it. Just go, and think about what I said. Stay away from Royal Sawyer and the police chief.

I'll give you the rest of the day off, but I expect to see you at the bakery for opening tomorrow. Otherwise, I might be forced to talk to West myself. Your grandmother was so disappointed when she saw how you'd stolen that money. When I tell her I found you here trying to take my cash and going through her jewelry box—"

I didn't wait for the rest. Leaving the uniform on the bed, I pushed past him and took off down the hall. His voice followed me. "Be smart, Daisy. Do what you're told and everything will be fine."

Be smart. I strode back to Main Street, my mind reeling, not sure what that even meant. *Be smart.* How? By doing what my father told me so he could keep trying to destroy Royal and I could stay out of jail?

That might be smart by Darren Hutchins' definition, but it wasn't right. I loved Royal. More than I'd ever dreamed I could love a man. He deserved so much more than being tied to a woman like me, one whose own father had been trying to destroy his business.

What was I going to tell Royal? And West? I had to call West. I should walk straight to the police station and tell him everything. Pulling my phone from my back pocket, I stopped the recording.

What did I have to tell West, anyway? The recording was mostly filled with threats against me. My father hadn't confessed to anything. Not really. It was my word against his. What if I went to West and I ended up in jail?

My dad was right about one thing. Technically, I'd stolen twenty thousand dollars from my grandmother.

Who was I kidding? There was no *technically* about it. Despite all of our plans, I was not a part-owner of the business.

I was an employee, and I'd transferred twenty thousand dollars from the business account to my own. Even if I had the contract, I'd still stolen the money. My intentions didn't matter here. That I'd thought of the money as half mine was irrelevant.

I'd taken money without permission. That was a crime. End of story.

I walked aimlessly with nowhere to go. I didn't want to be at my apartment with the two housekeepers from The Inn still working. I couldn't go see Royal, Hope wasn't home, and I had to stay away from the Sawyers until I figured this out.

I needed my car. With my car, I could go anywhere, if only for long enough to get my head together. Reluctantly, I turned in the direction of The Inn when I hit Main Street. I wasn't ready to see Royal, but my car was still there, parked in the employee lot.

And blocked in. Royal had blocked me in. His own car was parked behind mine, bumpers almost touching, leaving me no room to get out. Damn. I'd hoped to sneak away and drive until I had a chance to think. I wasn't ready to see Royal. If I wanted my car back, I had no choice.

I took the easy way out and texted him. I composed and erased the text twice before I settled on the right words.

Can you come move your car? Too annoyed.

I'm downstairs and my car is blocked in. Too distant.

Rough morning. I need to go for a drive. Clear my head. Do you mind moving your car?

Chapter Thirty-Five

ROYAL

Rough morning. I need to go for a drive. Clear my head. Do you mind moving your car?

The words were casual, but I didn't believe them. If she'd had a rough morning, why couldn't she talk to me about it? Why go for a drive?

Everything about her text felt off. I wasn't reassured when I found her standing beside her car.

Shifting her weight from foot to foot, she looked everywhere but at me. Something was very wrong.

"You okay?" I asked, moving in to pull her into my arms. A hug didn't fix everything, but it was a good place to start. To my relief, Daisy settled against me, burrowing her face into my chest and letting her breath out on a long sigh.

"No," she said. "I'm not okay."

"You want to talk about it?" Seeing her start to close down, I forged ahead. "Did you get lunch? I can order some food up to my office, and you can tell me about your morning, figure out how I can help."

She went stiff in my arms, pulling away and shoving her hair out of her face, not meeting my eyes. "Daisy, what happened?"

When she raised her face to mine, her beautiful brown eyes swam with tears. Frustrated anger surged through me. Her family couldn't keep doing this to her. "What happened?"

Daisy opened her mouth to answer, then snapped it shut. She wasn't going to tell me what was going on. I tried to tell myself to give her space, but I couldn't get there. She didn't need space, she needed someone to give her parents an ass-kicking. She needed her grandmother to stop enabling her son and stick up for Daisy.

She needed a lot of things, and she wasn't going to get any of them unless she was willing to stick around and ask for help.

"Why won't you talk to me?"

Daisy shook her head. "I can't. I want to, but I have to think. I can't tell you everything yet."

"Do you need to talk to West?" I asked carefully.

She shook her head, her cherry-cola curls bouncing in the light.

"Daisy, tell me how to help."

"Let me get my car out so I can go for a drive. I need to think. I need space, and I need to think. That's the only thing that's going to help right now."

Frustration built in my chest, insistent that I do something. Fix this. Daisy going off on her own wasn't a solution to any problem. "Something's changed. What happened? Why don't you just tell me, and we can work it out?"

"Because I can't," she burst out. "I can't tell you. I don't know what to do, and I need to think. Please, Royal, I need to go."

I stepped back, wrestling inside myself for control. "Why? Just tell me why."

"I can't!"

She stepped back too, putting distance between us. I didn't want Daisy over there. I wanted her here, in my arms. I crossed my arms over my chest to stop myself from reaching for her.

"You can't trap me here," she said, pressing her hands together so I wouldn't see they were shaking. "Do I need to call West to make you give me my car?"

"Maybe you should," I shot back. "Maybe he can get the truth out of you."

The stricken look in her eyes stopped me in my tracks. I was furious, hurt, so frustrated I wanted to punch someone, but Daisy had a point. She wanted to go, and I was stopping her.

I had the sinking feeling that if I let her go now, she wasn't coming back.

Stupid. I had no reason to believe that. People had bad days, and people went for drives to clear their heads. This wasn't the end of the world. It wasn't the end of me and Daisy.

"I need you to trust me," she whispered, tears staining her cheeks, her eyes frantic and so fucking hurt. I couldn't see straight past the pain in my gut at her misery. If I was any part of this, I had to stop.

"I trust you," I whispered back. "I do. I just want you to tell me what's going on."

"I can't. Not until I figure it out. Please."

She closed the distance between us and reached up, framing my face in her hands. "I love you, Royal. I do. So much. But everything is so messed up right now. I need some time."

My heart shattered. I knew what she meant by *time*. "No, Daisy. We can do this together. Just talk to me."

I hated to beg, but I would do it for her. Except begging wasn't enough.

"We can't do it together. I wish we could."

The sadness in her face was insurmountable. I wasn't going to talk her out of this. Ugly words rose to my lips, some bullshit about not waiting for her to figure herself out.

I kept my lips pressed together. She was killing me, but she was dying, too. As much as I wanted to strike out, I couldn't bring more pain to her eyes.

Daisy rose to her toes and pressed her mouth to mine, her lips moving, words barely audible. "I love you, Royal. I love you so much."

I pulled her to me, holding her there, kissing her, everything that was Daisy washing over me. Her taste. The vanilla scent of her skin. The soft brush of her curls. The low hum in her throat as our kiss deepened. Her mind was all fucked up, but Daisy's body still wanted me.

I thought about using that to get what I wanted. I could probably do it—seduce her and get her to talk. Maybe.

And if I did, I'd be betraying her trust.

Trust.

Everyone she trusted had screwed her over. Even J.T., staying away for so long and leaving her to face this on her own.

Our kiss felt like goodbye. It ended far too soon. From behind me, I heard a familiar screech. "Royal Sawyer!! This is your last fucking chance, you bastard!"

Daisy was already pulling away. I turned, tucking her behind me, and faced Vanessa. For a split second, I lost my words. I'd been about to tell her to shut the hell up, but her appearance threw me.

Her hair hung lank around her face, the gleam of the black strands replaced by grease and what looked like dust. Her porcelain skin was more like parchment, dry and dull. As far as I could tell, she wore no makeup. I'd never seen her without her signature red lipstick.

Even her clothes were wrong. She was in her usual designer gear, but she was wrinkled and sweat-stained. Vanessa was trouble on a good day. Right now? She was a disaster.

"Wait," I ordered her, turning to Daisy.

Daisy was watching Vanessa, her mouth dropped open, face leached of color. "What is it?" I whispered low enough that Vanessa couldn't hear.

"Who is that?"

"Vanessa. Ford's ex-wife. She's probably here to hit me up for money again."

Daisy started shaking her head, shooting a cautious glance at Vanessa, who paced behind us, only seconds from losing her faint control. "She's involved," Daisy breathed. "In what's been happening at The Inn. I can't tell you how I know, but I know. She's involved."

What? How did Daisy know Vanessa? I didn't have time to ask. Vanessa wasn't dangerous, but she was the last thing I needed dropped into the middle of my conversation with Daisy. Unfortunately, there was no way Vanessa was going to leave until she had her say. Again.

I dug in my pocket for my keys. "Here, take my car. Bring it back later. I don't care. You have enough going on without dealing with Vanessa."

Reluctantly, Daisy took my keys. I knew she'd rather have her own car, but that wasn't going to happen. Not yet. I had to deal with Vanessa, and Daisy wanted to go. She saw the logic and rose once more to her toes. Her mouth by my ear, she said, "Whatever happens, just remember I love you."

"I love you too, Daisy." I caught her as she tried to escape. She tugged on her wrist, but I held tight. Just one more thing I had to say. I reeled her back in and kissed her lips, then her cheek. "Whatever happens, whatever is going on that you won't tell me, just remember that I love you, too. No matter what."

A sob hitched in her chest, and she was gone, rounding the hood of my car and beeping the doors unlocked.

"No matter what, Daze," I called after her.

She nodded again as she started the engine, pulling out of the parking space with tears streaming down her face. Fuck. Not how I wanted that to go. At least she'd have to see me to return my car.

"Royal!" came the screech from behind me. I turned to Vanessa.

"What the fuck do you want, Vanessa?"

"Why, did I interrupt your lover's spat? I thought Darren told her to stay away from you."

"How do you know Daisy's father?" Puzzle pieces were rattling in my head. Daisy. Vanessa. Darren Hutchins. How did it all fit together?

"Not important. He's small-time. An idiot."

"I already knew that. Why are you here, Vanessa? You're banned from Inn property."

"I have one last offer for you Royal. Cash for information."

"What could you possibly know that would interest me?"

"I know who killed your father." She said it so bluntly I knew she was telling the truth. Or she thought she was.

"I didn't think you were that good a shot," I said, trying to play off the sudden tightness in my chest. Could she know?

Vanessa tossed her lank hair, the gesture losing most of its effect with her so disheveled. "Not me, you moron. But I know who did it. And how. And more importantly, I know why. But it's going to cost you."

I could play along. For now. "How much?"

"A million. Cash."

I waited for her to laugh and give me another number. No, she was completely serious. Was she insane? "I don't have a million in cash."

Another hair toss, this one accompanied by a sneer that almost did her justice. "You can get it. Between you, Griffen, Tenn—you can get it. I need the cash, or I disappear and you'll never know the truth."

I shook my head in denial, buying time while my mind raced. I could get the money if I had to. But this was Vanessa. What could she know?

"Fine. But we do the exchange after you tell West everything you know. I'm assuming for a million we get proof."

Vanessa's eye roll was impressive, especially considering how unimpressive the rest of her looked. "For a million you get who, how, and why. That's all. You can go dig up the evidence yourselves. Shouldn't be hard once you know where to look."

"Fine." I wasn't surprised she didn't have proof, but she wasn't getting her way without giving a little. "But we do the exchange in front of West. I'm not strolling around town with a million in cash."

"No fucking way."

"Fine." I shrugged and turned as if to go. Vanessa's hand shot out to grab my arm.

"Royal, think about what you're saying. I can give you what you want. You can get Ford out of jail."

"Unlikely, considering you don't have proof." I turned away again.

"Royal! Don't do this!"

I'd never seen Vanessa look desperate. Not like this. She was wound so tight, I thought she'd splinter if I touched her. The tiniest twinge of pity hit me.

"Look, Vanessa, I don't think you know anything useful. I think this is a last-ditch effort to scam some cash out of the Sawyers, and I'm not falling for it. If you think you know who killed Prentice, go see Griffen. I'm done."

Vanessa could go peddle her bullshit somewhere else. I didn't believe for a second that she knew anything about my father's murder.

I *did* believe that she was mixed up in the sabotage at The Inn. I wasn't ready to think about how Daisy knew that, but the kind of petty attacks we'd been dealing with were exactly Vanessa's style.

I turned again, this time really leaving, when Vanessa tried one more time. Her fingers locked on my sleeve, she begged, "Please, Royal. I need the money. I do know who killed Prentice. And he knows I know. I have to get away from him before he decides I'm next. I can't get anywhere near West Garfield. If he sees me talking to the police—"

If possible, Vanessa's face went even paler. I almost believed her. Almost. But not quite. She was a pretty package most days, but that package hid the opportunist beneath and I'd had my fill of those.

"Get lost, Vanessa. Try panhandling. Might work out better for you. If I see you here again, I'm calling West. Understand?"

Vanessa only stood there staring at me, unable to believe I'd turned her down. Tough luck. I didn't look back as I made my way into The Inn, ignoring her need to get the last word.

"You're going to regret this, Royal Sawyer."

"I already do," I said over my shoulder.

Not the part about turning down her generous offer of lies in exchange for a cool million. No, I regretted not running her out of town months ago. Years ago. If Vanessa knew who killed Prentice, she'd had plenty of time to come forward. Hell, she could have kept Ford out of jail. He'd divorced her, but I'd bet he would have forked over the cash in a heartbeat to keep his ass out of jail.

I doubted Vanessa knew anything about Prentice, but she'd said more than she meant to. In my office, I stood at the big window staring out over The Inn property into the mountains beyond.

Vanessa. Darren Hutchins. Daisy. The Inn. Puzzle pieces started to fall into place in my brain. Once I was sure I had the right picture, I picked up the phone and made a call.

Chapter Thirty-Six

DAISY

I DROVE AROUND FOR ALMOST AN HOUR UNTIL I FOUND myself at the trailhead to my favorite waterfall.

Easing Royal's lush sports car into the gravel parking area, I got out and began to walk up the familiar trail.

Everything was such a fucked-up mess. Not even the damp air on my cheeks or the emerald sway of branches above could soothe my raw heart.

My father was the one who'd been trying to destroy The Inn. How did he know Vanessa Sawyer? Had she hired him to do her dirty work?

Did it matter? I'd already learned my dad had a stupid grudge against Prentice Sawyer that he'd decided to extend to the whole family. Even if Vanessa was paying him, he'd seemed happy to jump in.

What did I do now?

Drive to the police department and ask to see West.

There it was. I knew the answer already.

My mother's face popped into my head, her eyes sad, accusing. What would happen to her if I told West everything? And Grams...

I'd been holding out hope that Grams would see the truth about my dad, kick him out, and things could go back to normal. If I was the reason her beloved son ended up in jail, she'd never forgive me.

If I turned my dad in, I'd lose my family.

And if I didn't, I'd lose Royal.

Finally reaching the waterfall, I climbed the last stretch of trail and slipped behind the narrow stream of water, taking refuge in the cool, damp shade of the rock overhang. Here I was hidden, the gentle spray masking the tears on my face.

It was a good place to think. One of the best. J.T. and I used to come here all the time in high school, to get away from home and adults and responsibilities. I hadn't come here alone in ages. It only made me miss J.T. more.

I settled back against the rock, damp soaking through my shorts and t-shirt, and tried to think. It was a waste of time. What was there to think about?

I had to choose: my family or Royal.

Right or wrong.

And when I lined it all up, it was so easy to see that there was really only one choice after all.

Easy to see and impossible to carry out. How could I do it and live with myself? How could I live with myself if I didn't?

And there was still the small matter of felony theft charges. If I turned my father in and he talked Grams into pressing charges, I'd be facing a future that included prison time at worst and a felony on my record at best.

I could be pissed at my dad all I wanted—for asking me to take the money, for never intending to pay it back, for threatening to press charges at all.

Except I was the one who'd taken the money. Me. My decision and my consequences.

And still, it all came back to one thing. What could I live with?

I'd made a bad decision in taking the money. No question there. But I couldn't fix that. The money was gone, and I wasn't going to get it back. I couldn't undo that bad decision, but I could avoid making a worse one.

My phone beeped with a text.

J.T.

Where the hell are you? Grams just got done crying all over my shoulder about you quitting the bakery. WTF?

Grams was crying? Ugh, that just made me feel worse. She was blind when it came to my dad, but she was still the woman who'd raised me when my own parents decided child-rearing was too boring for them. She'd given me a home. A trade. And love. She'd raised me with so much love.

One of our hearts was going to break. How could I choose to spare myself knowing the pain it would cause her? Could I ever be happy if it was at her expense?

I debated how to answer J.T. Unable to explain over text, I went for an interrogation instead.

Why are you home?

Classes were canceled. Power outage. Where are you?

At the waterfall. I had to think.

Do I need to come out there?

No. I'm headed home.

I might as well go back. Sitting under the waterfall hadn't solved anything. Now, I was wet on top of being heartbroken, confused, and angry. I dragged my ass back down the trail and let myself into Royal's car. The inside smelled of rich leather and Royal. I inhaled deeply, his scent a comfort.

Not a lot made sense right now, but I knew one thing.

I loved Royal. If I let him go, I'd regret it for the rest of my life.

I put the car in gear and headed back to town, no happier than I'd been when I'd left but a little closer to figuring out what I had to do. On the way back, Nelson's Farm Stand caught my eye, the baskets in the front full to bursting with summer berries.

Still turning over my troubles in my mind, I pulled in and bought pints of strawberries, blueberries, and blackberries. I couldn't resist popping a blackberry into my mouth after I pulled the car back on the road. Tart and sweet, the flavor of summer exploded over my tongue.

I still didn't know what I was going to do with my life, but I knew what I was going to do with the berries. I was going to bake a pie. I always thought best when I was baking and I still had some thinking to do.

J.T. was waiting in the kitchen of the apartment we'd shared over the bakery. He barely gave me a chance to come in before he jumped on my ass.

"What the fuck is going on, Daze? Why is all your stuff packed? How could you quit on Grams?"

I set the berries and Royal's keys on the kitchen counter before I turned to J.T. His familiar face was twisted with anger, his green eyes hard. I got it. He loved Grams almost as much as I did. She'd given him a home when his parents had kicked him out, had showered him with her love, just like she had with me.

"What did she tell you?" I asked, rinsing the berries under the sink.

"That you've been fighting with your parents and decided you couldn't work with them."

I went still for a second before slowly turning to face J.T. "That's it? That's all she said?"

He shoved his hands in his back pockets, eyes narrowing. "Pretty much. She started to cry as soon as she saw me, so I didn't get a lot. She begged me to talk you into coming back."

"Huh." I finished rinsing the berries and started to trim the tops from the strawberries. "So, she didn't say anything about partnering with Dad in the bakery instead of me?"

"No," J.T. said slowly. "She didn't mention that. You're kidding, right? Your dad's never done a day of work in his life."

"He's turning over a new leaf, I guess." I shrugged and concentrated on trimming berries. "He said she's making him a partner and leaving the bakery to him in her will with the stipulation that when he dies it comes to me. According to him, I'm an employee. Not even a manager. And he's my boss. I have to do what I'm told or get out. So, I left."

J.T.'s hands fell to his sides. "Why would Grams do that? She didn't give him access to the banking stuff, did she? The checkbook or the safe?"

I set aside the berries and got out the rest of the ingredients. "I warned her not to. I hope she listened."

"You need to talk to her—" he started.

"And you should know," I went on as if he hadn't spoken, "that I'm the reason we haven't started building the deck for outdoor seating or made any of the other improvements we planned."

I set the canister of flour on the counter and turned to face J.T. I'd lied to him for way too long. He deserved my full attention now that I was finally coming clean.

"Dad came to me in the fall and asked for a private meeting. Said he had a business plan, and he needed a little capital to get going."

"Aww, Daze." J.T. sank into a chair at the kitchen table. "Tell me you didn't."

"I did. And I used money from the bakery."

J.T. banged his forehead against the table. Once, then twice. Sitting up, he gave me his most pitying look and shook his head. "Daisy, babe, you're smarter than this."

"I know," I wailed, expecting to start crying again at the sheer relief of finally telling the truth, but I found myself laughing instead, shaking my head back at J.T. "I know I am, but he had spreadsheets, and charts, and a business plan. He was wearing a suit! He was so sincere, and I thought that this time, maybe—"

"Or maybe not," J.T. finished for me.

"Definitely not. Because when he came back and I started hounding him for the money, first he said he was working on it, and then he said it was *his* bakery and *his* money, and if I kept asking he'd press charges. Felony theft."

"Shit, Daze, that's low."

I turned from the table and started to weigh flour. J.T. shoved back from his chair and joined me. "Mixed berry pie?" he asked.

"Yep." I shoved the berries at him. "You can deal with these while I get the dough started."

"Might as well tell me the rest. You quit because Grams shut you out in favor of Darren?"

"Well, yeah. That and a bunch of other things. But I don't care about the job. Not right now. It's so much worse than just the bakery and Grams."

We worked side by side as I filled him in on the rest. By the time we were weaving the strips of crust over the top of the pie, J.T. was shaking his head again. "Sorry I yelled at you about Grams. I would have walked too."

"Yeah, I know. And I hate that I made her cry. I just... I can't stand by her side while she lets Dad have free rein on the business. She wants to hope he's changed, but we both know that's never going to happen."

I slid the pie in the oven and started a pot of coffee. I leaned into J.T.'s shoulder as we watched it drip into the glass carafe.

"What are you going to do now?" he asked.

I glanced out the window at the setting sun. "I don't know," I lied.

I knew what I had to do, I just wasn't ready to do it.

Not yet.

Chapter Thirty-Seven

DAISY

WE FILLED OUR MUGS AND WENT TO SIT ON THE SOFA AS we had so many times before. I sat beside J.T. and let my head tilt to rest on his shoulder. As I knew it would, his arm came around me.

We sat in silence, sipping our coffee. When he spoke, I thought he was going to tell me what to do about Grams or Royal. I was wrong.

"I've been seeing someone. At school."

I froze inside. This was what I'd been waiting for. For J.T. to talk to me like he used to. I tried to play it cool. "I figured that."

"His name is Clay. He's, uh, he's— I'm, um..." J.T. sucked in a quick breath. "I'm gay."

"I know, dumbass." I ducked my head forward to catch his eyes. "Is that what this has been about? You didn't know how to tell me?"

He shrugged a shoulder. "I guess? It happened so fast—"

A laugh burst from my gut, so big I almost spilled my coffee. I set the mug on the table and turned to sit sideways on the sofa, facing J.T.

"Fast? You call that fast? You got kicked out of your house for kissing a boy like seven years ago! And you haven't kissed anyone else since then! Fast?"

"Well, I mean…" J.T. shifted under my laughing gaze.

"Am I right? Clay is the first guy you've dated?"

"You know he is." J.T. relaxed a bit, finally getting that I wasn't mad, but I *was* going to give him shit. He'd given me enough over Royal. It was only fair.

"Fast," I muttered again, laughter still bubbling up. This time, J.T. laughed with me. "Is he nice? Is he good to you? I want to see pictures."

"He's amazing. He's funny, and sweet, and so cute. I swear—"

J.T. pulled out his phone and started to swipe for pics. I settled back into the sofa beside him, leaning into his side as I sipped my coffee and waited. When he showed me the screen of his phone, I grinned.

A handsome blond man stared back at me. A little older than us, maybe late twenties, with ocean blue eyes and golden stubble on his cheeks. He wasn't runway model handsome like J.T., but he was adorable, and the earnest affection in his eyes was all I needed to see.

"Do I get to meet him?" I asked. "Are you going to bring him home now that you told me?"

"I haven't told Grams," he said, and the caution in his voice made my heart hurt.

"Maybe you should wait until this thing with my dad is resolved. Grams won't care about you dating a guy, she'll be happy for you, but my parents will be assholes if they hear about it. Neither of you should have to put up with that."

We sipped our coffee in silence for a moment, finally in perfect accord after so many months of weirdness. Into the quiet, I said, "I'm glad you told me. I knew you needed time, so I didn't want to push, but you know I love you, right? You're my family. I don't care who you sleep with, I just want you to be happy."

"I am. Now that things are good with us, I'm happy. I'll bring him to meet you. Soon."

"Soon," I agreed.

"Can I keep the apartment after you move into Heartstone Manor? Or are you going to be too good for me once you're living in the big house?"

"I'm not moving into Heartstone."

J.T. just gave me a look, one dark brow arched above his piercing green eyes. "Sure, you aren't."

"I'm not. I don't know. I can't think about that yet."

"Then what are you going to do? You can't hide out in here forever, and I know you're not baking that pie for us."

"I'm not. But before I bring it to Royal, I have to call West."

J.T. leaned over and pressed a kiss to my cheek. "I knew you were a smart girl, Daze."

"Sometimes, I am. And sometimes, I'm a dumbass."

"We're all dumbasses every once in a while."

I pulled out my phone and opened my contacts. Before I could dial the police department, a knock fell on my door. I jolted, panic spiking through me.

J.T. stood. "Keep your phone in your hand. If that's anyone other than Royal or Grams, go ahead and call West. Especially if it's your dad. Got it?"

I nodded in agreement. I lurched to my feet, ready to bolt for the privacy of the bedroom to make my call if J.T. gave me the signal. He checked the peephole and laughed.

Swinging open the door, he let West into the apartment. "I swear, you have ESP or something. We were just going to call you."

"I talked to Royal," West said simply. "He suggested you might have some information for me about what's been going on at The Inn."

Maybe I should have been mad at Royal for talking to West, but I couldn't be. I should have called West myself the second I'd seen the Inn uniform in my father's room. I hadn't figured out exactly what to say or how to say it. Now I was out of time.

I poured West a cup of coffee and gestured to the table. He sat and waited. I sucked in a deep breath and said, "I stole twenty thousand dollars from the bakery. I gave it to my father for a business venture that turned out to be fake, and he said if I didn't come back to work he'd talk Grams into pressing felony theft charges against me. That's why I didn't call you a few hours ago."

I paused for breath. "Well, that and I'm afraid of what's going to happen to my family after I show you what I found."

West nodded slowly. "Why don't you show me, and I'll do my best to make this easy on you."

I sank into a chair at the table, J.T. by my side, and swiped through my phone for the pictures I'd taken in my dad's room. I told West everything. The missing contract with my father, that he'd pretty much admitted to the break-in, the meeting I'd seen and heard between my dad and Vanessa, and so much more. Together we listened to the video I'd taken earlier. There wasn't much to see, but there was plenty to hear.

When I was done, it was West's turn. "I already have my people looking for Vanessa. I'll go pick up your dad myself. If they know anything about Prentice's murder, I'll get it out of them. If your dad comes here, you call me. Do not open the door. Understand?"

"Yes, but what about the money? I didn't think of it that way at the time, but technically, I stole it from Grams." I should have kept my mouth shut, but the specter of felony charges dangled over my head.

West gave me a steady, calm look. "I have plenty of evidence against your dad and Vanessa, but I don't have any evidence against you. If your Grandmother provides it and presses charges, that's a different story."

"But... My dad said—" It's not that I was trying to get West to arrest me, but the idea of false hope was even worse.

"Daisy, I think you already know your dad is in a lot of trouble. He's making threats to save his ass, but they aren't going to work. He doesn't have any standing in the bakery right now. Only your grandmother can assess the bakery's finances and determine if there was a theft. And, honey," West gave a shake of his head, "Eleanor is not going to press felony theft charges against you. No way in hell."

I dropped my head to stare at the tabletop. I used to believe that, too. That Grams loved me best, that she'd always have my back. But now...

West reached out to take my hand. "Daisy, look at me." I did, and the kindness in his face was too much. A tear ran down my cheek, chased by another.

"I'm so tired of crying," I muttered, brushing the tear away with the back of my free hand.

"Hopefully, we'll get this sorted out with your father and you won't have to cry anymore. But I need you to listen to me for a minute, okay?" I nodded. "Your father is full of shit. He's an opportunist and a liar and no one in this town has any idea how he came from Eleanor. She did right with you, but your father is a waste of space."

West sighed and leaned back, letting go of my hand. "Darren talks a good game, and Eleanor loves him, so right now she's letting him turn her head. She's confused. But I promise you, she is not going to press charges against you. No fucking way."

The buzzer on the oven went off and J.T. took the pie out, sliding it onto a cooling rack. Turning to me, he said, "West is right, Daze. Grams was upset, and she doesn't get why you left because your dad is messing with her, but there's no way she'll press charges."

I scrubbed my palms over my cheeks. I was still wearing my damp clothes, my eyes were red from crying, and my hair was all over the place. Before I took the next step, I needed to get myself together. First, I had a question for West.

"Is Royal still at The Inn? Do you know?"

West raised an eyebrow at me, and I knew he was answering as Royal's friend, not as the chief of police. "He is. He's pretty miserable right now. Feels like shit for calling me and dragging you into this."

"He isn't the one who dragged me into this," I burst out. "I couldn't tell him." I choked on the words but forced them out. "I couldn't tell him it was my dad. I was so ashamed that my family did this to him."

West sighed. "Go see him. You're both idiots, feeling like crap over someone else's mess. Bring him something sweet and tell him you're sorry and everything'll be good. I promise."

"He's not mad at me?" I asked, feeling exactly like the idiot West said I was.

J.T. was the one who answered. "Why don't you go ask him yourself?"

"Good idea," West agreed. "Head over to The Inn and see Royal. Don't talk to your grandmother or your parents until I have your dad in custody, okay?"

"I won't, I swear."

Now that I'd unloaded the whole mess on West, I was more than happy to wash my hands of it. All I wanted to do now was make things right with Royal. I hated the way I'd left him in the parking lot earlier. I should have told him everything right away. It seemed like he'd figured it out mostly, but I owed him the truth.

West let himself out, reminding us to stay off the phone and lie low. My dad was probably at Grams' house finishing the dinner she'd cooked for him.

"We have just enough time while that pie cools to get you fixed up," J.T. said. "What did you do, stand under the waterfall?"

My hair was beyond saving. Too much mist from the water-fall and not enough product. Who was I kidding? There wasn't enough product in the universe to prevent a frizz explosion when I sat behind the waterfall. Usually, I wore a hat or wrapped it up, but today I hadn't been thinking. J.T. to the rescue.

I wasn't wasting the time it would take to wash my hair and start from scratch, so J.T. pulled it back from my face, turning the poof of frizz into a rounded bun. I swear if he weren't in culinary school he would have made an awesome hair-stylist.

A quick wash of my face, new makeup, and a sundress repaired most of the damage. My eyes were still a little puffy from all the crying I'd done in the past few days, but at least I no longer looked like I'd been dragged out from under a wet rock.

Almost ready, I pulled out my phone to text Royal. I was saving my apology for in-person, but I wanted to make sure he was still there.

> *I'm coming over to return your car and bring you a present. Are you in your office?*

He answered almost immediately.

> *I'm here. Are you leaving now?*

> *I'll be there in a few minutes. See you soon.*

See you soon.

That was the idea, but *soon* turned out to be a lot longer than I'd planned. All we had to do was drive to The Inn and walk inside. What could possibly go wrong?

As it turned out, everything.

Everything could go wrong. And everything did.

Chapter Thirty-Eight

DAISY

J.T. BLOCKED ME AT THE BOTTOM OF THE STEPS AND HELD out his hand. "You're way too upset to drive. Give me the keys."

J.T. was always good at making me laugh. "Right. You know I'm fine to drive, you just want to get behind the wheel of Royal's car."

"Guilty. Now hand over the keys. You know he wouldn't mind."

I dropped the keys into his outstretched palm and opened the passenger door, carefully setting the pie at my feet. Royal definitely wouldn't mind if J.T. drove his car, and I didn't care. It was a cool car, no doubt, but I'd had my turn and hopefully would again. All I could think about was getting to Royal.

I was halfway in the passenger seat when something thumped hard on the roof of the car, followed by a grunt.

"J.T.?"

We needed to get better lighting in the alley behind the bakery. All I could see was shadows, two of them, swaying and dipping in and out of the faint light from Main Street. Another grunt, this one of pain.

I shot out of the seat, stumbling a little in my sandals as I rounded the back of the car to get to J.T. He was struggling with someone the same height as him but more slender. Dark hair, pale face, and a flash of metal.

Vanessa, and she had a knife.

What the hell? Why would she go after J.T.?

I shifted my weight, looking for an opening, for any way to get her off J.T. With that knife flashing and the two of them in a combative dance, I couldn't get close. Physically, I was out-matched, but I had my voice and I had a phone. Somewhere.

Racing back around the car to find my phone, I started to scream. Main Street was mostly deserted this time of night, but someone had to be close enough to hear me.

Scrabbling for my phone in the passenger seat, I screamed as loud as I could. "Help! Help us, please! She has a knife!"

Over and over, I shouted and called, hoping someone would come. All I could hear from the other side of the car was their feet sliding on the pavement and grunts. Then a cry of pain.

J.T.—

No! I caught the reflection of my phone under the seat—I must have kicked it there when I jumped out. Grabbing the phone, I unlocked the screen. The police department's number was still pulled up. Thank god someone answered.

"This is Daisy Hutchins. I'm in the alley behind Sweetheart Bakery with J.T. Swift. Vanessa Sawyer attacked us. She has a knife and we need help."

The dispatcher gave a gasp as I identified our assailant. "Are you injured?"

"I'm not, but J.T. is, I think. They're fighting over the knife. I'm not close enough to tell."

A brief pause, then muffled sounds like she was talking with her hand over the phone. When she came back, her voice was calm. "Daisy, I have deputies on the way, and I'll get West as soon as I can reach him. Stay away from Vanessa and the knife. Go to the head of the alley so they can see where you are."

"I can't leave J.T. I'm sorry, I can't leave him. I think he's hurt. Please, hurry."

I dropped the phone and came around the back of the car to see them still grappling over the knife. Vanessa's face was twisted with rage, the knife flashing in what little light there was, seeming impossibly bright and sharp as she yanked her arm down and buried it in J.T.'s shoulder.

"No!" The scream was torn from me. I launched myself over the back of the car, not thinking, just seeing that long knife, hearing J.T.'s cry of agony. Vanessa wrenched the knife out and stabbed again, her momentum carrying them to the ground. She rolled on top of him, bringing the knife down once more, this time stabbing deep into his side.

It was dumb, I know, but I threw myself at her, knocking her off J.T. as we rolled. I lost track of the knife, lost track of everything. I only wanted her away from J.T.

She fought me, all long limbs and sharp nails, the knife nowhere to be seen. Her fist came around and struck my cheek, pain exploding, slowing me down just enough for her to roll me on my back and pin me.

"I have to," she muttered, her long, dark hair everywhere, her eyes wild and her face sheet-white. "I didn't want to do it, but I have to. He said to get rid of Royal. If I took care of Royal, I could go."

She closed her talon-like hands over my shoulders, yanking me up and slamming me down so my head smashed into the pavement. I twisted, trying to roll over, to see J.T., to get away from her before she found the knife. Where were the deputies? Where was West?

All of a sudden, I understood. She thought J.T. was Royal. Same height, same dark hair. Royal's car. Someone sent her to kill Royal. Whatever was going on, it was a whole lot bigger than sabotaging The Inn. This was murder. Like Prentice.

"That wasn't Royal," I screamed, hoping I could penetrate her insanity long enough to get the message through. "You stabbed J.T. Let me go so I can take care of him. Royal isn't here." I hoped with everything I had that he was somewhere safe, far away from Vanessa and her knife.

Vanessa went still on top of me. Her head cocked to the side like a deranged bird as she seemed to process what I'd said. "Not Royal? This is his car. He was with you." As if that explained everything.

"I borrowed Royal's car, remember? Let me go so I can take care of J.T. Let me go!"

Instead, she leaned in, pinning my wrists to the pavement, grinding them into the rough surface until I felt my skin tear and the wet heat of blood. No more words from her, just wide, crazy eyes and utter stillness. She was slender but a lot taller than me and fueled by madness. I twisted and bucked, kicking my legs to get her off, but she was unmovable.

"J.T.?" I called. "Can you hear me? Are you okay?"

A faint groan from behind me, and nothing else. J.T. Oh, God, J.T. What had happened with my father and The Inn was bad enough. If my problems got J.T. killed, I'd never be able to live with it. He was just starting his life, had finally found someone to love.

I couldn't let Vanessa do this to us. Royal was waiting for me. What if he came looking? What if she got to him before West's deputies could find us? I yanked at my wrists and life rushed back into Vanessa.

She let go of my wrists, her hands closing over my shoulders as she dragged me up and slammed me down onto the pavement, again and again, the blows to the back of my head scrambling my thoughts.

She was muttering, every word worse than the one before. "Have to find Royal. Once I deal with Royal, I'm free. Kill Royal and I'm free."

"J.T.!" I screamed again. "Someone help us!"

"Shut the fuck up you little bitch!" Vanessa let go of my shoulders to deliver a ringing slap across my face. Damn, that hurt. Her hands closed around my throat and she squeezed. Hard.

I scrabbled at her arms, clawing, pulling, desperate to get her off. My lungs burned for air, no scream escaping my open mouth. Lights flashed, my head buzzed. Thunder rolled in my ears and everything went dark.

I blinked my eyes open to find Vanessa gone. I couldn't have been out much longer than a few seconds. Two deputies were by the hood of the car, wrestling with Vanessa. The thunder hadn't come from the sky, it had been pounding feet. Help had arrived. I could only hope they weren't too late.

I rolled over, crawling to J.T.'s prone body. Even in the dim light of the alley, I could see the blood. Too much blood. His shoulder was a mess, and the knife was still buried in his side, all the way to the hilt. I wasn't touching the knife. I'd probably do more damage taking it out when I didn't know what I was doing.

Dragging myself to sit by his head, I gathered the skirt of my sundress and pressed the wad of cloth to his shoulder to stop the bleeding. The best I did was slow it. He was running out of time. Pressing harder, I spoke to him, trying to hold him with me. "J.T., hang in there. It's going to be okay. Everything is going to be okay. Just stay with me, J.T."

No response. Nothing. I glanced up to see the deputies cuffing Vanessa as she twisted and pulled in their hold. I yelled down the alley, "Did you call an ambulance?"

"On the way," one of them shouted back.

"Did you hear that?" I asked an unresponsive J.T. "You just have to hang on a little longer and the ambulance will be here. Just hang on. Please, please, hang on."

I wanted to be done with crying, but hurting all over and covered in my best friend's blood, tears were all I had. I shut out everything else and leaned on the blood-soaked pad of fabric, pressing on his shoulder and praying I wasn't making it worse.

Knees hit the pavement. Arms came around me. Royal. I turned my face into his neck and wept harder.

His hands came over mine, nudging me to the side as he leaned on the pad I'd made of my skirt, pressing it into J.T.'s shoulder. "I went down to the parking lot to wait for you. I saw the lights and started running."

I choked back my tears enough to fill in the blanks. "Vanessa thought he was you. Someone told her to kill you. She stabbed him. Twice in the shoulder and once in his side. The knife is still in there. You have to be careful Royal. You shouldn't be here—"

I could feel the hysteria taking me. I was covered in J.T.'s blood and now Royal was out in the open when someone wanted him dead. He couldn't be next. Not Royal. "You have to go. She was trying to kill you. You have to go, Royal. Go to Heart-stone where you'll be safe. You can't— You can't—"

"Shh. It's okay, sweetheart. There are cops everywhere. Look up and see. We're safe. And I think the ambulance just got here. Everything is going to be okay."

I did as he said, raising my head to see two more officers had joined the two who'd caught Vanessa. The first two were leading her down the alley to their vehicle, lights still flashing red and blue. How had I missed those? All I could see was J.T. and the blood.

More lights had joined them. The ambulance. Finally.

Everything was a blur of voices and hands. Strangers in blue nudging me back from J.T., asking if I was injured. I couldn't focus. My head ached, my vision was blurry. Royal pulled me to my feet, taking most of my weight, and led me off to the side, away from the paramedics working on J.T.

"Where are your keys, Daisy?"

My keys? Why did he need my keys? "In the car, I think. On the floor. Passenger side."

He leaned me against the wall and disappeared. A spike of panic went through me. I didn't want Royal out of my sight. He'd appeared like a dream. Maybe he was one. Maybe—

And he was back, unlocking the alley door to the bakery.

He flicked a switch, flooding the doorway with light, and led me into the alcove just inside. Under the glow of the light bulb, Royal ran his hands over my body.

"I'm okay," I offered weakly.

"You're not okay." His voice was brusque, but his hands were gentle. "You're covered in blood. We need to get you to the hospital."

"J.T.—"

"The paramedics are working on him. As soon as we get you checked out, we can focus on J.T."

That gave me something to hold on to. "Okay, then take me to the hospital."

"I'm on it. Stay right here." Holding my arms, he lowered me to sit on the steps and disappeared again. This time I didn't panic. Much. Royal was back a minute later. "One of the deputies is going to give us a ride. We'll get there the same time as J.T. You ready?"

I started to nod, then stopped at the pain in my neck and head. "Ready." A deputy I didn't recognize led us to his vehicle at the end of the alley, and we slid in the back.

I stared blindly out of the window facing the alley, watching as two paramedics jogged beside a stretcher, rolling it to the ambulance.

J.T.

If they were jogging, he was still alive to save.

Chapter Thirty-Nine

DAISY

WE PULLED ONTO MAIN STREET AHEAD OF THE AMBU-lance and Royal picked up his phone.

"Griffen. I need a favor. Vanessa attacked Daisy and J.T. We're on the way to the hospital. Can you come get her keys and then go by Daisy's place and get her a change of clothes?"

"My bags are packed," I whispered. "On my bed. He can just grab them and I can find something."

Royal's grin flashed for a second, and I knew exactly where he planned to bring my stuff after all of this was done. I didn't have it in me to argue. I was too tired, too scared, and most of all, I wanted to be with Royal.

Wherever he was, that's where I'd be. In the end, it was that simple.

"She seems okay," Royal said to Griffen, "but I want to get her checked out, and Griffen—Vanessa stabbed J.T. She told Daisy she was trying to kill me. Daisy had my car. Vanessa must have thought J.T. was me in the dark. She's in custody, but be careful."

He hung up. I rested my hand over his, squeezing his fingers in mine. I didn't have the energy to sit up, but I had to tell him. "It's not your fault. You know that, right? What Vanessa did isn't your fault."

"She was after me," he said, his voice rough. "J.T. was in the wrong place—"

"Not your fault," I repeated. "She said someone told her to kill you." I tried to remember her exact words, but it was a blur. "She said he told her to get rid of you and she'd be free."

"Did she say who 'he' was?" Royal's voice was tight, his muscles stiff.

"No. She was rambling, and I was trying to fight her off, so I didn't hear everything."

"It's okay. You're alive. That's all that matters."

"And J.T.," I said, unable to erase the picture of him, blood everywhere, eyes closed. He'd been so still.

"And J.T.," Royal agreed.

We were at the hospital sooner than I expected. Those flashing lights on top of the car really cut down the travel time. The deputy escorted us into the ER, taking the lead at the front desk.

"I have a witness to a crime here. I need her in a room. I'll be on the door. She's with the victim, he's right behind us in the ambulance."

The twin doors crashed open and J.T. was wheeled through, the paramedics on either side met by people in scrubs, the paramedics shouting things I didn't understand. All I knew was that if they were rushing, J.T. was still alive.

It was a slow night in the ER. The nurse had us in a curtained-off room a moment later, the deputy standing outside. Royal didn't want to wait for the nurse to come back and check me out. He grabbed a handful of paper towels from the sink and wet them before he got to work cleaning me up.

I reached for them, mumbling, "I can do it," but Royal waved me off.

"No, you can't. Just sit there and let me take care of you."

I didn't fight him. I was covered in drying blood, and I hurt all over. I wanted a hot bath and to know J.T. was going to be okay. For the moment, I wasn't going to get either of those things.

Royal didn't get very far cleaning me up before a nurse hustled in and pushed him aside. Griffen poked his head in while the nurse was making noises over the scrapes on the back of my wrists.

Royal stepped out for a minute. I could hear them talking in low voices on the other side of the curtain, but I missed what they said. It didn't matter. Royal would tell me later if it was important.

The nurse poked and prodded, checked my vitals, bandaged the cut on the back of my head, and cleared me to go. All my injuries were superficial. Even the headache was fading.

After the nurse left, the deputy poked his head in. "West is on his way. He wants you to stay here until he can take your statement."

West showed up ten minutes later to find Royal and me side by side on the bed, my head on Royal's shoulder, my hand in his. I recoiled at the sight of West. I liked him usually, but the last thing I wanted was to relive those horrible minutes in the alley behind the bakery.

He went first, giving me time to get my bearings.

"Vanessa is in custody, and she's not talking. She asked us to call Cole Haywood, and he's not going to let her tell us anything. I need you to run me through everything you can remember."

I did, closing my eyes and trying to recall every single thing she'd said, even if I'd only caught a fragment. Anything that would help West find out who had sent Vanessa after Royal. And why. He asked me probing questions, most of which I couldn't answer, then clicked off his recorder and shut his notebook.

"Your dad skipped town," he said. "I caught up with your grandmother at home. He cleaned out the cash she had stashed in her jewelry box, along with some of her jewelry. There's a warrant out for him and for your mother as an accessory. I was out looking for them when I got the call about what happened in the alley. Do you want me to call Eleanor?"

I didn't have to think about that. Grams did not need to see me like this. "No. Please, don't. Griffen is bringing me clean clothes. I need to change and get cleaned up before I call Grams. Have you heard anything about J.T.? They won't tell us anything."

West shook his head. "I only know that he's in surgery. You're going to wait here?"

"I'm not going anywhere until I know he's going to be okay." Something occurred to me. "I need to make a call, someone he's close to will want to know what's going on. His phone was in his pocket. Can you find it? Please? He'd want me to call and I don't have the number. Or my phone."

"I'll see what I can do." West disappeared through the curtain, leaving us alone.

"Where's your phone?" Royal asked.

"Somewhere near your car. Or in your car. I'm not sure. I dropped it. Stupid dress didn't have pockets."

Sometimes women's clothes sucked. How come we never got pockets? My mind was drifting, the shocks of the day finally catching up with me. I leaned my head against Royal's shoulder.

"We baked you a pie," I rambled. "Mixed berry. To say sorry for being such a jerk before. I should have told you what was going on with my dad."

"It's okay, sweetheart. I knew you needed time."

"I thought I did." I turned my face into his shoulder, breathing deep of his scent, soaking in the heat of his body. I was terrified for J.T., but my heart was calm.

I knew who I wanted. Who was important. Royal. And the fact that he'd given me the time I needed even when it hurt him? If I didn't already know he was the one, that would have done it.

"I didn't need time," I said. "I just needed you."

Royal was silent for a long moment, his voice so rough when he tried to speak he had to clear his throat. In the end, his arm came around me, holding me tight to his side. "Love you, Daisy. So much."

"I love you, too." I did, more than I knew I could, so much that my heart hurt from letting that fierce emotion run wild. I'd spent too long being afraid of loving him, afraid of being hurt, of doing the wrong thing. If I'd known how good it would feel to just love him, I would have done it sooner.

I closed my eyes for a minute. Possibly I drifted off. There was a lovely line of drool on my chin when West came back, but I admit nothing.

Before I could ask, West said, "No word on J.T. He's in surgery, and he's hanging in there. That's all they can tell us for now."

"Thanks, West." I took the phone he handed me and unlocked the screen. Royal and West talked in the background, but all I could think about was Clay. This wasn't how I wanted to meet J.T.'s boyfriend. I had absolutely no doubt J.T. would want me to call him. Well, that wasn't true. J.T. might want to spare him the worry. But if the tables were turned J.T. would want to know.

It was easy to find Clay's number since he was at the top of the call list. I tapped his name, nerves fluttering in my belly. A low male voice answered, warm with welcome. "Hey, I didn't expect to hear from you tonight, thought you had plans with Daisy."

I cleared my throat. "Uh, this is Daisy, actually. Sorry to take you by surprise but, uh—"

"What's wrong?" he asked, his warm voice sharp with a thread of worry.

"J.T. and I were attacked. He was stabbed. He's in surgery. I thought you'd—"

"What hospital?" Clay demanded.

"County Regional. I'm in the ER right now, but as soon as I can I'll head to the waiting room closest to where J.T. is. I'll text you as soon as I know where that is."

"I'll be there in an hour."

"Hey, Clay!" I called, knowing he was about to hang up.

"Yeah," he barked, impatient. I got it, but I had to say one more thing.

"Drive safely. Seriously. J.T. will kill me if you rush and get into an accident on the way here. He's hanging in there, and he'll be in surgery for a while. Drive safe."

"Yeah," he grunted. "See you soon."

"He's still going to speed," I murmured as I set the phone down.

"Probably," Royal agreed. "I would. But since you reminded him, he'll be more careful."

The curtain on my room slid open and Hope was there, Griffen behind her, a stack of clothes in her arms. "I have your things." She turned an eagle eye on Royal and then Griffen. "Get out, you guys, and let her change in privacy." Royal started to object. Hope leveled a sharply pointed finger at him. "Go."

He grumbled as he kissed my cheek, but he went. "I'll be just outside."

"I won't be long," I promised.

Chapter Forty

DAISY

I WAS STILL STRUGGLING TO SIT UP WHEN HOPE wrapped her arms around me in a long hug.

"He's going to be okay," she said, her words more a prayer than a promise.

"I know," I lied, holding on to her with everything I had.

I didn't know. We knew nothing except that we loved J.T., and he was clinging to life. All we could do was wait.

Hope helped me change into jeans and a t-shirt, urging me to add a sweatshirt despite the warm temperatures outside. "It's freezing in here. They have the AC cranked like it's July. If you get hot, you can always take it off."

It felt good to be in clean clothes. Hope handed me a fresh scrunchie and I redid my bun for the second time. It wasn't the fashion statement J.T. had made it, but it would do.

Royal was waiting when I came out. "No news on J.T., but I found out where we can wait." I wasn't expecting Griffen and Hope to follow us.

"Hope, you should go home. This could take a while. I'll call as soon as we know anything," I said.

"No way. We're staying."

"Tenn is on his way," Griffen added with a nod at Royal. Tears sprung to my eyes at the way Royal's family was here for him. For us.

I couldn't bear to think of my own family. My father and mother gone, leaving Grams heartbroken and betrayed.

Grams. She'd want to be here. She loved J.T. like he was her own. I still didn't have my phone, but I had his. I tapped the screen, waking it up and then clicking it off as I thought about what I had to do.

I was still angry at Grams, but J.T. was far more important than my anger. I had to call her.

I was still thinking when Hope asked, "Are you hungry? Or do you want tea? Chocolate? We're going to the cafeteria to get something."

I shrugged. I was vaguely aware of being hungry. J.T. and I had never gotten around to eating dinner, but the thought of food wasn't appealing. I was too worried to eat. Hope wasn't interested in my denials.

"I'll get you something anyway. You can always eat it later." They left, Griffen's arm around Hope, her leaning into him, talking softly.

Royal took my free hand in his. "When are you going to call Grams?"

"As soon as I work up the nerve," I admitted.

"She loves you, Daisy."

"I know. I love her too. I'm just—" Scared. Pissed off. Overloaded. Totally without words. What did I say to her?

304

In the end, I kept it simple, clicking open J.T.'s phone and dialing before I could chicken out.

Grams sounded tired when she answered. "Hello? J.T.? Is everything okay?"

"Grams, it's me. I need you." Words spilled out about J.T., and where we were, and what had happened. Once I heard her voice, a dam broke loose inside me. I was still hurt, still pissed, but I loved Grams more than anything. Even with Royal by my side, I needed my Grams, and she needed me.

I hung up, telling Royal, "She's on her way." That done, I texted Clay directions to the waiting room we'd taken over. Hope and Griffen were still gathering provisions from the cafeteria, but Tenn showed up just after I hung up with Grams, his eyes worried when he saw us.

"Any news?" he asked as he slouched into a chair near Royal.

Royal shook his head. "Not yet. Might be awhile. Griffen and Hope went to get food. If you want anything, just text them."

"No, I'm good. Everyone sends their love."

"Everyone?" Royal asked with a raised eyebrow.

"Well, not Bryce. But everyone else," Tenn admitted, the side of his mouth curving up. After a moment, he sighed. "I should have talked to Vanessa, given her some money."

I was already shaking my head as Royal said, "Don't. Don't second guess. This wasn't just about money. Vanessa told Daisy someone ordered her to go after me. We don't know who, but this afternoon she told me she knew who killed Dad. Not too much of a stretch to think it's the same person."

Wait, what? Why hadn't he mentioned this earlier? "She told you she knew who your father's killer was?"

"She claimed to know and said she'd tell me for a cool million. Cash."

I whistled. "Do you have a million in cash?" I had to ask.

Royal's teasing grin was the sweetest thing I'd seen in ages. "I could get it, but even if I did, I wouldn't give it to Vanessa. And now, I think the money was more about getting me alone to make the exchange. Somewhere she or whoever's behind this could get to me."

I shivered. What had happened to J.T. was bad enough. I couldn't stand imagining the same thing happening to Royal.

Grams made it to the hospital before Hope and Griffen got back from the cafeteria. Still wearing her house slippers, hair falling out of its usual braid, gray eyes bleak, she made a beeline straight for me, arms outstretched.

I jumped to my feet. My heart broke as Grams dropped her arms and stopped, uncertain of her welcome. Whatever problems we had, they weren't bigger than this crisis, and they absolutely weren't bigger than our love. This woman had raised me, been there for me at every hard moment in my life until the last few weeks. I wasn't going to turn from her now. No way.

I barreled into her arms, my head on her shoulder, exactly where it had fit so perfectly since I was a little girl. She smelled of lavender and vanilla. Grams. Her strong arms came around me, hesitant at first, then closing tightly, holding me to her as her breath hitched.

"Oh, Daisy, my girl, my sweet girl." She rocked me from side to side, murmuring, her tears falling down her cheeks to drop on mine. Drawing in a deep breath for strength, I hugged her tight, my arms steel around her.

It struck me that this time Grams needed *me* to comfort *her*. We had issues to work out, but none of that mattered right now.

For the first time in memory, Grams was fragile, on the edge of breaking, her heart too sore to comfort me. After all these years of love and support, it was my turn to comfort her.

My heart swelled as I rocked her, stroking a hand down her braid, murmuring, "It's all going to be okay, Grams. Shh, it's okay. J.T.'s going to come through this, and we're all going to be okay. I promise."

We both knew I couldn't promise any such thing, but I said the words anyway. J.T. was going to be okay. He had to be.

When she was cried out, I settled Grams into the seat beside me, handing her the honeyed tea Hope brought me. Neither of us wanted the turkey sandwich, but Royal and Hope glared at me until I ate half. I knew better than to think I could fight both Royal and Hope if they were teamed up against me.

The sandwich was dry and had too much bread, but I felt better once my stomach was full. The cookie wasn't one of mine, but it didn't hurt either. Done eating, Grams still sipping her tea, we sat in silence for a while, everyone tensing every time the door at the end of the hall opened. None of the white-jacketed doctors were there for us. Ditto for every figure in scrubs who strode through. We sat, and we waited, worry winding tighter with every quiet minute that passed.

When her tea was empty, Grams rose to throw out the cup, standing so slowly I imagined I heard her bones creaking. She'd always been so vibrant, but now I saw the weight of age dragging her down. I hated my parents for bringing her to this.

I was going to be fine. I had myself and my friends. Most of all, I had Royal. I couldn't see the future, but I knew Royal would be a part of it. This love was forever. I didn't know what was going to happen next for me considering I was homeless and unemployed, but I knew Royal and I would get through it together.

Grams sat slowly, easing herself into the chair. "Daisy," she said, hesitant. I hated hearing that reserve in her voice. We'd always been so open with each other.

Chest aching, I took her hand in mine and squeezed gently. "Grams, it's okay."

"It's not," she retorted, a little of her usual fire sparking in her voice.

"Grams—"

"No, let me say my piece."

"Okay," I conceded, stomach twisting with sudden nerves. I wasn't ready to talk about my parents or what they'd done. What my father had done. Beside me, Royal took my other hand in his, anchoring me. I let out the breath I'd been holding, ready for whatever Grams had to say.

"I didn't do right by your father," Grams started. I shoved back my instinct to disagree. Biting my lip, I forced myself to stay quiet and let her speak.

"I see you biting your lip, little girl. I know you want to stick up for me, but this time, you're wrong. I did a better job with you, but I didn't do right by your father. I was so young when I got pregnant with him. Young and foolish. I thought I could make it work, and I did, mostly. But I was more a playmate for him than a mother. I gave him everything he wanted that I could afford, and by the time I realized it hadn't done him any good, it was too late. I ruined that boy."

I couldn't stay quiet any longer. "Grams, his choices are not your fault. Maybe you spoiled him, and maybe you weren't the best mom at sixteen, but he's a grown man. He has a wife and a child of his own. He is not your fault. None of this is your fault."

A little voice in my head reminded me that she was going to cut me out of the bakery. Maybe that part was her fault, but it was her bakery. I wasn't going to throw out a lifetime of love over one bad decision.

Chapter Forty-One

DAISY

I KNEW TOO WELL HOW MY FATHER COULD TALK A SEN-sible woman into total idiocy. Hadn't I fallen for his act, too? All he had to do was put on a suit, show me a few spreadsheets, and I'd written him a check for money that wasn't really mine. So freaking stupid.

I'd be the biggest hypocrite in the world if I blamed Grams for falling for his crap when I'd done exactly the same thing.

Grams started to speak, but I cut her off. "Is he sorry for everything he did to you? Did he apologize? Leave a note? Express remorse in any way?"

Grams shook her head.

"Then I don't think you should be beating yourself up for any mistakes you made years ago. This isn't on you."

Her head shook again, a tiny rueful smile on her lips. "Oh, Daisy girl. You'll understand when you have children of your own. Your father's made some bad choices, and he's not welcome in my home any longer, but he'll always be my boy."

I sighed. "I know."

"But if I see him, I'm calling West. He's my boy, but I'm not protecting him. Not anymore." She leaned past me to look at Royal. "I didn't know, Royal. I swear to you, I had no clue what he was up to. I'm so sorry—"

"Eleanor, don't. You don't have anything to be sorry for," he said, his eyes kind.

"I do. But we can talk about making that right later."

"Later," I agreed. "We need to get through tonight first."

The doors at the far end of the hall slid open. We all leaned forward, hope and terror warring inside us. Not a doctor. A man, tall and broad, with messy blond hair and golden stubble on his cheeks. I instantly recognized him from the pic on J.T.'s phone.

Rising to my feet, I crossed the waiting room. "Clay? I'm Daisy."

He looked down at me, his throat working, hands hanging loosely at his side. On impulse, I leaned in and hugged him. "No word yet. We're still waiting. Come sit with us."

Clay returned my hug with a squeeze of one arm, clearing his throat. "I don't want to impose—"

I ignored his protest, taking his hand and leading him to a seat beside Grams. Pointing around the room, I made introductions. "This is Grams, Royal, Royal's brother Tenn, his other brother Griffen, and Griffen's wife Hope—who should be home in bed but refuses to leave."

"You're all here for J.T.?" Clay asked, sounding a little dazed.

"He's Daisy's," Royal said simply. "Makes him family."

"Clay is J.T.'s," I explained to the group, nudging Clay into the seat beside Grams.

As I expected, Grams' eyes lit. Giving Clay a brilliant smile, she raised an eyebrow at me. "Why didn't I know about this?"

"Because J.T.'s a dork."

That was all the explanation Grams needed. Turning to Clay, she took his hand and squeezed. "I hate the circumstances, but I'm so glad to meet you. That boy and his secrets."

"I've heard all about you and Daisy." Clay swallowed hard. "J.T. loves you a lot."

"It's mutual," Grams said. "Daisy brought him home when they were thirteen, and he's been mine ever since. Tell me how you two met. Are you in the culinary program at Tech, too?"

"No ma'am. I've been working in the small business incubator they have there, first with my brewery and now as an advisor. We ran into each other on campus and hit it off."

Grams' smile was almost blinding. I knew she wouldn't care that J.T. had a boyfriend, she'd only care that he was happy and loved. Based on the way Clay had rushed to be here, I knew J.T. was both.

I leaned into Royal, resting my head on his shoulder. "I hate the waiting," I said, keeping my voice low so I could eavesdrop on Grams and Clay.

"I know. Try to close your eyes, get some rest."

I made an inelegant sound in the back of my throat. A nap was not going to happen. I was drained from everything, and I'd been up since before dawn. I still wasn't going to sleep.

"Fine, then tell me about your packed bags. Are you going to move in with me?"

I glanced up to see his blue eyes trained on my face, emotion swirling through them. Nerves, humor, hope, and love. Royal felt it all and I wanted to give the same back.

"I was planning on it. Thought I'd bring a pie to bribe you."

"I can always be bribed with pie. Or cake. Cookies..."

I squeezed his hand and laughed. "I know. I figured I'd sweeten you up with the pie before I asked for half of that closet."

I was mostly joking. First, I didn't have nearly enough clothes to fill half of Royal's closet. Neither did he. His suite wasn't the most luxurious in Heartstone Manor—he claimed that honor belonged to Griffen and Hope—but it was larger than my own place by far. I wondered if Savannah and their cook would let me play in the kitchen. I'd figure it out later.

I opened my mouth to ask when the door at the end of the hall opened and a tall, thin woman in scrubs came out. She looked strained and tired. "J.T. Swift?"

I stumbled to my feet, Royal standing beside me. Everyone else did the same. "That's us. We're here for J.T. Is he okay?"

At that moment, I was afraid to hope, terrified she was going to say he was dead. I couldn't read her face, saw only the lines fatigue had drawn into her forehead, the circles beneath her eyes.

Please, please, let him be okay.

"He's stable." My heart kicked back to life and I took a breath. Stable. He was stable. Stable was good.

She went on. "No visitors yet, he woke from anesthesia, but he's asleep now. You can see him in the morning."

"Is he going to be okay?" I asked.

She gave me that measured doctor look that told me she wasn't going to make any promises. "He came through surgery well. The knife made a mess but didn't damage anything vital. He lost a lot of blood, and he's going to be off his feet for a while, but, assuming things go well over the next twenty-four hours, he should make a full recovery."

I sagged with relief, Royal's arm the only thing holding me upright. "When can we see him?"

"Come back after nine am tomorrow. He needs to rest and I want to take another look at him before we move him to a regular room. Then he can have visitors."

Grams turned to Clay. "You can come home with me and stay in J.T.'s old room, or Daisy can give you the keys to the apartment over the bakery." She tilted her head at me. "You're going home with Royal?"

"That's the plan," I confirmed. To Clay, I added, "I can give you the key to the apartment, but you should go home with Grams. She'll be coming straight back here in the morning, and she makes a killer breakfast."

Grams nodded in agreement. "I will and I do." Turning to me, she said quietly, "I'm going to stop by the bakery on the way home, put up a sign saying we're closed tomorrow. After we see J.T., can we find some time to talk?"

"Of course, we can. I'll call you in the morning."

Grams left, towing Clay behind her. She'd feel better with someone to take care of. Normally, that would be me, but I was going home with Royal. Tomorrow, I was going to take care of Grams, whether she liked it or not.

My dad had hurt both of us, but I had Royal. Grams had had too many shocks in a short period of time. My parents betraying her, me quitting the bakery, J.T. in the hospital... I didn't know what my future held when it came to our working relationship, but she was my Grams.

I'd be there tomorrow and every day I was lucky enough to have her, to make sure she knew how much she was loved.

For now, it was time to go home. I turned to Royal, but he was already on it. "Tenn's going to give us a ride home. That okay with you? Griffen and Hope have your things from the apartment."

"Sounds great." Suddenly, I was exhausted, one blink away from falling asleep. I let Royal tug me toward the elevators at the end of the hall.

"Ready to sleep now?" Royal asked, a laugh hiding in his voice.

"Yes, please." Standing in the elevator, I let my eyes slide shut, my face buried in Royal's chest, snuggled into his arms. "I'm going to pass out right here. Now that I know J.T.'ll be okay, there's nothing keeping me awake."

"Nothing?" Royal asked with a raised eyebrow and a wicked quirk at the side of his mouth. My body hummed but couldn't kick into gear. At the regret I knew was all over my face, Royal burst into a full laugh. "Maybe tomorrow," he said, rubbing my back.

"Definitely tomorrow," I murmured into his shirt.

He dropped his head, his lips at my ear so no one else could hear, and detailed exactly how he planned to wake me up. It was almost enough to bring both my brain and my body back online.

It was definitely enough to guarantee I had very nice dreams. And I did. Dreams that came true as I woke on the crest of orgasm with Royal's mouth between my legs.

I was suddenly very, very glad I'd agreed to move in, even if it might only be temporary. I wanted to wake up with him every day for the rest of my life. We hadn't quite gotten around to talking about forever, but this was a good start.

He moved over me, inside me, his body and mine creating a perfect circuit, a connection that my heart knew was forever, no matter what we had or hadn't discussed.

We didn't need to talk. We knew what we wanted. The details could come later.

Epilogue: Part One

DAISY

*I*T WAS EASY TO SAY THE DETAILS COULD COME LATER. Pinning them all down was a lot more complicated. J.T. was stuck in the hospital for almost a week before we could bring him home. Grams insisted he recover at her house, and between Grams and Clay hovering, J.T. was on his feet faster than anyone expected.

He loved Grams, but by the time he was up and around, J.T. was eager to move back into the apartment so he and Clay could have a little privacy. I didn't blame him.

Despite the number of Sawyers living in Heartstone Manor, the sheer size of the place meant I wasn't having any issues with privacy. I wasn't wild about the longer commute to the bakery, but otherwise, I loved living at Heartstone. Probably because I loved living with Royal.

Which didn't explain why I hadn't fully committed to the move. My mail still arrived at the apartment mailbox, and while I'd moved my clothes, there were plenty of things I still hadn't packed. Books, knickknacks, the prints and photographs I'd collected over the years. Royal wanted all of that in our rooms at Heartstone. I was dragging my feet.

And yes, I was back at the bakery. I needed to talk to Grams about everything that had happened, but I was dragging my feet there, too. The confrontation with my father had made a few things clear. One of them was the realization that though I loved working with Grams with all my heart, I didn't want to spend the rest of my life as an hourly worker when I was doing the work of an owner.

My father had shown me just how little security I had the way things were now. I didn't want to quit on Grams, didn't want to leave the bakery I'd grown up in. I wasn't ready to abandon our dreams for the future.

I also wasn't going to strong-arm Grams into giving me a piece of the business. She'd started Sweetheart Bakery on her own when my father was only a child. It was hers to share or keep to herself, and considering everything that had happened with my father, I could understand Grams being a little low on trust.

All of that left me backed into a corner. If I left the bakery for good, I wasn't sure I had any prospects in Sawyers Bend. The town wasn't big enough for two bakeries, and I couldn't bring myself to think about competing with Grams. Not to mention my lack of start-up capital.

We did have plenty of restaurants in town, and I was sure Royal and Tenn would give me a job at The Inn, but after so many years basically being my own boss, I wasn't looking forward to punching a time clock for someone else.

I'd tossed around the idea of starting a small catering and delivery business, but I couldn't seem to work up much enthusiasm. Instead of doing anything about it, I'd drifted from day to day, worrying about J.T. and going through the motions at the bakery.

Royal was the only part of my life that excited me. I loved our life together, loved waking up beside him every morning, the sleepy, sexy smile that crossed his lips when he opened his eyes and saw me lying next to him.

It was everything else I wasn't sure about. And loving our life together, I didn't want to look for work anywhere but Sawyers Bend. I pushed the worry away for another day. I had prep to finish before I could leave, and Royal had planned a date night. I didn't want to be late.

I had no clue what he had in mind, but I'd learned my guy was all about the romance when he wanted to be. For my part, I'd made a chocolate raspberry tart for two. If it didn't fit his date night plan, we could always eat it later.

"Are you almost done back here?"

Grams' voice took me by surprise. I flashed her a bright smile, hoping it was enough to mask the awkwardness that lingered between us. "Almost. Just have to wipe down the last worktable."

"I'll do it later," Grams said, taking a seat at the clean side of the worktable in question. I didn't see the manila envelope in her hand until she set it in front of her. "Come sit with me a minute. I'd like to talk to you before you go."

See? Awkward. We'd never had this kind of restraint between us. I hated it, but I didn't know how to fix it. I didn't even know what was wrong. Not really. Grams swore she wasn't upset about the money I'd given my father.

Her giving the bakery to him still stung, I won't lie, but I didn't hold that against her. Really. Maybe a little. But not enough to make things weird. I'd do almost anything to have Grams back the way we were before.

I sat, folding my hands in my lap, my mind racing to figure out what this was about.

Grams cleared her throat. "I went to see Harvey last week. This whole process took longer than I expected. First, I want to apologize for what happened with your father."

"Grams, you don't need to apologize, I understand. He's your son and—"

She cupped my cheek in her hand, her gray eyes swimming with tears. "He is, but you're my baby girl. I gave him everything I could, and I finally understand that'll never be enough. But you, Daisy, I gave you everything I have, and you gave me back more in return."

"I love you, Grams," I said, my own eyes blurred with tears. I hated my dad for letting her down. "I'm sorry I—"

"No, Daisy. You don't have anything to be sorry for. Nothing," she added when I would have objected.

Clearly, she'd forgotten about the twenty grand I'd taken from the business. Even if she wasn't sorry for that, I was.

"I love you so much," she said, "and I rely on you. Too much. So much that I took advantage."

"Grams," I tried again.

"Daisy, just let me get through this. I know you have a date tonight."

At that thought, I snapped my mouth shut. I did have a date, and if I didn't stop interrupting her, neither of us would get out of here.

"I went to see Harvey," Grams went on when it was clear I was going to shut up. "I changed my will. I'm sorry to say your father and Sheree are no longer included. When I go, everything I have will go to you, except for a few personal bequests, including J.T."

"Grams—"

Her eagle-eyed stare had me closing my mouth. Okay, I'd wait until she was done. But what more could there be?

"You don't have to do anything about the will, that's signed and safe with Harvey. I do need you to read this, and if you want to, sign it."

Grams opened the manila envelope and slid a stack of papers in front of me. It took me a few seconds to realize what they were. A partnership agreement. My fingertips hovered over the first page, afraid to touch it.

Grams cleared her throat and started to talk again, this time a little hesitant. "We never talked about you quitting. I don't know if you want to stay, or if you're just waiting for me to get back in the swing of things. But if you want to stay, I want you to do it as my partner. 50/50, even split. If anything happens to either of us, the bakery goes to the surviving partner. If either of us wants to leave, the other has first chance to buy out the other's share."

"Really?" Hot tears spilled over my cheeks. I didn't want to leave the bakery. No way. I wanted to stay and work with Grams. I just wanted the assurance that my dad wasn't going to sweep back in and take it all away. Not that he could considering that pesky warrant, but it was more the uncertainty.

I hadn't expected this. I'd wanted it, but Grams had been so reserved...

She nudged the papers closer to me. "I should have said something earlier, but I wanted these first. So it wasn't another promise. I wanted to show you this is real."

"And all I have to do is sign them, and we're partners in Sweetheart Bakery?" It seemed too good to be true.

"Read them first, but yes. If that's what you want."

"It is, it really is, but Grams, what about the money?"

"The money you gave your father?" I nodded. "We're writing that off as a bad investment and moving on. Your heart was in the right place. But let's agree, no major withdrawals unless we both sign off."

I swallowed hard, blinking back my tears. "That sounds like a good idea. I'm going to read these now."

I did have that date to get to, but I couldn't bring myself to do this later. Grams and I would both feel better once these papers were signed and we could put all of this behind us. Grams rose to finish wiping down the last worktable except the spot where we were sitting. I sent Royal a quick text telling him I was running a few minutes late and got to reading.

The partnership agreement was straightforward and exactly as Grams had described. When I was done reading, I looked up to see Grams hovering. I wanted to sign for me because this was what I wanted most for my career, more than anything else. And I wanted to sign if doing so would take that hesitant look off Grams' face. I wanted my teasing, loving, slightly crazy, hippie Grandmother back. Not this worried shell of herself.

"As soon as I sign this, we're partners?"

"Harvey has to file it for us, but basically, yes. Daisy, is this what you want? Are you sure? If you wanted to follow J.T. and go to culinary school—"

"I don't. I want to stay here and run Sweetheart with you. I want to add that outside seating, maybe next summer, and try pop-up lunches. I want this, Grams."

Tears filled her eyes. "I want this too. I don't know what I was thinking with—"

I shot up a hand. "Stop apologizing. I know how persuasive he is. Do I need to remind you about the money? If you're giving me a free pass on that, you can give yourself one for falling for his crap. We were both dumb, and we won't be dumb again."

I dropped my hand and braced it against the papers, holding them still to sign on the last page with a flourish. Shoving the papers in front of her, I handed her the pen. "Your turn, partner."

With a watery smile, Grams leaned over and signed. When she was done, she wrapped her arms around me, rocking me back and forth. "You *are* my baby. From the moment you were born you were mine, and you always will be. Now, go home to Royal and get ready for your date. I have that tart you made all boxed up and ready to go."

"I love you, Grams, no matter what."

"I know you do, Daisy girl. But not as much as I love you. Now get out of here."

I wasn't going to argue with my grandmother. One more tight hug and I bolted for the door, checking my phone to see if I still had time for a quick shower. I had a date to get ready for.

Epilogue: Part Two

ROYAL

*D*AISY WAS FLOATING ON AIR WHEN SHE GOT HOME from work, her grin lighting her whole face. Good thing. I needed her in a good mood tonight. I had plans for us, and a smiling Daisy was a good start.

"What happened?"

"I'll tell you in a minute, just have to change first."

She was in and out of the shower in a flash and so tempting in her flannel bathrobe I thought about changing my plans and dragging her off to bed right then.

Not going to happen.

Hope and Savannah would kill me after they'd pitched in to make tonight happen.

"So, where are we going?" Daisy asked, still smiling.

"You'll figure it out." I smiled back, absurdly happy just to have her here, living in my space, waking up with me and falling asleep in my arms. The past few weeks had been better than any dream. Daisy's parents had wreaked havoc, but they were long gone. Vanessa was in jail, J.T. was on the mend, Daisy was back at the bakery, and we hadn't had an incident at The Inn since the day Vanessa was arrested.

Everything should have been perfect. It was. Almost. Taking Daisy's hand, I led her out the back door to the gardens behind Heartstone Manor.

"Are we going where I think we're going?"

"Wait and see," I teased, though we were going exactly where she thought we were going. While the rest of the family had explored the watchtower, secretly, I thought of it as ours.

"Are you going to tell me what has you in such a good mood?"

Daisy's smile was almost blinding. Swinging our clasped hands between us, she spilled. "Grams brought me a partnership agreement for the bakery! Harvey drew up the papers for her. 50/50 partners."

I stopped in my tracks, closing my hands around her waist and swinging her into a high circle. "That's amazing. I knew Eleanor was going to come to her senses. And it's what you wanted."

"Exactly what I wanted. I convinced myself it wasn't going to happen. She's been so weird lately."

I took Daisy's hand again, and we continued down the path to the watchtower. "A little weird is normal after everything that went down."

"True. And she said she forgave me for the money I took." Daisy sounded surprised. I wasn't. Eleanor might have been swayed by Darren for a while, but she loved Daisy too much to hold one mistake against her.

"Now everything is perfect." Daisy sidled closer to me, tipping her head against my shoulder as we walked. Not quite perfect, but close. Now that Eleanor had made Daisy a partner, there was only one thing missing.

Candlelight welcomed us as I pushed open the door to the watchtower. Protected by an ancient glass globe, the light swayed in the breeze from the open door, changing the familiar room into something out of a dream.

Scents drifted from above, savory and sweet, drawing us up the curving staircase. Daisy climbed through the trap door first, stopping at the top to take in the room, her mouth open in surprise.

"When did you do all of this?" she asked in wonder.

I followed her into the top level of the watchtower, grinning in satisfaction at the scene I'd created with the help of Hope, Savannah, and—oddly enough—Finn. Flowers filled the room. Roses, lilies, daisies, and everything in between. Some of the arrangements were formal, some little more than wildflowers stuck in a jar, but more than anything, they were abundant. As in every available surface was covered with flowers. Every surface but the bed and the small table set for two.

I moved to the bottle of champagne chilling in a silver bucket. "Champagne?"

Daisy's eyebrows shot up. "Yes, please."

I wrestled with the bottle, popping the cork and catching the foam in a glass while Daisy strolled around the room, sniffing the flowers. She came to a stop beside the bed, freshly made with a mountain of pillows and a fluffy white duvet.

I handed her the glass and cleared my throat. Why this should make me nervous, I didn't know. Daisy was living with me. Maybe she hadn't finished moving out yet, but what did that matter?

I tried to tell myself that, but it did matter. I wanted more. I wanted it all. It was too soon for everything—we hadn't been together long enough for that— but I needed to move us one step closer. I just had to hope I wasn't going to scare her off.

"Let's sit at the table," I said. I'd planned this out, but now that we were here, my plan seemed forced and awkward. I sat, waiting for Daisy to do the same. She did, dropping into my lap instead of the seat across the table.

That would work. Not like I was going to shove Daisy off my lap when that was exactly where I wanted her. Clearing my throat again, I reached into the picnic basket Savannah had left on the table and pulled out an envelope and a small velvet box. Daisy eyed the box with a flare of alarm in her brown eyes, then narrowed those eyes on the envelope.

"What's that?"

I handed her the envelope. She opened it slowly, brow furrowing as she read it. "A change of address form?"

Printed from the DMV website, it was the form she'd need to permanently change her address to Heartstone Manor. "I want you to move in. For real."

Daisy laid the form out on the table, smoothing her hand over it, back and forth, saying nothing.

"You can do it online, I think, but I wanted to give you this, to show you—" I shut up. Where was all my charm? The change of address form had seemed like a good idea at the time. Watching her squint down at it, mostly it just felt lame.

I wasn't expecting her to lean in and kiss me softly, her champagne-flavored tongue tasting mine. When she pulled back, she was smiling.

"I'm sorry, I've been dragging my feet. It wasn't about you. At all. I was just worried about everything with the bakery and if I was going to have to find work somewhere else. I didn't feel like I could settle in until I knew I had a job."

"Just for the record, I don't care if you have a job."

"I want to support myself, Royal. I'm not—"

I leaned in to kiss her, stopping her words. "I know. And I get it. I really do. But life isn't always smooth, and I'll love you through the hard times along with the good. Job or no job."

Daisy didn't answer me in words. Setting her champagne on the table, she framed my face in her hands and kissed me. Thoroughly. I was breathing hard when she pulled back to say, "I'll go to the DMV on Monday and change my address. Maybe after I'm done you can help me pack up the rest of my stuff from the apartment."

"Sounds great to me," I agreed.

"What's in that basket?" Daisy asked, shifting on my lap to brush against my erection. It never failed. Kissing Daisy always made me hard. "Can it wait until later?"

My cock insisted it definitely could not wait until later. It took me a second to realize she meant the food. "Finn cooked us dinner, and yes, it can wait." Truthfully, I wasn't sure if it could, but it was going to.

Daisy's eyebrows shot up. "Finn cooked for us? Finn doesn't cook for anyone."

"I know. I had to beg and bribe him with a favor to be redeemed later."

"From the smells coming out of that basket, it was worth it." She leaned in for another kiss. I hated to do it, but I held her off.

"One more thing." I set the velvet box in front of her. Reading the alarm in her face, I covered the box with my hand. "It's not what you think. I'm not dumb enough to try to give you an engagement ring when I'm still trying to get you to finish moving in."

A sheepish smile curved her lips. "Sorry, it was knee-jerk. So, it's not a ring?" The smile faded. "Not that I want a ring. I mean, I do, someday, but it feels too soon and—" She rolled her eyes, shaking her head at herself. "Shut me up, will you?"

"Never." I loved listening to her, even when she made no sense. Except she *was* making sense. "I want to give you that kind of ring. But not yet, not until you're ready. We can wait on that, but I wanted to give you something from me. I never got the idea of promise rings. It always seemed like a cop-out. Why not just pull the trigger and get engaged? Now I get it. You're mine. My woman. My love. Forever. I want you to wear that promise, to have that from me." I flipped open the box.

A delicate ring of yellow gold gleamed against the black velvet, the center pearl glowing in the candlelight, surrounded by petals fashioned of tiny yellow diamonds.

A daisy. She reached for it, then snatched her hand back. "Can I—"

Pulling it from the box, I slid it on her finger. It was a perfect fit. I owed J.T. a thank you for that. Holding her hand in mine, I turned it back and forth, watching the sparkle of the diamonds, the glow of the pearl. This ring was Daisy, the fire of diamonds and the serene calm of the pearl.

"It belonged to my Great-Great-Grandmother, Lady Estelle Ophelia Sawyer. My brothers and sisters helped me look through the jewelry, and when I saw this, I knew you had to have it. Not just because it's a daisy. It reminded me of you. As delicate as the pearl and as strong as the diamonds. Will you wear it?"

She closed a fist around the ring. "I'm never taking it off." Shifting on my lap, she went in for another kiss. Dinner could wait. Scooping her up, I left our champagne on the table and carried Daisy to the bed.

Laying her across the white duvet, I looked down at my future. Her warm brown eyes, the explosion of pink curls, her wide smile. She radiated love. For me. She was what I'd been waiting for my entire life.

We were what I'd been waiting for. Together we could do anything.

I set about stripping her bare, needing to show her exactly how much I loved her. Daisy was ready for me, her eager hands making quick work of my pants before I managed to get her shirt off. We rolled across the bed, laughing and loving until our dinner was cold and we'd sated ourselves on each other.

I got up to bring the champagne to the bed and looked back to find Daisy sprawled across the duvet, gorgeously naked, a smile of satisfaction spread across her face. I didn't know what the future held for us, but with this woman by my side, I knew it would be everything I'd dreamed.

Daisy and I might have our forever figured out, but for everyone else… Things were still up in the air.

We slept in, for us. Grams was opening the bakery, and Daisy and I were still lazing in bed as the first beams of sunlight crested the mountains, turning the treetops emerald and burning off the dawn mist.

We took our time getting dressed, pulling on clothes between kisses, reluctant to leave our cozy love nest for work and real life. Unfortunately, we hadn't packed breakfast or coffee. Stomachs rumbling, we set out for the house, hand in hand.

As we walked, I caught Daisy turning her hand in the light, watching the diamond petals flash and glow in the early morning sun. I loved the sight of that ring on her finger almost as much as I was going to love sliding on the engagement ring I'd already picked out.

If she loved Lady Estelle's daisy ring, she was going to adore the diamond I had in mind for her. Later. We had time. Now that she'd agreed to move in and wore my ring on her finger— even if it wasn't an engagement ring—I could be patient.

I expected the house to be quiet when we snuck in the back door. Breakfast was served as a hot buffet most days to accommodate the widely varying schedules of the Sawyers. Those of us who worked outside the house usually hit breakfast early, though not this early.

Then again, what did I know? I'd been leaving before dawn with Daisy for the last month. Maybe the rest of the family had turned into early risers.

Despite the cacophony of voices from the front hall, I doubted it. Daisy and I bypassed the dining room, dropping our picnic basket at the top of the stairs to the lower level, and headed straight for the crowd assembled just inside the front door.

Griffen stood there, his hair rumpled from sleep, Hope in her robe beside him, her face pale and eyes wide. I glanced to Tenn and saw the reason for her expression. He stood beside a tall redhead I didn't recognize. The redhead's teeth were gritted, her finely wrought features torn between fear and annoyance.

"Hey guys," I said, trying to figure out what the hell had gone wrong now. "Since when are you all up this early?"

Tenn raised an eyebrow at me. "Since I found Vanessa's body this morning when I came back from my run."

Daisy and I both stared at him, his words not sinking in. Vanessa had made bail a few days before, but she'd since disappeared. We'd kept an eye out for her to resurface but otherwise hadn't given her much thought.

"Vanessa's body?" I asked. "She's dead?"

"Shot in the forehead, just like Dad," Tenn confirmed.

"And who's she?" I asked, looking at the redhead. The redhead in question rolled her eyes to the ceiling, her impatience almost disguising her nerves.

"Her?" Tenn asked. He raised his arm and hers followed with a metallic jingle, the handcuff connecting them shining silver. "She's my alibi."

ARE YOU READY FOR TENN'S STORY?

Visit IvyLayne.com/SchemingHeart
to see what happens next!

Never Miss a New Release:
Join Ivy's Reader's Group
@ ivylayne.com/readers
&
Get two books for free!